PRAISE

CRAZY FOR THE SWEET CONFECTIONS BAKER

2015 RONE Award for Best Sweet Contemporary Romance

"A delectable contemporary romance ... **Characters with depth and heart,** and a cast of side characters that need to be seen in later books. A must-read!" - *InD'Tale Magazine*

"**This story sucked me in** on so many fronts. First, the bakery, and then the mouthwateringly delicious goodies described throughout the book. And no, I'm not talking about the cupcakes or the eclairs. I'm talking Graydon Green, the famous ex-hockey player. Wowza!" - *Cindy, Goodreads reviewer*

"**Loved... Loved... LOVED Crazy for the Sweet Confections Baker!** I could not put it down! I loved all the characters and the relationships they had with each other. The book was just amazing! I can't wait to read the next book in the series!" - *KJ's Book Nook*

"This was a delightfully fun and engaging read. **Lots of charm, wit and intrigue!**" - *Stephanie, Goodreads reviewer*

"**This is sassy classy writing at its finest.** The story grabs you from the first page and doesn't let go." - *Barnes & Noble reviewer*

When an author can draw me in, and make me feel that **I would like to actually meet and be friends with the characters in a book**....then that author has done a great job!! I loved this book and I can't wait til the next book is out! - *Terri, Amazon reviewer*

This story reminds us all why it's so great to fall in love, and why it's worth overcoming all the obstacles to stay there. A sweet tale! - *Reader23, Amazon reviewer*

CRYSTAL CREEK

CRAZY FOR THE *Sweet Confections* BAKER

DANYELLE FERGUSON

Published by Wonderstruck Books

Kansas City, KS

ISBN-13: 9780998088648

Cover and book design by Danyelle Ferguson

Cover design © 2022 by Danyelle Ferguson

❄ Created with Vellum

DANYELLE FERGUSON BOOKLIST

CRYSTAL CREEK SERIES:
Confessions to the Girl Next Door
Crazy for the Sweet Confections Baker
Saving Dr. Weston Blake
A Best Friend's Guide to Love
How to Woo a Billionaire in Ten Days

STAND-ALONE NOVELS & ANTHOLOGIES:
Once Upon a Wish
With a Kiss Anthology
Timeless Romance: Kissing a Billionaire Anthology
Carol of the Tales & Other Nightly Noels
A Christmas of Hope

To my sweetie, John.
Thank you for the kitchen timer you gave me for Christmas, and
helping me put it to good use with word war sprints and editing
marathons. My taste buds thank you for all the delicious, gooey ice
cream sundae rewards as I met my goals. But most of all, thank you
for loving me just the way I am.
I love you more.

Chapter ONE

*L*ife as a single chick sucked. Well, not all of it. Rachel loved designing cakes at the upscale bakery she co-owned with her best friend. Kicking butt at local and state cake competitions made work all the sweeter. No, there were lots of great elements about life in general, but the search for The Guy was exhausting. Was it really too much for a girl to ask for interesting conversation not centered around sports, a guy who laughed at corny jokes—possibly even himself at times—and a kiss with some zing? Major zing would be most appreciated.

She'd had visions of left-handed sparkle in the not-so-distant future with Nico Giambiasi. Instead she sat at Brisket and Noodles, one of Kansas City's popular BBQ restaurants, decked out in her favorite clingy jeans, an emerald top that contrasted nicely with her deep red hair and killer heels, trying to absorb the bomb her boyfriend just dropped.

"Are you serious? You're married?" Rachel pushed her hair back over her shoulder, although she was tempted to wrap it around her fingers and pull hard to see if this conversation was real or just a horrible dream.

"It's not what you think, darling." Nico reached across the table, but she moved her hands to her lap.

"Really? We've been dating for three months! What am I supposed to think?" She searched his face for signs of something she must have missed, but all she saw were dark good looks. She leaned back in the seat and placed a hand over her stomach, trying to hold back the bubble of hysterical laughter gathering within. Dimly, she heard him talking, but couldn't focus on the words. How could this be true? Sure he left for extended trips, often flying back to Italy where the company he worked for was based. But married? Never in a thousand million years would she have guessed he was spoken for in a very permanent way. Had all the time they spent together really been one big tangled web of lies? There should be a cell phone app that monitors your social calendar and sends a flashing neon text message after ten dates with a reminder that it's probably time to apply the one thing the male species ever got right—the Boy Scout motto. 'Be Prepared' and locate the nearest emergency exit.

Then she heard something that made her sit up straight. "Stop. Say that again." She shook her head. She couldn't have possibly heard him right.

"I said if it weren't for the kids, I would have left Denita long before I met you."

"Your kids?" she squeaked. The image of a little boy covered in dust and dirt and a sweet girl holding her baby doll with no daddy to play with popped into her head. Nico was lucky the table wasn't preset with sharp knives. The jerk. She leaned forward and lowered her voice. "You make me sick." She pushed back from the table and stood to leave, but he grabbed her arm and pulled her close.

"You need to listen, Rachel." Anger sharpened his features. Her heart pounded against her chest as she attempted to step away but he pulled her closer still. "Sit down. I'm not finished yet."

She reached for a glass of water, intending to throw it in

his face, but he took the goblet from her. "Please, that is so cliché."

Her nails bit into the palm of her hand, then the next thing she knew, her fist connected with his nose. Pain shot up her forearm, all the way to her elbow. *Holy mackerel.* She had never hit anyone before, but thankfully her brothers made her learn how to do it properly.

Nico gasped and released her, bending over to cover his face. She took the opportunity to snatch her purse and get away, quickly weaving between the tables toward the front of the restaurant. *Well, Rachel,* she thought, *this is what you get for meeting people online. Didn't Mom tell you there were a bunch of loonies out there? But did you listen? Of course not.* As she neared the foyer, Nico yanked her around to face him. A trickle of blood ran down from his nose. A wave of queasiness washed over her when he reached up and wiped it with the back of his hand. He looked at the smeared blood, then shoved his hand into his pocket before returning his attention to her.

"Where do you think you're going? You came with me and you'll leave with me." People waiting to be seated stopped talking and stared at the drama unfolding before them.

"Let go of me, Nico. You're causing a scene," she said quietly. Instead, his hand tightened on her arm, making her wince. What was he doing? He had always been charming and sweet—until tonight. Was it all a masquerade?

"Excuse me, but I believe the lady asked you to let her go."

The deep voice came from over her shoulder. Nico glanced up and his eyes widened, then narrowed. He slowly released her arm.

Rachel automatically stepped away, but bumped into a solid chest. She moved to the side and looked up . . . and up.

Beside her stood one of the tallest men she'd ever seen. She was an average girl who could hit 5'8" with the right heels on, but still, her head barely came to the middle of his chest. He turned and blocked Nico from her.

"Are you okay, miss?" he asked in an unexpectedly gentle voice. She forced herself to nod, but couldn't seem to make her vocal cords work. He studied her for a moment, then gave a return nod. When he turned around, she saw Nico's face harden with resentment and a shiver ran down her spine.

"Rachel," Nico said tightly. "This is enough. I'm taking you home, *now.*"

"I believe she's changed her mind. You can say goodnight." Her rescuer motioned to the front door.

Nico looked as if he might push the issue, but instead turned away and pulled his coat on. "I'll call you tomorrow."

"Don't." She couldn't stand the thought of being near him. If she didn't get away from him soon, her roiling stomach would force her to the nearest restroom or trash can.

"I'll call you tomorrow," he repeated, then shoved the door open and stormed out.

Married. He's married, married, married.

"Excuse me," the man said, stepping to her side. "Perhaps you'd like to come into the office while you wait for a cab?"

Rachel tightened her grip on her purse, trying unsuccessfully to quiet the jumbled confusion in her head. "Yes, thank you. I'd appreciate that."

"Max, please call a cab and let me know when it arrives."

The restaurant host gave a slight nod in acknowledgment,

then she followed the man down a short hallway and into a masculine office. Simple black framed pictures of hockey players and teams lined the wall behind the desk. He motioned to the black leather couch sitting in front of a large mahogany desk. "Please sit while I get you a drink."

She sank into the soft, buttery leather and closed her eyes, concentrating, searching for the calm she needed to make it home before falling apart. She could keep herself together. She *would* keep herself together. She opened her eyes to find the manager standing before her with a glass of ice water. She'd noticed his height, but didn't realize how *big* he really was. Medium brown hair fell forward onto his forehead, his shoulders were wide and everything else was all muscle. The combination of being in the small office and him standing near made her claustrophobic. She thanked him, then took a sip, but didn't relax until he took a few steps back and leaned against the edge of the desk.

"I'm Graydon Green," he said. "And I take it you're Rachel." He extended his hand toward her.

"Yes, Rachel Marconi." Warmth tingled where his rough palm rubbed against hers and she pulled away. "I really appreciate your help, Mr. Green."

"Please, call me Graydon. Do you need some ice for that?" He motioned to her hand.

She held it out in front of her. There was some redness around the knuckles and it still hurt a little, but she shook her head. "I've never hit anyone before. Not even my stupid brothers when they cut the hair off my Barbie dolls." She flexed her hand a few times, then transferred the water glass to it. The iciness felt good as it seeped into her hand.

"It looks like you did a decent job for your first try."

She twisted the glass around, listening to the clink of ice

against glass. *Calm*, she repeated to herself. *Find something else to focus on.* She looked at the decor. "So, who's the hockey fan?"

His whole body tensed and became unnaturally still before relaxing. The moment passed so fast, she wasn't sure if she had really seen it or if it had been her imagination.

"The guys in my family. Any time we all get together, it's the only thing that can be on TV without someone complaining." He hesitated, then asked, "Do you like hockey?"

She shook her head. "Not really. But my dad and brothers follow almost everything—football, golf, soccer, bowling. I think I've interrupted them during a few hockey games. Personally, I think it's too violent." She looked again at all the hockey pictures, sure she had offended a die-hard fan. "Well, it's not just hockey. I feel the same way about football."

"Says the girl who just punched her boyfriend in the nose," Graydon said, a small lopsided smile made a dimple appear in one cheek.

Rachel snorted. "Believe me, he deserved it."

He remained silent, looking at her in a way that made her feel like he was weighing her comments. She met his gaze as they contemplated each other. Then she blurted out, "What is it with guys and lying?" He jolted in surprise. She continued before he could answer. "Seriously. Why do men think it's okay to cheat?"

Graydon held his hands out, as if defending himself from an ambush. "Just because I'm a guy doesn't mean I understand why others make the choices they do." He lowered his hands to grasp the edge of the desk. "To answer your question, I don't know. Maybe they grew up with dads

6

who cheated or didn't have someone around to teach them the right way to treat a woman." He shrugged. "I do know there are lots of good guys out there."

"If there are, I haven't discovered proof of their existence."

He leaned slightly forward. "Is that what tonight was about?"

Rachel turned her head away. She would never tell a stranger the truth. But how could she tell her family and best friend that she unwittingly became 'the other woman.' The one wives whisper about and plot revenge against. She gripped the glass of water, pondering how her life had taken this turn.

"My parents have been married for almost 40 years," she said. "These days, it seems like a miracle if a couple stays together long enough to celebrate their 10th anniversary." Their eyes met, hers moist while his were contemplative. "What happened that people don't love and respect each other through all the bumps anymore?"

The question sat in the silence of the room, dangling like a dead man at the end of a rope. Rachel's stomach tightened in a knot, creating a combination of queasiness and the urge to laugh at the horrendousness of the situation. She had gone from a startling, relationship-altering bomb being dropped to spewing her inner-most gut-wrenching questions about men and relationships to a total stranger.

She fidgeted in her seat, desperate to change the subject. Suddenly, it clicked in her mind who he reminded her of. "Has anyone ever said you look like that guy from The Pacifier?" His forehead scrunched in confusion. That should have been her clue to stop, but instead verbal diarrhea took over. "You know, the movie about the military guy who ends up babysitting. I'm terrible at remembering celebrities." She rubbed her forehead, trying hard to come up with the name that seemed to be on the edge of her memory. Anything to keep her mind distracted from tonight's disaster.

He cleared his throat. "You mean Vin Diesel?"

Her head snapped up. "That's it!"

"You think I look like Vin Diesel?"

"Yes! Well, other than you actually have hair and I guess he's on the short side and you're rather tall," she tilted her head, not able to stop the rambling. "But your faces are similar and you're both freakishly muscular—um, I mean . . ." Heat flooded her cheeks. His lips were thin and his eyes crinkled at the corners while mirth danced in the brown depths. "I'm sorry. I tend to put my foot in my mouth, or let it out as the case may be, but—" She didn't even finish the sentence before he began to laugh. Great. Where was the duct tape when you needed it?

A light knock caught her attention. She turned to see the restaurant host standing at the door. "Your cab has arrived, miss."

Escape. The emergency exit she so desperately needed finally appeared. She gathered her things, then stood and bumped into Graydon.

"I'm sorry," she mumbled, hurrying out of the room.

"Wait." He followed her down the hall. She almost made it to the front entrance without speaking to him again. "Here, let me get the door for you." He reached around her and grabbed the handle.

Sure, anything to get me out of here faster. She brushed past him to the cab waiting at the curb, but paused when she thought she saw Nico's car parked at the corner. *Has he been waiting for me all this time?* She squinted to see if it really was him, but the car was parked in a poorly lit area of the street. The evening's darkness made it difficult to tell if someone sat inside or not.

Once more, Graydon materialized, this time to open the cab door. She wanted to slide in and escape, instead she turned toward him one last time. His expression was calm and warm. Chocolate. His eyes reminded her of melted chocolate just before mixing it into ganache. She blinked, then refocused. For a brief moment, gratitude pushed her desperation and anger aside.

"Thank you for helping me earlier." She started to move, but he took her hand and helped her into the cab, then briefly squeezed it before he stepped back.

"I hope you come back soon, Rachel Marconi." He closed the door and waved the driver on.

She turned in her seat. Graydon stood at the curb, hands in his pockets, watching her ride away. She faced forward and sighed. The night flashed through her mind like a bad movie rerun.

Well, one thing's certain. I'm an idiot. She wiped at the tears falling down her cheeks, pulled her cell out of her purse and hit speed dial. *But at least I'm an idiot who has Ben & Jerry's and a best friend to share it with.*

Chapter TWO

"*B*est shot between the eyes wins. Deal?" asked Kristen.

"Deal," Rachel said, as she and her best friend drew their arms back, darts ready to fly. Her focus was intent on the 4x6 color picture pinned to the dart board. The lying jerk's cheerful face mocked her own red blotchy one as Kristen counted down.

"Three . . . two . . . one!"

Rachel threw her dart straight and true, but was dismayed by the *ping* sound as both darts bounced off the picture and fell to the basement floor.

"No way," she said, then bent down and picked up another dart, throwing it even harder. It, too, bounced off and landed on the floor. She picked up another, then another, throwing each of them with more determination, but all she got was a pile of darts beneath the target. Finally, she flopped onto the couch behind her, leaned her head back and fought to control the anger, bitterness and sadness all warring against each other. She didn't want to cry anymore, especially after going through enough tissues to make the floor look like a snow storm had blown through.

"These darts must be defective." Kristen turned it around, trying to figure out what could be wrong. "Honey!" she yelled upstairs.

A tiny smile came to Rachel's lips as faint thumps sounded on the floor above. Kristen's husband, Todd, appeared at the top of the basement stairs.

"I'm almost done making your sundaes. What's up?"

"Your darts are defective. Why did you buy ones that don't work?"

Sure enough that got Todd's attention. If there was one thing she had learned from growing up with a bunch of sports fanatics, it was that equipment of any kind had to be in perfect working condition.

He clomped down the stairs and took the dart from his wife. He carefully looked it over, then asked, "What's wrong with it?"

"It won't stick. What kind of dart doesn't stick to its board?" She gestured to the opposite wall.

Todd looked from the board back to his wife, then leaned closer and asked, "Were you trying to shoot the dart at the picture?"

"Of course," she replied.

"Then it works." Before Kristen could interrupt with more questions, he held up the dart and pointed to the tip. "Sweetie, these darts have plastic tips. Remember, you didn't want me to buy a regular set so Daphne wouldn't get hurt if she found one of them. Plastic tips won't break through a picture."

"Oh." She took the dart back. "You don't happen to have any regular ones do you?"

He shook his head. "Of course not, 'cause if you discovered them under any other circumstance, I'd be in the dog house." Then he gave her a loud smooch on the cheek and headed back upstairs.

"Well, that just stinks," Rachel said, as Kristen sat next to her. "I was really looking forward to putting pock marks all over his disgusting face." They both stared at the picture, trying to decide what to do next. She heard her cell phone beep, signaling another call. She wondered how many phone messages Nico had left and if her voicemail reached its max yet. She didn't even want to think about how many messages were piling up for her to sort through later. Man, she hoped the chocolate arrived soon.

"I know!" Kristen said. She jumped up from the couch and pulled out the side table drawer. Rachel didn't see what Kristen grabbed before she ran over to the dart board, took down the picture and stabbed it. That's when she saw the pen in Kristen's hand.

"Where did you get this picture printed? This has got to be the thickest photo paper I've ever seen," Kristen said, pulling the pen back out.

"Dork head brought it back from Italy." Rachel grabbed another pen from the drawer and joined her friend, stabbing the picture over and over.

"Dork head? Come on, you can do better than that."

"I could but it wouldn't fit your PG kiddy guidelines," she replied, then stabbed the picture.

"Yeah. I never know when Daphne will pop up. We'll have to figure out a code name."

When it was sufficiently full of pock marks, they pinned it back up to the dart board. Rachel bent over, picked up one of the fallen darts, and made one last stab—right between Nico's eyes.

"Yes!" They did a little dance and gave each other high-fives.

They turned to find Todd, his mouth slightly ajar,

standing next to the couch. He held huge bowls filled with Chocolate Lava sundaes. He slowly set them on the coffee table and backed away from the girls. "Well, um . . . here are your sundaes. I think I'll go back to upstairs where men are safe."

"Thank you," Rachel called, as he thumped up the stairs. She turned to Kristen, who was already sampling her sundae. "I think we've officially freaked out your hubby."

"Hmm, maybe. But I doubt it."

They returned to the couch with their bowls. A mutual silence filled the room as they dug into the rich chocolate treat. Rachel thought about the very first time they shared these sundaes together. Ironically, it was after a terrible blind double date set up by a friend from culinary school. Together, they baked a batch of homemade fudge brownies. Then they created brownie sundaes layered with several scoops of Ben & Jerry's Phish Food ice cream, rich hot fudge, and topped with a mountain of real whipped cream, lightly sprinkled with shavings from a half-eaten Hershey's chocolate bar. Hence, the Chocolate Lava sundaes were born, to be eaten only after horrifying date experiences or in celebration of something absolutely wonderful. The last time they shared them was when Kristen's daughter, Daphne, turned two-years-old.

Rachel sent up a prayer of thanks that many more sundaes had been made for celebrations rather than their original purpose—chocolate therapy for the broken hearted. The sundaes also marked the beginning of their dream to open a dessert shop together. She looked at the large framed picture from the opening of their shop, Sweet Confections. They still looked about the same, Kristen with her shoulder-length brown hair and deep blue eyes. The only noticeable change in Rachel was her thick auburn hair now reached past her shoulders, which made it easier to twist up and clip when she was baking. Sweet Confections just celebrated its fifth anniversary and was one of Kansas City's best bakeries.

So much had changed in their personal lives since then. Rachel studied the gooey chocolate on her spoon a moment, before asking Kristen the question weighing heavily on her mind.

"How am I going to tell Mom I've been dating a married man?" She looked away from her friend's compassionate expression. "Last week, I told her things were getting more serious and he might possibly be The One. You should have seen the smile on her face, Kristen. The mere thought of her almost *ancient* daughter finally saying *I do* made her glow like white twinkly Christmas lights. And now . . . I don't know how to tell her." Her throat closed up around her words. She turned her attention back to her now-melted ice cream which looked blurry as tears filled her eyes, then fell into the chocolate concoction.

Kristen took the bowl and set it on the coffee table, then she wrapped her arms around Rachel. "First of all, twenty-eight years old isn't even close to being ancient. And second of all, your mom is going to have a cow, but she'll get over it. The thing you really need to remember is that a man does not define your worth as a woman."

Rachel pulled back and wiped tears from her eyes. "You're right. I know you are, but sometimes it's so hard to feel that way. I'm going to turn thirty in a little under two years and I feel like my life is never going to amount to anything more than cake and sugar frosting."

"You have an incredible gift that makes others happy. Do

you want to take back all our clients' smiles when you create something they could only put into words? You may not see it right at this moment, but you have a wonderful, full life. Just ask your nephews. They'd never trade you for anyone else."

She couldn't stop her lips from forming a small smile at the mention of her boisterous nephews. "Yeah, well, they love the desserts I bring to our family dinners."

"See? All that cake and sugar frosting isn't such a bad thing, is it?" Kristen teased and bumped her friend's shoulder with her own.

"No, I guess not." Rachel looked over at her friend and asked one last time, "So, any other thoughts on how to break the news to my mom?"

She shook her head. "Although a few prayers asking for divine intervention wouldn't hurt. Well, that and your chocolate torte topped with fresh strawberries might help the news go over better." Kristen reached over and grabbed a mint out of the candy bowl on the side table.

She tilted her head back and stared at the ceiling tiles. "Why didn't I ever date Todd? I could be you right now."

Kristen coughed as she choked on her mint. When she could breathe normally again, she looked at Rachel as if trying to figure out if she was serious or just teasing. "If I remember correctly, you thought perfecting your vanilla-bean pound cake was more interesting than any of the guys we knew, including Todd."

She tipped her head to the side, considering her friend's comment. "Hmm. Maybe I should have paid closer attention." Then she glanced at Kristen and allowed a tiny smirk to appear. "Who knows how things might have turned out had I let loose my full arsenal of feminine powers?"

"Whatever!" Kristen grabbed the pillow beside her and gave her a solid *thwump* upside the head.

Rachel caught the pillow before Kristen could smack her a second time. "Yeah, you're right. I'll stick with the vanilla-bean pound cake."

Chapter THREE

*R*achel pulled into her parents' driveway, turned off the car, then stared at the two-story stucco house looming in front of her. She gripped the steering wheel, trying to build up enough nerve to walk in. Through the window, faint shouts came from the backyard. Obviously her nephews were getting their energy out before being summoned to the dinner table.

She replayed the events of the last twenty-four hours in her mind. Nico's declaration, her uncomfortable conversation in Graydon's office, then staying up until the early morning hours with her best friend. She finally fell asleep, only to have dreams of Nico repeating, *I'm married*, over and over. She wished she could permanently forget she was single. How awesome would it be to never have anyone ask who she was dating or pat her hand and make some pitiful comment about today's young men being blind? An escape seemed to be exactly what she needed.

Instead she and Kristen whipped up a dark chocolate cake and a batch of peanut butter icing. It certainly wasn't the chocolate torte topped with fresh strawberries Kristen recommended, nor the Raspberry Jelly Roll sitting in her refrigerator at home. She contemplated going to her townhouse, but was afraid of what she might find when she got there.

That morning, Todd deleted over thirty-something text messages from Nico and erased all the messages in her cell's voicemail. Because really, what could he say to make her feel any different about the situation? Did he think there was some excuse that would change her mind about pursuing a relationship with a married man?

Even if he did, he was dead wrong.

Pathetic. She turned her head and listened to her nephews' shouts once more. She should have spent more time paying attention to guys during her college days. At least then there was a better variety to choose from. She never thought she'd end up as one of those older girls skimming through the left-overs, hoping for at least one good guy in the batch.

Rachel looked up at her parents' house. She should get inside before someone discovered her sitting in the driveway. That would only cause questions to start flying before she was ready to answer them. She took a deep breath and exhaled. *You can do this*, she thought, walking up the sidewalk to the front door. *It's only dinner with my crazy family. They probably won't even remember I had a date with Nico last night.*

Just in case, she stopped with her hand on the knob and prayed God would be merciful and let her mother have temporary amnesia in regards to her social calendar for once. She straightened her shoulders and entered the house.

"Hi, everyone. I'm here!"

From the entry way, she could see her father and brothers —Christopher and Adam—squished together on the couch, shouting at something on the TV. She waved to them, trying to remember which sport played at the beginning of October. Soccer? Basketball? She could never keep them straight.

She passed the living room, went through the dining room and into the large sunny kitchen. Her mother removed a casserole dish from the oven and set it on the counter. From the wonderful smell, she guessed they were having either stuffed shells or her mother's incredible manicotti. Her sister-in-law, Eva, pulled open the sliding glass doors and called for the boys to come in to wash their hands. Eva moved aside as Jordan, Malone, and Stockton ran through the door.

"Aunt Rachel!" Little five-year-old Stockton threw his arms around one of her legs.

"Whoa there, buddy! You almost knocked this super yummy cake out of my hands." She ruffled his hair with her empty hand then inched toward the counter to set the cake down, all while her nephew continued with his monkey grip. As soon as both her hands were free, she pulled him into a bear hug, squeezing him as much as she could until he gasped for air. Not all kids with autism liked to be held, but Stockton craved it. It always calmed him down, and maybe he was on to something, because she started to feel better, too. Perhaps this wouldn't be so bad after all.

"More Aunt Rachel! More!" he begged. She gathered him close for another squeeze. When she released him, he leaned his head on her shoulder and giggled, running his dirty fingers through her loose auburn hair.

"How's my favorite buddy doing?" she asked.

"Good. I love Thomas. I have a new James, too. Wanna see?" He was completely fascinated with Thomas the Tank Engine and had quite the collection going. He even named her car Percy because it was small and green.

"I'd love to see your new James, but right now I need to help Grandma get dinner ready. Can you show me after we eat?"

"Eat! Eat! I need to wash my hands." Stockton scrambled

back down then rushed off to the bathroom. Rachel saw her mother set the hot dishes on the table. Definitely manicotti. She could feel her mouth watering already.

"You're late. Your mother's been asking about you for the last hour," said her other sister-in-law, Faith, as she handed her a green salad. "Toss that for me, please. I'll grab the dressings out of the fridge. So, where were you?"

"I spent the day with Kristen's family and lost track of time." She shrugged, hoping it looked casual, then grabbed some tongs out of a drawer and tossed the salad a few times.

Faith got the dressings and came to stand next to her. "Hmm. Really?" Rachel could feel prickles on her back as Faith stared at her. Before she could ask anything else, Rachel changed the subject.

"How's Emery? I didn't see him when I came in."

"He's doing great! I can't believe he's three months old already. He did the most amazing thing yesterday. I was holding his rattle out to him, 'cause you know he's just been swinging his arms at it. But yesterday, he actually grabbed it! With both hands! And then he stuck it right in his mouth. It was so awesome, Rachel. I wish you could have seen it."

She couldn't help but smile as Faith's excitement bubbled. They carried the salad and dressings to the table, then shooed the kids away from the rolls.

"Boys! It's time for dinner," her mother yelled over the sound of the TV. The game was promptly turned off—the magic of DVR meant they could pick up where they left off later—and her father and brothers appeared for the meal.

A brief chaotic scramble ensued while everyone found their seats. Once they were settled with one of her parents on each end and all their children and grandchildren sandwiched in between, her father said a blessing. Then the chaos started once again, but in a more organized manner. Dishes were passed as the family talked over each other, sharing about their week, fun stuff that happened at school and which teams were rising in the ranks.

"Go, Chiefs!" Adam cheered, reminding her that it was football season. Of course, this started a whole round of booing from others as they each put in plugs for their favorites and made bets about which two teams would make it to the coveted Super Bowl. The cajoling continued through the majority of the meal and helped her relax. She thought her prayer had been answered until her mother asked the question she'd been dreading all night.

"So, Rachel, how is everything going with Nico?"

Rachel bobbled the plate she held and barely escaped with a few drips of sauce on the tablecloth. She handed her nephew's dinner back to him.

"Sorry, Jordan," she said, then turned toward her mother. Time seemed to slow, but she knew nothing had changed. Everyone still talked over each other and continued to eat. She hoped to make it through this conversation with as little notice as possible. "I guess he's doing okay. Actually, Nico and I aren't seeing each other anymore."

Disappointment crossed her mother's face. "What do you mean?"

The conversation at the table grew quiet, although everyone continued to eat and listen. All the attention made her tongue thick and she stumbled over her words. "We just aren't. Things didn't work out."

She hoped it would stop there, but as usual, her mother pushed the subject. "You aren't getting any younger, you know. Maybe you can patch things up."

Rachel sighed. She wasn't going to be able to avoid it.

"Actually, I didn't have a choice. I found out Nico already has a wife and family back in Italy."

Suddenly, all motion at the table stopped. Wide eyes turned toward her in a mixture of disbelief and wonder. Her father's mouth gaped open. She hated it. Hated the feeling that it was all her fault. Knowing they wondered how she could be so stupid.

"Excuse me." She hastily shoved out the chair and rushed into the kitchen, searching for her purse. She needed to leave, to escape before the weight of failure crushed her.

"Rachel, wait."

Great, her mother had followed her. Would the torture never end? "I have to go. I'll talk to you later." She found her purse, but before she could leave, her mother took her arm, turned her around, then wrapped Rachel in a hug.

"I'm sorry, sweetie," she said.

Rachel gasped, then wrapped her arms around her mother and fought for control over the emotions rushing through her. This was not the reaction she'd expected. The good old Italian crossing, a little mama mia, and a rant that went on long enough for her children to all wish they had been born deaf. Yes, that was the typical Mom reaction at the Marconi house. But the hug, the warmth, and understanding undid her. Her mother stroked her hair and continued to murmur until Rachel calmed down. She pulled back and cupped her daughter's face.

"It will be okay. You'll figure this out. You're like your father that way. Always moving forward, making nasty bumps into something good." She brushed the hair back from Rachel's face. "Why don't you take a deep breath, then we'll go back in."

Rachel steeled herself to face the rest of the family. When

they returned to the dining room, the kids were the only ones eating while the adults picked at their food.

"Eat." Her mother motioned to the table. "I didn't make all this food to go to waste."

Her father cleared his throat. "So, I hear the Kansas City Coyotes had a good game last night." It took a few seconds, but finally her brothers caught on.

"Yeah, I saw that game. They had a couple of great body slams," Adam said.

"Hey, Grandpa! Did I tell you I start DG's Hockey Camp next week?" asked Jordan.

Rachel didn't even try to follow the conversation. Eva reached beneath the table and squeezed her hand, then joined the conversation with the rest of the boys. Her father winked and she gave him a little smile before returning to her dinner, although she didn't have much appetite left.

The rest of dinner and dessert passed by in a blur. When the boys started to clear the table, Rachel grabbed her keys, said a quick round of goodbyes and slipped out of the house. She had just unlocked the car when she heard the front door slam. She sincerely hoped her mother had not followed her outside for another little chat.

"Hey, Rachel, hang on a second," called Eva. Rachel turned and leaned back on the car door. "With all the craziness at dinner, I never got a chance to talk to you. I was wondering if you might be able to help us out in two weeks. The kids are out of school for Parent-Teacher Conferences. We had originally planned that I'd be home, but some work meetings were rearranged and our schedule got messed up. Anyway," she said, taking a deep breath and sweeping her dark hair back from her face. "Jordan needs a ride to camp Thursday and Friday morning. Could you possibly help?"

"Sure, let me check my schedule." Rachel dug in her purse and pulled out her phone. She scrolled through her week, looking at the number of cakes and other desserts she had scheduled. "It looks like it should be fine. I have some birthday and anniversary cakes, but the bulk of my work is for the Partridge wedding and that isn't until Saturday evening. What time does he need to be at camp?"

"Check in is at 8:30. I hoped it would be early enough for you to run him to the arena then get to the shop without being too late." Eva slid her hands into her back pockets.

She quickly typed the info and set a reminder alarm. "I'll double check with Kristen, but it shouldn't be a problem."

"Sounds good."

Rachel nodded, then moved to open her car door. "Well, I'll talk to you later then."

Eva snagged Rachel's shirt sleeve. "Hang on a sec. Are you okay?"

Her eyes stung as she avoided Eva's gaze, focusing instead on the house across the street.

"I'm so sorry, Rachel. I don't know how you found out, but he's a first-class jerk who doesn't deserve any of your tears. I know that doesn't make it any better, but it's the truth."

Rachel barely choked out thanks. Eva squeezed her upper arm, then stepped back. "You're welcome. I better get back inside and hold down the fort before the boys get too crazy. I'll call you later."

Then Eva ran back to the house and Rachel slid into her car. On the drive home, a Carrie Underwood song came on. She cranked up the radio and sang along, wishing she could undo the past three months. When she arrived home, she cued the song up on her iPod, hit repeat and listened as it pounded out of the speakers. She grabbed a trash bag, went through each room and got rid of everything that reminded her of the cheating schmuck. Out with the pictures, postcards and movie stubs. She even tossed the fuzzy sweater he brought back from Italy. When the bag was full, she went out to the garage and threw it in the trash. *Gone. Gone. Gone. Out of my life,* she thought, letting the lid slam closed with a satisfying thud.

She went back into the kitchen, washed her hands, then poured herself a glass of lemonade. She curled up on a chair at the kitchen table with a notepad and holder full of pens, ready to put all this behind her and reprioritize her life.

My Goals
1. *Check on my Food Network Challenge application. Hound them until I compete and WIN!*
2. *Ditch the romance novels and check out some new suspense authors.*
3. *Buy more Kick Butt music.*
4. *Consider dating again.*

Rachel sat back to review the list. She grabbed a Sharpie out of her pen holder, then drew a thick red line through the last item on the list: ~~Consider dating again.~~ Finally satisfied, she recapped the pen, then lifted her glass in a toast to herself.

"To the new and improved, single, independent and awesome Rachel Marconi."

Chapter FOUR

he next day at work, Rachel signed a form and sent off yet another flower delivery man to the local children's hospital. This morning, she discovered her entire front porch overflowing with pale pink roses. As tiny as her porch may be, there were a whole heck of a lot of flowers. Some were in vases, others in baskets, and still more in floral boxes. On the front door, she found one little card that read, 'Please meet with me so I can explain. I love you.'

Had the gesture been from another man—or more precisely, an eligible man—she probably would have turned into a mushy puddle and signed the dotted line for forever right then and there. But knowing Nico was married made her stomach turn inside out. She couldn't leave them there for the whole neighborhood to gossip about, so she loaded them into her car and delivered them to Children's Mercy Hospital on her way to work. The volunteers were wide-eyed and amazed as they helped unload all the beautiful flowers sent by an anonymous benefactor—or at least that was her story. She wondered what they thought now as more flowers came every hour. It had to stop soon, didn't it?

"Shawna, could you please take care of the rest of the deliveries? I don't want to be interrupted again."

"Sure, Rachel. No problem," replied the college employee as she served customers samples of Oreo Truffles.

She took a moment to look over the front shop. The minty green walls were accented with pictures of Sweet Confections desserts in deep brown frames. It reminded her of mint chocolate chip ice cream. The two cute cafe tables were filled. A mom shared a cupcake with a preschool-aged daughter and a set of women were drinking coffee and munching on goodies while they chatted. The shop was perfect when they opened five years ago, but their clientele had grown so much, they really needed to move to a new location. She sighed. She just hoped they could find what they envisioned in Crystal Creek. She and Kristen loved the little Kansas City suburb nestled on the edge of city and country. She needed to remind Kristen to chat with their Realtor friend, Victoria, when she attended the next Crystal Creek Women in Business meeting.

She returned to the kitchen where Kristen was busy mixing ingredients for cake batter. "Why can't he take a hint? I told him not to contact me. Doesn't he get it?" She took out her frustration as she kneaded and rolled out fondant for a baby shower cake.

"Well, let's see. He's a guy, Italian, and conceited. Those three things combined tell me he's not going to give up easily. Look on the bright side, all those kids probably love being surrounded by their own little garden."

"Ugh. Pink roses used to be my favorite. Now they make me want to puke."

Kristen burst out laughing. "Don't worry, you'll find a new favorite flower."

Rachel pouted as she checked the fondant thickness. Satisfied it was just right, she picked it up and draped it over the cake. She smoothed it, making sure there were no cracks. Mrs. McMullen, who was hosting her daughter's shower, wanted a big splashy cake to display surrounded by five dozen little pastel pink and yellow rubber ducky cakes. Oh, how she hated working with pourable fondant. But at least that was done and now she could work on the best part—the display cake.

It was a replica of an old-fashioned bath tub with sugar bubbles brimming and sudsing over the edge. She enjoyed designing, then taking the drawing and sculpting a masterpiece—all out of yummy, delicious cake. She was sure Mrs. McMullen's friends were going to drool in envy, but the first bite of cake would make them devoted fans of the bakery. Any cake could look pretty, but not many taste as buttery, creamy, and irresistible as a Sweet Confections cake.

The phone rang, breaking her concentration.

"Hey, Rachel, can you get that?" Kristen asked, as she poured cake mix into pans.

She dusted her hands off on her apron, then picked up the wall phone receiver. "Sweet Confections, this is Rachel."

"Darling, don't hang up. I just want to talk to you for a few minutes."

The sound of Nico's voice made her stomach clench. "I don't think you have anything to say that I want to hear," she said icily.

"Please, sweetheart, let's talk. At least let me explain my side of the story."

"Honestly, Nico, I don't think I could handle seeing you without giving you a black eye. Do you know what I realized? I kissed a married man. It made me feel so disgusting, I considered washing my mouth out with peroxide. If I actually thought it'd help, I would have done it, too. I want you to stop calling, stop sending flowers and leave me alone.

Because no matter what you say, I cannot, *will not*, have a relationship with a married man. Do you understand?"

She heard a deep sigh on the other end of the line. "Baby, don't do this. We need to talk, then you'll understand and we'll be together. I can't let you go, Rachel."

"You don't have a choice." She firmly set the phone back in its cradle, severing her relationship with Nico.

"Now that's the Rachel I remember." Kristen slipped her arm around her friend's shoulders. The phone started to ring again. "That's probably him. Do you want me to answer it?"

She shook her head and picked up the receiver. "Sweet Confections."

"She cheated on me first," Nico said, his voice filled with anger.

"Does that make it okay for you to cheat? Or to drag me into this situation without any thought to how I might feel?"

"I love you, Rachel. I'll leave her, I'll—"

"It's too late for any of that, Nico. No matter what changes you make at this point, you'll always be the guy who cheated on his wife. There's no justification for your actions and I'll never forget how you lied to me. Never, Nico. Don't call me again." She hung up the phone, then waited. It didn't ring again.

Kristen tugged on Rachel's apron strings. "I think we need a celebratory lunch," she glanced at her watch. "In about an hour when the cakes are out to cool. My treat."

Rachel felt the first genuine smile form since Saturday. She did it. She was able to tell Nico off and she felt great about it. "Excellent idea. I'm suddenly craving Red Lobster."

Kristen quirked her brow. "Of course you are. You always pick the expensive restaurants when I treat."

"Hey, you did say it's a celebration. How can you celebrate without seafood?"

The knots in her shoulders that weighed her down all morning finally lightened as they wrapped things up to a stopping point, then untied their aprons and prepared to leave. *Everything really was going to be okay. One way or another, life was getting back on track.*

Chapter FIVE

"So, hockey camp, huh?" Rachel asked, glancing over at her nephew, Jordan, who was practically bouncing on the passenger side of the car.

"It's gonna be so cool, Aunt Rachel! I can't wait to meet DG. He's the coolest! I have a list of moves I want him to teach me."

"I hope none of those moves involve body slams," she said, wincing at the thought of her nephew being shoved against the rink walls.

"They're called body checks, and no, we're not allowed to do that yet."

"Yet?" She repeated, pulling the car into the arena parking lot.

"Yeah. They make us wait until we're twelve before we can do any of the really fun stuff."

She gulped and tried not to give into the desire to turn the car around and take her nephew as far away from the camp as possible. "I don't suppose you'd rather come to the bakery with me today? I'll make anything you want."

"No way! Your cooking's awesome, Aunt Rachel, but there's no way I'd ever miss DG's camp."

"Not even for triple chocolate chunk cookies?" she asked, knowing they were Jordan's all-time favorite treat. He didn't even miss a beat before shaking his head and reaching for the car door. She sighed, exited the car and accompanied her nephew inside.

The arena lobby was full with kids of all ages. She dodged hockey sticks, hoping to make it to the registration table without getting a concussion.

"Name please?" asked the man behind the table. He was a bit taller than her with curly black hair and wore a long-sleeved hockey shirt with the DG Foundation logo across the chest.

"Jordan Marconi." She glanced over at her nephew, who appeared to be frozen in awe. She looked back to the man in front of her, not sure who he was, but assumed he must be important. She smiled. Oh, the emotions his little hero-worshipping heart must feel.

"Here's your packet. It has more details about the program each day, what skills Jordan's group will work on, and the game schedule for the last day of camp." The man handed her a thick manila envelope. "Now, if I could have you sign Jordan in here, Mrs. Marconi, then he can go meet his group."

She didn't bother to correct his assumption. It wasn't the first time she had taken a nephew somewhere and been mistaken for his mother. She leaned over and signed the form.

"Thank you," he said. "Don't forget pick-up is at 5:30." Then he looked down at her nephew. "See you on the ice." He winked. Rachel took hold of her still-frozen nephew's arm and pulled him off to the side where they could talk.

"Do you know who he was?"

"I have no clue," she said, smiling at Jordan's wonder.

"That was Amelio Masorti from the Kansas City Coyotes. He's one of the awesomest hockey players ever! Not as awesome as DG, but still . . . Wow! I can't believe he's here!"

"I'm glad you're excited. Now, listen, I have to go. Should we put this packet in your backpack? That way it won't get lost." He turned around so she could put the packet inside, then re-zip it. "Alright, buddy. I guess that's about it. Do me a favor and don't get hurt, okay?"

He rolled his eyes when she ruffled his hair.

"Okay." He shuffled his feet, anxious to get started.

"Have a great time. I'll see you tomorrow morning."

"Hey, there's Mike from my team. Bye!" Jordan said, then turned and hurried over to his friend. She shook her head, chuckling at her nephew's excitement, then turned to leave and start her work day.

Graydon blinked his eyes. Was that really Rachel from the restaurant? What was she doing at his hockey camp? And who was that kid she was with? Her son? He watched as she weaved through the crowd, making her way toward the door. He lost sight of her at one point, but then saw her appear again just before pushing through the arena doors.

"Graydon, did you hear what I said?"

He reluctantly turned his attention away from Rachel back to his PR manager, Sheila. "I'm sorry, I thought I saw someone I knew and got distracted."

She pushed her dark bangs out of her eyes, then smoothed out her DG Foundation shirt over her jeans which hugged her curvy Hispanic body. "Well, if it was someone here for camp, you'll see them again later."

Graydon felt a spark of hope. He'd have to figure out a way to see Rachel during pick up. Maybe even get a chance to talk to her.

"Now, let's get back to the schedule for today." Sheila consulted the clipboard in her hands. "Channel 5 and Fox News are coming at 3 pm to get footage of the kids practicing their skills. They both plan to interview you. Channel 5 will be first, while Fox News gets their footage shots. Then we'll swap."

"Good. Hopefully that will keep Tobyn and Lisa from sparring," he said, speaking of the two competitive sports anchors.

"I already gave the security team instructions to let me know when they arrive so I can set them up on opposite sides of the rink."

"It sounds like you have everything under control." He rested his hand on her shoulder. "Thanks for all your hard work, Sheila. I couldn't have put this camp together without your help."

A faint pink tinged her light brown cheeks. "You're welcome, Graydon."

He squeezed her shoulder, then let go. "I'm lucky to have such great friends working at the DG Foundation. I better head over to the rink and get everything started. I'll see you later this afternoon."

He nodded to Sheila, then turned in the direction of the rink. He thought about the speech he prepared for the camp attendees and reviewed the points he wanted to address before camp officially started. He also made a mental note to watch for the boy who came with Rachel. Maybe he could get an opportunity to talk with him and figure out a way to ask about her.

He walked to the box where his cousin, Zack, waited. When Graydon saw his hair, he couldn't help but laugh.

"I hope your new do isn't permanent or your mom is going to skin my hide." He picked up his skates from the bench, then sat and began the process of switching sneakers for skates.

Zack ran his hand through his shaggy light brown hair which was streaked with the Kansas City team colors. "Not to worry," he said. "They're some hair chalk thing. Laura came up with the idea. She thought the kids would like it. There's no way I want to spark Mom's wrath on my wedding day."

"Well, if it was Laura's idea, then you must be safe. You definitely landed a great girl there. Are you ready for Saturday?" He finished tying his skates and stood, testing the tightness around his ankles.

"Definitely." Zack handed him the microphone. "We'll have to talk more later. You ready to start this shindig?"

He nodded, then stepped out onto the ice. The voices of over one hundred kids echoed around him. Part of him was awed so many came to his camp. Each year the numbers got bigger and the kids weren't just from Kansas City, but from all around the country. He looked into the sea of faces and felt the weight of responsibility settle on his broad shoulders.

Hockey had always been something he loved. As a young kid, gliding onto the ice was like magic and the first time he picked up a hockey stick and pushed a puck around had been like coming home. While he dreamed of becoming a professional player someday, he didn't think he'd ever actually make the dream a reality until his high school team won the state title. Following that came college scholarships, which led to being scouted out by the pros.

While the money was nice, he felt a strong responsibility to be a good role model, especially for the younger fans dreaming of going pro as he did at their age. After he blew his knee out, he had been sad to leave the sport he loved so much, but another part was ready to move on. Working with kids and giving back to the community gave him an extra burst of energy to get out of bed each morning.

He held up his hand to quiet the chants of 'DG, DG, DG'. He raised the mic, ready to dive into camp. After welcoming the kids, laying out the house rules, and going over the schedule for the day, he released the participants to join their team coaches.

Graydon spent the morning working with the various junior camp kids who were in elementary school. Each group had been divided up by age, with the youngest kids learning better skate skills and basic hockey techniques up to the older kids who focused on more advanced play techniques. During their non-ice time, each group worked on team building activities, good sportsmanship and just some good old fun.

And he finally met the mystery boy. He discovered his name was Jordan Marconi and he played a mean game of hockey for a nine-year-old. Graydon enjoyed challenging him on the ice and gave him a few extra tips to polish his turns and puck control. He wasn't able to find out anything more about Rachel. He just couldn't figure out a good way to ask, "Hey, you know that woman you came to camp with? Is she your mom or what?" Even a nine-year-old would see through a question like that. No, he'd just have to wait until pick-up and hope for a chance to chat with her again.

He'd wondered about her ever since that night at Brisket and Noodles. He told himself it was because he'd worry about anyone in that kind of situation. But he couldn't explain why he spent more time thinking about how cute she looked when she was flustered or how she caught him off-guard. After the brief glimpse of her this morning, he admitted that if she really was single, he'd like to see her again, talk to her. Maybe explore if there was enough interest to ask her out on a date.

Who was he kidding? Of course he wanted to ask her out on a date.

But he was also confused. After saying how much she disliked violent sports, why would she let her son attend the camp? And why his camp? She didn't seem to know who he was that night, but was it just a ploy? It wouldn't be the first time a woman had been less than honest with him.

Similar thoughts swirled through his mind throughout the remainder of the day. He shoved them aside to concentrate on the TV interviews and working with the kids. But now that it was time to let the kids go for the day, he searched the stands for Jordan while Amelio gave the attendees some final instructions and thoughts for the night. He located the boy just before the kids were let loose to find their parents. Graydon left his place in the box and met Jordan partway up the stands.

"Hey, Jordan. Did you enjoy your first day of camp?" Graydon asked, walking beside him toward the lobby.

"It was awesome, Mr. Green. I worked real hard on how you told me to make my turns better."

"I noticed that. You've made a lot of improvement in just

one day. And hey, you can call me Graydon or DG, if you'd like."

"Really? That would be cool, but my parents say I should always call adults Mr. or Mrs. So I'll have to ask them. Hey! There's my dad!" Jordan hurried over to a tall, dark-haired man. Graydon pushed down the disappointment that it wasn't Rachel.

"Hi, I'm Graydon Green. You must be Jordan's father." They clasped hands. *Good grip*, he thought, then rested his hands on his hips.

"Adam Marconi," Jordan's father replied.

"Jordan is doing great with his hockey skills. I was very impressed with him today."

A huge smile spread across Adam's face. He ruffled Jordan's hair, similar to how Rachel had earlier, Graydon noticed. Then he pulled his son close to his side. "Really? Good job, buddy!"

"Camp was awesome! Mr. Green taught me a few tricks and I'm on the same team as Mike, too!"

Graydon needed to figure out how to ask about Rachel and had decided to ask straight out when Sheila appeared at his side.

"I'm sorry to interrupt, but you have a phone call and another interview to prepare for." She gave him an apologetic smile.

"Oh, okay. Well, I guess that means I better go. I'll see you tomorrow, Jordan. Will I see you at drop off, too?"

"No. Rachel will bring him in the morning, but I'll be here to pick him up after work."

"Great! I'll see you tomorrow then. It was nice to meet you, Adam."

"Let's go, buddy." Adam and Jordan turned and walked away, the father's arm draped over his son's shoulders.

Sheila touched his arm, pulling his attention back to her. "You can take the call in the office. I'll meet you in thirty minutes to drive you to the radio station for your interview there."

Graydon made his way back through the crowd to the office. He still didn't know how Rachel fit into Jordan's life, but he couldn't help plotting a way to meet up with her tomorrow.

Chapter SIX

*T*he next morning, Graydon was going over some last-minute details for the day's schedule with Zack and Sheila when drop-off began. The second day always had less confusion since the parents had been through the routine. Graydon had a clear view of the table where Jordan would check in.

"What time do you need to leave to get ready for your wedding rehearsal tonight, Zack?"

Sheila's question broke through his search. "That's right. Tonight's the family dinner, isn't it?"

Zack landed a hard punch on his upper arm. "That better not be a surprise, cuz. The dinner is at your restaurant."

"I didn't forget, and don't worry, our chef is ready to ooh and ahh your future in-laws. Chef Mike has all the decorating and set up well in hand . . ." He trailed off when he saw a flash of red hair back toward the entry doors. He lifted onto his toes to try to get a better view.

"What are you looking for?" Sheila asked, looking out at the sea of kids.

"More like *who* is he looking for," Zack replied.

"Who? What do you mean?" She looked between the two men.

Graydon got a good view of Rachel and Jordan, then stepped away from Zack and Sheila. "I'll be right back." He dodged through kids, saying brief hellos as he made his way over to where they stood in line.

"Hey, Jordan. Are you ready for another day at camp?" Graydon heard the happiness in Jordan's voice, but his attention was glued to Rachel. She looked up and he saw her clear green eyes widen in genuine surprise.

"I've been practicing the moves in my head, like my coach talked about, and practiced on roller blades in my driveway most of last night. I can't wait to show you." Jordan replied. "Is it okay to head over to the rink now?"

"Sure," he said, still not breaking eye contact with her. "I'll see you over there in a little bit."

"Great. Bye!" Jordan said as he hurried off.

She blinked, then turned to Jordan. "Be careful!"

"I will," he called back, making his way quickly through the crowd.

Rachel turned back to Graydon. He could tell she was still flustered by the way she fidgeted with her purse. The line had moved forward, but she hadn't noticed.

"Hi, Rachel. How are you?" He loved the way her eyebrows and forehead crinkled, like she was still trying to figure something out. Then he had a horrible thought. *What if she doesn't remember who I am?* His heart sped up, thudding against his chest.

"Hello again, Graydon," she finally responded.

Tremendous relief coursed through him. *She does remember me.* He grinned, then gestured toward the line.

"Oh!" She stepped forward, then glanced up at him. "What are you doing here?" Her face turned red. It was like it caught on fire and almost matched her hair, reminding him of that day in the office.

"I'm here with the hockey camp. How about you?"

"I'm just dropping off Jordan. Not that I want to. I think his dad is nuts for letting him play hockey, but he won't listen to me. But apparently you really like hockey. At least I remember there were lots of pictures in your office and you did say you're a fan." She moved forward again and he stayed with her. "I'm sorry. I'm rambling. I'm just so surprised to see you. So, um, are you here to help the camp? Catering from your restaurant?"

"Something like that." Graydon reasoned it wasn't *technically* a lie. The restaurant was providing the daily lunches. It just wasn't his primary role.

"Oh. Well. Jordan's been super excited about the hockey camp. All he's been able to talk about is meeting this DG guy. It's been DG this and DG that all the way here. I thought DG was like some kind of company or team initials or something. But apparently it's the guy's actual name and really, what kind of ridiculous name is DG? Sounds like some kind of rapper wanna-be." She finally reached the sign-in table and stopped talking long enough to sign the form in front of her.

The sweet scent of vanilla wafted around him, reminding him of warmth. He couldn't keep the smile off his face. She was a gem, but if her red hair was any indication, she wasn't going to be happy if he didn't come clean about who DG really was. She finished the sign-in, then stepped out of line next to him.

"Rachel—" he began, but was interrupted by Sheila.

"Graydon, Amelio needs to talk to you."

He wanted to tell her to go away, but couldn't be rude to her like that. Now, if it was one of the guys that would be different. Still, she had rotten timing. "I'll be there in a few minutes."

"He said it's important. Something about wanting to change today's schedule."

"Listen," Rachel said. "I need to get to work. It was nice to see you again, Graydon." She turned to leave.

"Wait, Rachel—" He started after her.

"Graydon!" Sheila called.

"Just a minute." He half turned toward Sheila, then turned back around in time to see Rachel push through the doors and leave the arena.

Dang it! Frustrated, he shoved his clenched hands into his pockets. He didn't even get a chance to really talk to her. He didn't know if she was Jordan's mom or get answers to any of the other million questions he wanted to ask. He was trapped between a conflicting desire to run after her and probably freak her out; or stomp his foot, although it definitely wouldn't be good to act like a two-year-old in front of camp kids. Instead, he took a deep breath and released it before turning to face Sheila again. *Calm,* he reminded himself.

"Did you say Amelio needed me?" He tried to keep the frustration out of his voice.

She looked slightly wide-eyed, but recovered quickly. "Yes. He's waiting for you down on the ice."

He took one last look toward the doors. He'd see Rachel again tomorrow. Just focus on today. He turned and started down to the rink. Yes, the ice was the perfect place for him to be right now. It always made everything better, put things into perspective when he glided across the smooth, frigid surface.

Zack was waiting for him in the box with his skates. "So, who was the hot chick you were talking to?"

He glared at him. It didn't seem to bother Zack though.

"You're getting married tomorrow, remember? You're not supposed to notice other women."

"What? Do I look dead to you? Just 'cause I'm getting married doesn't mean I don't know what other women look like. It just means I don't ogle and follow them around like a puppy anymore."

"Does Laura know you think that?" he asked, pulling the lace strings tight.

His cousin fidgeted from side to side. "Ah, no. And you don't need to enlighten her either."

Graydon finished tying his laces, then stood to test out his skates.

"You know, she looked familiar." Zack said, a thoughtful expression on his face.

"What?" He was ready to pounce on any information Zack might have about this woman who was the main preoccupation of his thoughts lately.

"I'm not sure. She just looked like someone I've seen before." Zack looked out at the rink. "You better go. Amelio is waving you over."

Graydon looked into the rink where Amelio stood with the master clipboard and microphone, then into the stands at the kids waiting to begin. He couldn't let them down. "You and I need to talk more later." He pushed all his thoughts and questions to the side, then stepped onto the ice, forcing himself to concentrate on the day ahead.

Rachel eased her aching body onto the couch. It had been a long day, but she finished all the pastries for the Knowlton-Partridge wedding the next day. The cake was baked and cooled. Once the portable pastry case was packed tomorrow, she would spend the rest of the day frosting and decorating the wedding cake for the evening reception.

Wanting to take her mind off work for the rest of the evening, she picked up the remote and scrolled through the movies on her DVR, searching for a good comedy. After about a dozen pages filled with either pointless plots or sexual innuendos, she finally found a funny chick flick. *Can't go wrong with Sandra Bullock,* she thought, pressing the rent button on her remote.

"Now for dinner. What shall it be tonight—pizza or Chinese?"

She walked into her kitchen and went through the stack of take-out menus hidden under her kitchen towels. After placing her order for a Meat Trio pizza, she tucked the menus back in place. She never knew when her mother might stop by. It was best to avoid her mother's lecture about what a waste culinary school was if her daughter couldn't cook her own dinners. Her mother didn't understand that after cooking all day for other people, sometimes—okay more often than sometimes—she didn't have the desire to pull out a skillet and cook when she got home.

She settled back onto the couch and was only fifteen minutes into the movie when the phone rang. She tensed, hoping it wasn't Nico again. She had been deleting messages all week long. She relaxed when she saw her brother's name and cell number on the caller ID.

"Hi, Adam," she answered. "What's up?" As much as she loved her brother, it was usually his wife who called. Figuring their conversation would be short, she left the movie playing.

"Hey, sis. I heard from Jordan that you got to meet 'The Man' today at drop off. I just wanted to see what was up. You know, what he said about Jordan?"

"Who?" she asked, thoroughly confused.

"The Man. DG – the head of the hockey camp. You know, the guy whose name is on all the t-shirts." Her brother laughed on the other end of the phone line.

Yeah, ha ha, Adam. Like I can't read. She rolled her eyes. "Adam, I have absolutely no idea who you're talking about. Jordan must be confused. I was talking with someone, but he wasn't this DG guy. He's the manager or something over at Brisket and Noodles. And his name's not DG. It's Graydon."

"Graydon Green?"

"Yeah," she replied, surprised her brother knew Graydon's last name. "Do you know him?"

"Rachel, Graydon Green *is* DG."

"What?" She sat up, sending the remote clattering to the floor. She scrambled to find it, then hit the pause button, certain she couldn't possibly have heard him right. It almost sounded like Adam just said that Graydon Green—the guy who rescued her that horrible night with Nico—was this DG hockey player guy. That just couldn't be. Could it?

"Sheesh, sis, what rock have you been living under? DG stands for Double G, as in Graydon Green. The commentators got tired of getting tongue twisted, so they nicknamed him DG. I can't believe you didn't know who he was! So tell me, what did he say?"

Her head felt like it was swirling. This just could not be happening.

"You still there?"

She shook her head to clear it, then replied, "Um, yeah. He really didn't say anything about Jordan, other than saying hello to him and me. Then Jordan ran off to meet up with his team."

Ding dong. She had never been more grateful for a speedy delivery.

"Listen, Adam, my pizza just got here, so I have to go."

She quickly got off the phone, grabbed some money from her wallet and opened the door. The delivery man left with a big smile on his face and with what she assumed was probably a huge tip.

She set the pizza box on the coffee table and flopped onto her couch, trying to absorb what she had just learned. Graydon Green, aka DG. A famous hockey player. *Former* hockey player, she amended. Then she thought back on their conversations from the night at the restaurant and this morning. Her face flooded with warmth as she remembered all her comments.

Personally, I think hockey's too violent.

Yeah, Rachel, and he's probably the guy who does the body slamming—oh sorry, body checking. Just the thought of bodies crunching on the cold, hard wall made her cringe.

Has anyone ever said you look like that guy from the movie The Pacifier?

She groaned. No wonder he laughed so hard. He probably got a real kick out of that one. For all she knew, he actually knows Vin Diesel and called him up to tell him about the nut case who just left his office.

What kind of ridiculous name is DG? Sounds like some kind of rapper wanna-be.

Yep. The pièce de résistance. She totally dissed the guy's professional name. Right to his face. Was he shocked or did he think it was funny that the little naive chick didn't know who he was?

She dropped her head into her hands. Why couldn't the earth open up and swallow her? She could only imagine what a complete and utter idiot she must have sounded like. Why didn't he say something? Was he some rich guy who thought it was funny to see what the village idiot would say next?

Frustrated and annoyed, she sat up and opened the pizza box lid. She was stressed and her coping method for stress was food, either cooking, baking or eating. It didn't matter, because they all worked wonders on her poor, tortured, humiliated soul.

After seeing Graydon again this morning, she had considered stopping by his restaurant to say hello. But now, she was *never* going back to Brisket and Noodles. And since she was done with hockey camp drop-offs, she didn't have to worry about looking like a fool in front of him ever again.

Mr. Graydon Green, who she mistakenly thought was a good guy, was nothing but a class A jerk, who apparently found other ways to hurt people now that he was retired from the ice.

She bit into the cheesy meat combo, switched her chick flick out for a popular action film, and vowed she was finished with men. Kaput. At least for the next thirty years. Maybe when she hit her sixties, she'd find some nice widower to date. Until then, bah humbug on men!

Chapter SEVEN

"Congratulations, Zack," Graydon said as he shook his cousin's hand. The cacophony of noises from the guests surrounded them in the reception center. Graydon turned to Zack's new bride and pulled her into a hug. "And you, Laura, have my most sincere sympathies."

"Hey!" Zack pretended to be offended.

Graydon pulled back from the hug and admired the glow of happiness radiating from her eyes. "You look absolutely beautiful. Zack is a lucky man. Now remember what I told you at the wedding. If he doesn't keep you happy, just give me a call."

"I'll do that. I'm sure he'll need some sense knocked into him occasionally." Her eyes crinkled with laughter as Zack pulled her out of Graydon's arms.

"Honey, you don't need any help in that department. You do just fine on your own. See you out on the dance floor, cuz." Zack grinned and slapped Graydon on the shoulder, then moved away. He noticed they didn't make it very far before another well-wisher stopped them.

"Hey, Gray," said a chirpy voice behind him.

He rolled his eyes before turning to face his teenage cousin. "Hey, Chloe. Did you enjoy the wedding?"

"It was, like, awesome. Don't you just love the bridesmaid dresses? I love the chocolate and pink theme.

And, like, Zack's friend Mike looks so hot in his tux. I'm glad he was my escort for the wedding instead of TJ, cause, like, TJ's girlfriend is totally giving Marina the evil eye, which is totally unfair, cause you know it was so not Marina who got to choose which groomsman she got paired up with. Some people are just so lame. Don't ya think?" *Chomp, chomp, smack.*

He nodded and tried to keep up with Chloe as she continued talking ninety miles an hour and snapping her gum. He liked Chloe when she was little. She was quite the chatterbox, making him laugh at silly things she said, but once she hit her teenage years, she went from chatterbox to speed demon talker. She could probably out talk an auctioneer and make about as much sense, too. After a few minutes, trying to keep up gave him a headache.

"Oh hey, the music's starting!" Chloe bounced beside him. *Chomp, chomp, smack.*

He hoped that meant she was going to join the crowd of people gathering out on the dance floor, but he wasn't that lucky.

"So, like, do you think they'll play the Macarena? And hey, did you know that song is about a cockroach? Seriously, why would anyone write a song about something so disgusting? But, like, the line dance is fun, so I guess that makes up for it."

"How's school?" He broke in, not even bothering to correct her and hoping to change the subject before she started going off about The Chicken Dance.

Chomp, chomp, smack. "Ugh! I had no idea being a sophomore would be so freakin' hard! I totally hate Advanced Algebra. I have no idea why the teachers think we have to know all that stuff, cause, like, everyone says you never use it after you graduate. It's such a waste of my time. But I totally love . . ."

He listened as Chloe continued talking about homework, her new friends, and how nasty the lunches were. As he listened with half of one ear, he looked around the reception. He spotted his grandmother seated at a table with his parents and siblings. He made a mental note to work his way over there as soon as he finished talking with Chloe, which would hopefully be sometime in the next millennium.

"So, like, have you checked out the food yet?" She broke into his thoughts. "There's tons of it! Fruit, sandwiches, and the best-ever desserts."

His stomach rumbled. "You know, Chloe, that actually sounds pretty good. Maybe I'll head over there."

"Okay! I'll come with you." Her chatter continued, although she changed the subject to getting her drivers permit in a few weeks. *Dear God, save us all.* He made another mental note to talk to Aunt Sarah about which cars would be safest to buy for Chloe. Just when the food buffet finally came into view, Graydon froze in his tracks.

Right across the room was Rachel Marconi. He had looked for her this morning at hockey camp, but Jordan's dad had dropped him off. He thought about her on and off all day, wondering if he'd see her again. He even debated about searching for her phone number online, but now here she was behind the buffet table, arranging desserts.

Chomp, chomp, smack. Chloe bumped into Graydon. "Oh hey, look, there's Rachel," she said.

He snapped his head around to look at his flighty cousin. "You know her?"

"Well, duh. Of course I know her. She taught my culinary arts club all about cake design and decorating."

Graydon couldn't wrap his mind around the fact that 1—Chloe knew the mysterious Rachel, and 2—Chloe was in a culinary arts club. He didn't think she was interested in cooking. He made yet another mental note to ask more about that. Pretty soon he was going to need to get out his Phone to keep track of everything. More importantly, back to picking her brain about Rachel, which really wasn't that difficult since she just kept on talking anyway.

"She's, like, the best cake designer ever. I totally kept telling Laura over and over again to check out Sweet Confections. And when she and Zack finally did, they were, like, wow! And I was, like, I told you so!"

So that's why Zack thought she looked familiar. Then he smirked. He knew just how to get the information he needed.

"Yeah," he said, "Zack mentioned he knew her and that she has a kid who plays hockey."

"What? Rachel so totally doesn't have kids. She's not even married. Zack's such a dork. My friend, Emily, babysits for Rachel's brother, Adam. And, like, she says their three boys are cute, but they can be such twerps, too. Which is why I so totally don't babysit. That and it just doesn't pay enough money for all the hassle you have to deal with."

Tweet, tweet.

"Oh hey, that's my cell." Chloe pulled out her phone, but where she'd been hiding it, Graydon had no clue. "Sweet! It's Brianna. Talk to you later, Gray." She walked away, her thumbs moving just as fast as—and quite possibly faster—than she could talk. Graydon shook his head, then refocused his attention on the dessert bar.

His gut clenched with anticipation as he approached the table. Rachel had her back turned, talking with another woman. While he waited, he took a moment to take in everything about her—from her auburn hair twisted up with one of those funky claw clippy things his sisters liked to how appealing her curvy figure looked in the pink shirt and black pants. He wondered if she still smelled like vanilla. About the time a goofy grin spread across his face, she turned back to the table and saw him.

Another look of surprise crossed her face, but then she turned away from him. Before she could walk away, he said, "Hi, Rachel. I missed you at hockey camp drop off today."

She paused. For a second, he thought she might ignore him, but instead she slowly turned and approached with a wide, friendly smile.

"Good evening, Mr. Green," she said, tilting her head to the side. "Oh, I'm sorry, should I call you DG? That is your name, right?"

Uh oh. Busted. "Yeah, about that, I was going to—"

"No worries," she waved her hand as if swatting away a fly. "After all, a famous hockey player like yourself couldn't possibly be expected to remember his own name. You've probably taken one too many hits to the head. You should consider seeing a doctor about that."

"Let me ex—"

She once again cut him off. "You must be hungry. I'm sure skating around with a bunch of kids has worked up quite the appetite. Have you ever tried a mini-chocolate swirled cheesecake with fudge cracker graham crust, DG?"

"Um, no," he replied a bit nervously.

She picked a cheesecake up then turned it around, admiring it from all angles. "That's a shame. Here, this one is perfect. Just for you." She extended the small cake toward him, then grasped his hand, and put the cheesecake in his palm. Only it was topside down and she smooshed it in circles until cheesecake filling oozed between his fingers. She slid her hand out of his, then smiled. "Enjoy."

"Rachel!" said another woman wearing a Sweet Confections pink shirt. "What—"

But she turned and walked past the two other servers, then through a doorway leading to what Graydon supposed was the kitchen.

"I'm so sorry," said the woman in front of him. Her name tag read Kristen. "Let me help you clean that up."

"If I could just get a napkin?"

She dashed away and he looked back to the doorway Rachel had disappeared through. Once he cleaned off his hand, he assured the fluttery and embarrassed Kristen that he was fine. Then he walked around the buffet table, past the gaping employees, and through the doorway, intent on finding Rachel and clearing up this misunderstanding.

And maybe, he thought, with a smile on his lips, *even convince her to go out on a date.*

Chapter EIGHT

*R*achel rushed past the servers in the kitchen, slammed her hands against the exit door bar, and burst into the alley. She turned to look at the door as it banged shut behind her and realized Kristen had the caterer key, which meant she was locked outside. The anger that was already brewing inside reached a boiling point. She kicked the door. It felt so good, she turned and kicked the dumpster beside her a few times. The sheer physical impact sent jarring vibrations up her legs.

"Stupid, stupid, stupid, Rachel." She leaned against the brick wall and rubbed her eyes with the heels of her hands. Just breathe. She sucked in the cool night air. In and out. She tried to calm down. Tried, but couldn't dissipate the frustrated feelings within her.

So, Mr. Famous Hockey Player missed her during drop off today, huh? And of course he was 'going to tell her' who he really was. What else did she expect him to say once he knew the game was over? Well, at least that was the last she'd ever see of the jerk.

She closed her eyes and leaned her head back. The exit door opened and shut with a quiet click.

"I don't want to talk about it, Kristen," she said, without opening her eyes. She heard feet shuffle and step toward her.

"Then it's a good thing I'm not Kristen."

Her eyes popped open. Graydon stood just across from her. His expression was difficult to read, but she could only imagine he must be furious. She should apologize. He's a guest of their clients after all, but man, she didn't want to. Instead of feeling contrite, she wanted to lash out.

"What's the matter? Need another sample of cheesecake?" she asked sweetly, ready to start a word spar.

"Why? Do you have more stashed out here?" He looked around the alley.

She rolled her eyes. He was all show and no real substance. "Not unless it's in the dumpster."

"Well, that's too bad. I didn't get a chance to taste the last one." He stepped closer, making her flatten her back against the brick wall. He shoved his hands in his pockets, then leaned his shoulder against the brick wall beside her. "How about we talk and straighten out some things."

She folded her arms in front of her, determined not to give in. The heat radiating from his body crowded her. "Talk then."

"You know, for someone who says she doesn't like violence, you sure seem to hit and break things a lot."

"What can I say? Liars bring out the worst in me."

He shifted so he was also leaning his back against the brick wall. "I don't know what actually happened between you and that guy at the restaurant, but I'm sorry I didn't get a chance to tell you that I'm not just Graydon Green."

She jolted in surprise. Of all the things she expected to come out of his mouth—annoyance about the cheesecake or excuses about why he didn't tell her who he was—an apology was not one of them.

He took a deep breath, then continued. "That first night we met, you intrigued me."

"Really? Which part did you like best—when I was humiliated in front of the entire restaurant or when I thought you looked like Vin Diesel?"

"Actually, it was your feelings about hockey and football."

He really had taken one too many hits to the head. A professional hockey player—albeit retired—just implied he liked that she thought hockey was too violent. She took a few steps away, then turned to face him. It should be illegal for jerks to look so good, she thought, taking in the way his tux fit his tall, very fit and fabulous body. She blinked away the distraction and focused on the topic at hand. "Why didn't you tell me who you really were?"

For the first time since their conversation began, he looked away. A stab of something grabbed at her stomach. She craned her head, meeting his brown eyes again.

"I am Graydon Green. I never lied about that. The other —being DG—comes with mixed reactions. When I first went pro, I loved the attention, pictures splashed across the sports sections, everyone who wanted to be around me. It took a few years, but eventually I realized all those people weren't necessarily my friends. I've had a few relationships that ended up being more about the spotlight than actual interest in the real me. Since then, I've been . . ." He paused for a brief moment. "Cautious would be the best word, I guess."

She understood caution. Since the breakup with Nico, she wondered how she'd know if some guy was being honest or feeding her his best line. If she could be fooled once, it could happen again. She looked toward the end of the alley, not wanting to get too caught up in his story. Just because he had a sorry sap story didn't mean she had to forgive him.

He shrugged and captured her gaze. "I liked that you

didn't know who I was. You didn't try to make yourself look good or dole out compliments to pump me up."

She was caught off guard when he stepped forward and tucked a piece of hair that had fallen out of her clip back behind her ear. It was such a gentle touch, but the effect was anything but sweet. Tingles sparked a pull of . . . something she didn't want to define. He dropped his hand and the warmth that flowed between them suddenly cooled. She shivered and rubbed her arm, at the same time pulling her shield back in place. "That's a nice little story you have there, DG, but you still haven't answered my question."

Surprise crossed his face. He stepped back again, putting more distance between them. The openness that had been on his face now shuttered closed.

"I *was* going to tell you, but my assistant interrupted me. Then you left before I could stop you. Besides, I didn't know if you had orchestrated the whole thing."

"What thing?" she shot back, defensive.

"I saw you that first day. After everything you said about violent sports, I couldn't understand why you would bring a child—who I thought was your son—to a hockey camp. And not just any camp, but *my* camp."

"You thought Jordan was my son?"

"You both have the same last name and no one ever said you weren't his mom. Believe me, I tried to find out."

She was curious and a bit flattered. No, she corrected herself. She wouldn't let herself be pulled into another web of lies.

"I thought maybe you would pick up Jordan at the end of the day and I'd get a chance to talk to you. But his dad showed up instead. He never said if you were his wife, ex-wife, girlfriend or what. But he did say you'd drop Jordan off the next morning." He folded his arms. "So, I waited for you to show up. I wanted to see your reaction when we met up again."

A lump formed in her throat. "And?"

"You seemed genuinely surprised to see me. It eased some of my doubts. I hoped you'd drop Jordan off again this morning, so we could talk. Maybe see what happened after that. So, who's Adam?"

After what? There could be no after. "He's my brother. I was just helping out for a few days."

The back door swung open and Kristen stepped out. She looked back and forth between the two of them. "Rachel, we could really use some help inside again. They're getting ready to cut the cake in about fifteen minutes."

"I'll be right there." She smiled weakly, sending a silent apology to her friend. She owed Kristen a huge explanation, which she would get as soon as the event was over.

Kristen nodded, turned and went back inside.

Graydon moved closer to her. "Listen, we both need to get back, but I'd like to get together. Maybe have dinner and talk, figure things out without any additional interruptions or misunderstandings."

Exhaustion washed away the anger. "There's a part of me that would like to, but a bigger part of me is still tied in knots about, well, everything that's happened these last few weeks. This just isn't a good time for me."

Wow. Did she really give him the ultimate cop-out line ever?

"What if we got together as friends? Get to know each other better. I won't even try to steal a kiss, no matter how tempted I may be."

His smile was devilish. She chewed on her bottom lip,

debating the possibilities. Finally she shook her head. "Being friends is great, but I just don't have the energy to put in anything more. I need to focus on my own life and goals right now."

He slowly nodded. "I understand. Friends, though?"

She grasped his extended hand and they shook on it. "Friends. Now let's get back inside."

Kristen had lodged a cardboard box between the door and jam. Graydon pulled the door open and together they entered the kitchen. She ignored the inquisitive looks from the staff. They stopped near the doorway to the reception room.

"One last thing, if you change your mind about getting together, call me. No pressure." He squeezed her hand, then returned to the reception. He joined a group at the family table and she realized he wasn't just a guest, he was part of the wedding party's family.

Uh oh. Not good. She looked over at the buffet tables and saw Sarah Partridge, the groom's mother, heading her way with a silver haired older lady just behind her. *I am so screwed.*

She pasted a smile on her face, ready to suck up. "Mrs. Partridge, hello! Your son and daughter-in-law look just gorgeous together. Congratulations."

"Don't try to distract me, missy." Mrs. Partridge's cheeks were flushed. "Whatever possessed you to pull such a horrible stunt with my nephew?"

"I'm sor—" She didn't even get two words out before Mrs. Partridge interrupted.

"Absolutely disgraceful! I expected professionalism from such a highly recommended bakery."

"Oh, shush, Sarah." The silver-haired woman elbowed Mrs. Partridge, then shook hands with Rachel. "I'm Ellen

Partridge, Graydon's grandmother. Now, don't you let Sarah fluster you, sweetheart."

She was caught between Graydon's grandmother and his sputtering aunt. How did she get herself into these situations? Oh yeah. Men.

Ellen leaned closer. "It's actually rather nice to see someone deflate his fat head."

"Mother!" Sarah's hand covered her mouth, eyes wide.

Ellen turned toward her daughter. "Just relax, Sarah. Graydon's a big boy and can take care of himself. Now, go enjoy your son's wedding reception." She winked before she herded Mrs. Partridge away. Rachel looked past them and saw Graydon not far away, watching the interaction. He smiled, nodded, then returned his attention to his family. She narrowed her eyes, still not sure what to think about Graydon and his offer of friendship. Then again, maybe it was an empty offer since she refused to go on a date. Maybe it's his way of smoothing over the rejection. 'Let's be friends' had a lot of different connotations. Feeling better about things, she shifted her thoughts to Sweet Confections and prepared for the bride and groom to cut the cake.

Rachel was grateful for all the extra hands they hired for the evening. Break down and clean up took a lot of work.

While boxing things up, she mulled over the glimpses of Graydon she saw this evening.

The comfortable Graydon visiting his family, dancing with his grandmother, and teasing some of the teenagers. There was another side she thought of as his professional side. What he told her about reactions didn't just apply to twitter-pated chicks, but to all his admirers. There were the awe-struck fans nervous to meet him, shake his hand and ask for his autograph. Then there were people who tried to act cool, as if talking with a celebrity was something they did every day. And finally, the boastful, macho guys bragging about their glory days, most likely from high school based on their current physiques.

She felt a whole new level of empathy—no, sympathy would be a better word. She really did pity him for how difficult it must be to lead two conflicting lives. She understood why he hesitated to tell her he was also DG. Which was different from Nico, who deliberately lied to her so she would date him.

Kristen came to stand next to her as she boxed up the last dessert stand. "I think this is it," she said. "I told the extras they could pack up and head home. They'll stop in on Wednesday for their paychecks."

"Sounds good." Rachel folded the box top closed. "I have some grapes and sandwiches in the cooler. Are you ready for dinner?"

It had become tradition that at the end of long events, the two women ate a second light dinner. They were silent as they put together their sandwiches. Her shoulders were tense while she waited for Kristen to say something about what happened with Graydon. Finally, she decided to jump in.

"Sorry about what happened tonight." She picked the bread crust off her sandwich.

Kristen cocked her head to the side. "What did happen? I've never seen you act that way toward a guest before."

"Remember the guy who helped me the night Nico and I broke up?"

"The restaurant guy? The one you found out is actually a hockey player?"

Rachel quirked her eyebrow and continued looking at Kristen, who abruptly leaned forward.

Kristen's eyes widened. "You mean *that* was him?"

Rachel nodded, then took a bite of her sandwich.

"That big buff hunk of man is . . ." her voice trailed off.

"The guy who rescued me and lied to me all at the same time? Yeah." She took another bite, munching while Kristen continued to process the situation.

"I was worried when he followed you outside. I kept my head close to the door just in case you yelled for help."

"You were listening?" Rachel's question came out squeaky.

"I couldn't actually hear what you were saying. Just the mumble of your voices. But I figured it was enough that if you started yelling for help, I could jump out and karate kick him."

"Kristen, the guy is huge. I doubt a karate kick would take him down."

"Unless it was well placed in a certain sensitive spot," she replied and winked.

"Oh my." Rachel shook her head. "I love you, you know that right?"

"Yep. Which is why I didn't follow him out there and kick

your butt right along with him. Really, I could not believe it when you smeared whatever it was all over him."

"Cheesecake and I only smashed it into his hand. Be grateful it wasn't his face."

Kristen almost choked on a grape. "Now there's a great visual. What happened outside?" Kristen listened attentively while she spilled all the details. "So when are you going to call him?"

"What do you mean?" Rachel brushed some crumbs off her pants.

"You are going out with him, aren't you?"

"I don't think so. I'm still topsy turvy about all the other drama. Nico's still calling and leaving messages on my voicemail constantly. Between dealing with that and running the shop, I don't know if I have any additional energy to devote to anything or anyone else."

"Whoa, first of all, why didn't you tell me Nico was still calling you? We can get a restraining order, you know. Make it official."

Rachel shook her head. "I don't want to do that. He'll give up eventually. He has to at some point. Until then, the delete button will be my friend."

Kristen pushed her brown hair behind her ear. "Fine. I'll let you wait for now. But if he doesn't stop soon, I'm going to convince you to do more. Second, I think you should call Graydon." She put her hand up. "Just hear me out. It's been painful to watch you deal with all the Nico crap, but you can't dig a hole and hibernate. Why don't you give the guy a chance? Just go out to talk and get to know each other. He's asking you to dinner, not to hop the next flight to Vegas."

Rachel started to interrupt, but Kristen reached over and squeezed her shoulder. "Just think about it."

Chapter NINE

he shop doorbell chimed when Graydon entered
Sweet Confections. It had been two weeks since
Zack's wedding and the conversation with Rachel in the back
alley. She said she wanted to be just friends, but as he
continued to get to know her, the desire for more than that
grew.

"Back again, I see," Kristen was behind the counter,
packaging up cupcakes for a customer.

"I just can't stay away from all the sweets," he teased
with a wink.

During his past four visits, Graydon found an ally in
Rachel's best friend. She helped coax Rachel into
conversations, and bit by bit, her meddling paid off.

So far, they covered all the basics—who grew up where,
family size, jobs, schooling—and moved on to more fun,
quirky subjects, such as weirdest themed Harley motorcycles
they've seen. Rachel won with a story about a Mickey and
Minnie themed bike by a Harley/Disney fan. He doubted her
until she pulled a picture of it up on her cell phone. It was a
bit blurry but definitely a Disney-themed Harley. At least it
wasn't a bunch of princesses. He shuddered in horror at the
thought.

When the customer left, Kristen leaned over and rested

her elbows on the counter. "Looking for anything, or should I say anyone, in particular?"

He grinned, then rested his hip against the edge near the register. "So, best friend, what do you think my chances are of getting a yes if I ask Rachel out for dinner?"

"Yes!" Kristen exclaimed, pumping her fist into the air. Graydon grinned at her reaction. "Well, not actually a yes to you," she went on. "But I'll work on her." Kristen waggled her eyebrows.

Graydon laughed heartily and soon Rachel came through the swinging doors leading to the kitchen. Her red hair was clipped up as usual, but a few tendrils had escaped and caressed her cheek. He wished he could reach out and tuck it behind her ears. Maybe trail his fingers down her throat to see if her skin was as soft as it looked.

Patience, he thought.

"I thought I heard you," she said, eyeing the two of them suspiciously. Then she focused in on Kristen. "What devious plans are you trying to cook up this time?"

"Me? Devious?" Kristen replied, placing her hand on her chest with the most angelic expression on her face. She backed up to toward the kitchen. "But you are right. I need to get back to cooking something. Nice to see you again, Graydon." She winked then disappeared into the kitchen.

Rachel turned to face him, tapping her finger on her chin. "I don't know if I trust you two."

He folded his arms and played along. "I'd say go with your instincts."

She crossed over to the counter, tilted her head, looking into his eyes for a brief moment. Her green eyes sparkled with mischief. "My instincts say you're going to purchase quite a few treats today."

God, he loved her sense of humor. He rubbed his hands together. "Well, let's see today's choices."

She led him down the display case, describing each of the delectable treats inside. He chose a dozen almond-lemon shortbread cookies and a half dozen flaky apple turnovers drizzled with caramel sauce.

"So, what's today's trivia going to be?" she asked when she finished ringing him up.

"No trivia today. I need to get back to the office." He couldn't help but feel elated at her disappointed look. "But I do have a question."

She smiled. "Just one?"

He nodded. "Just one. Would you have dinner with me this week?"

Her eyes widened and her mouth made an 'oh' shape. Surely this wasn't that much of a surprise. She had to know how he felt about her—right?

She tucked the stray bit of hair behind her ear, avoiding his gaze. "Um, listen, Graydon—"

He tucked his finger beneath her chin and brought her gaze up to meet his. "It's just food and conversation, Rachel. Nothing to be afraid of." She sucked in her bottom lip and nibbled on it. He swallowed his desire to share the nibbling and used his thumb to release the lip from her teeth. "Just think about it, okay?"

She nodded, then stepped back. "Thanks for coming in."

He knew a dismissal when he heard one. But he wasn't discouraged. She just needed time—and her best friend to nudge her along. "Thanks for the goodies," he said, lifting the bag off the counter. He wished her a good day, then left. He looked back over his shoulder after the door closed and saw her watching him go, once again chewing on her bottom lip. Kristen came out of the kitchen, drawing Rachel's attention away from him.

He smiled. Let the meddling begin.

"Just think about it," Rachel mocked. For the last week, Graydon was all she thought about. She went back and forth. Should she call him or not? Gack! The pull between yes and no was excruciating. After burning two batches of peanut butter chocolate chunk cookies, Kristen shooed her out of the kitchen with strict orders not to return until she made the phone call.

She grabbed her cell and went out into the parking lot. She paced back and forth in front of her car, then leaned against it. *My hands are a sweaty mess.* She wiped them on her pants, then activated the phone.

It shouldn't be so hard to push seven little numbers. She hesitated with her thumb poised over the last button. Finally she pushed it. Her hand trembled as she put the phone to her ear. She waited, but nothing happened. Did she dial wrong? She pulled the phone away from her ear to look at the display, only to realize she had not pushed the send button. A nervous giggle bubbled up as she tapped the final button, then jumped slightly when the line began to ring.

Calm down, Rachel. You're making a phone call, you ninny.

"Good afternoon, Brisket and Noodles. This is Max. How may I help you?"

"Um, hi. Is Mr. Green—I mean, Graydon—available?"

"May I ask who's calling please?"

"This is Rachel Marconi."

"One moment, please."

A classic Springsteen song filled the line. Her chest tightened in anticipation. She pressed a hand to her stomach to suppress the flutters that made her midsection all tingly.

"Hello, Rachel? I hoped I'd hear from you."

Just hearing his voice soothed away her worries. She smiled, confident she had made the right decision. "Hi," she squeaked. She cleared her throat and tried again, hoping to sound normal this time. "Hi, Graydon. Well, to be honest, I didn't have much choice. Kristen kicked me out of the kitchen for burning my second batch of cookies. I guess I've been too distracted to be much use."

He chuckled on the other end. "I hope thinking about getting together was the reason for your distraction."

"Just a little," she replied, feeling lighthearted. Wow. What a difference from thirty seconds ago. "So, is dinner still an option?"

"Would tonight be too soon to get together? I'm scheduled to be here for the next four nights."

She considered her schedule for a few seconds. "That should work. Usually later in the week I spend more hours at the bakery to get the weekend orders and events ready. So tonight would probably be best for me too."

"Great! How about if I pick you up around six-thirty?"

She agreed. "Oh Graydon, just one more thing."

"Sure," he replied.

"Promise we won't go to a hockey game or any other sporting event."

His deep chuckle rumbled in her ear. "I promise."

They said goodbye and she closed the phone. She lifted her face to the sun shining down from the sky, feeling excitement for the first time since her breakup with Nico. That had to be good, she tried to convince herself. A sign that she was healing and life was getting back on track.

She pushed away from the car and walked back to Sweet Confections. Once Kristen got a good look at Rachel, a huge grin broke out across her face.

"Looks like someone has a hot date," Kristen said. "When and where? I want details."

"Not a date," Rachel reminded her. "It's just friends getting together to eat, and it's tonight. All I know is we won't be going to any sporting events."

"Sounds perfect. Now, get back to work. Those cookies don't bake themselves, you know."

Rachel tied the apron around her waist and returned to the batch of peanut butter chocolate chunk cookies. She stirred the dough, then began to hum as she dropped spoonfuls of the delectable mixture onto baking sheets, all the while wondering what that evening might bring.

Rachel put the finishing touches on her lip gloss, then

checked her reflection in the mirror. Since she didn't know the itinerary, she decided to go for a casual chic look with dark, boot-cut jeans, a black tank top edged with lace and topped with a short-sleeved thin turquoise cotton cardigan that had a flowy cut. It was flattering and hid a bit of her extra curviness. Her auburn hair hung loose past her shoulders. She was so used to having it pulled up at the bakery, she forgot how feminine it felt to wear it down.

She did one last turn in front of the mirror, then grabbed her purse and went into the living room to wait. She sank into her favorite chair, but couldn't relax. Instead her foot bobbed up and down over her crossed leg.

"Ugh! This is worse than waiting for a prom date!" She jumped up and began to rifle through her desk. Not finding anything interesting, she went into the kitchen where she deposited the mail each day. Sorting mail was a good way to waste a few minutes.

"Junk, junk and more junk mail," she muttered, throwing the flyers into the recycling bin under her sink. "Ooh, the electricity bill. How exciting."

She sat the envelope aside, then glanced at the clock. Six twenty-five. Only five more minutes. A zing pulsed through her. She forced attention back to the letters in her hand. She threw away a few more flyers, then stopped when she came to a letter with an Italian postmark. She turned it around in her hands a few times. There was no return address, but it could only be from one person. *Should I open it or just throw it away?*

Ding dong.

He's here! She set the envelope on the counter to deal with later. She walked to the front door, took a deep breath, exhaled then opened it.

And wow, did he ever look incredible. Her gaze traveled across his broad shoulders, over the charcoal gray sweater layered over a red plaid shirt. Then lower to his dark jeans which fit just right around his hips and legs. It should be illegal for a man to look that good.

Graydon tucked a finger under her chin and brought her gaze up to meet his.

"Hello," he said, amusement sparkling in his chocolate brown eyes.

Heat infused her cheeks. She must look like a hussy checking him out. "Um, hi, Graydon. I'm sorry. Um . . ." She stumbled over her words. His thumb brushed against her cheek.

"You're beautiful when you blush," he said, holding her captive with just his eyes.

Man, I'm doomed. Her cheeks flared with more heat. "It's one of the curses of being a red-head," she replied, then stepped back. "Please come in. I just need to grab my purse, then we can go."

She led him into the living room. He wandered around the room while she retrieved her purse. It was small, but neat and contemporary. Not frilly, but it definitely had a feminine feel. Not exactly décor for a sports celebrity though.

"I like your house. It's bright, but comfortable."

They paused on the doorstep while Rachel locked up. Then he took her hand and linked it through his arm.

"So, how was your day? Did you burn any more cookies?" he asked, leading her to his truck.

She laughed. "No, but if I had, I'm sure Kristen would have banished me from the kitchen."

"I'm glad you didn't." Graydon opened the truck door and helped her in. Once he was settled behind the wheel, he turned toward her again. "By the way, I forgot to ask if there's anything you don't like to eat."

"I'm pretty open. What did you have in mind?"

"There's a really great Thai place on the other side of town."

"That sounds great. I've had a long-standing love affair with Thai since culinary arts school. One of my roomies visited there on vacation and came home with some great recipes."

On the way, he turned on the radio and they took turns playing around with the stations, laughing about songs they liked, others they didn't, and some they thought were just plain odd. When they pulled into the parking lot for The Thai Place, Rachel was relaxed and glad they had gotten together.

Inside, they were seated at a quiet table in the back corner. The lighting was dim, lending an air of intimacy. She admired the colorful glass jars lined along the wall shelves.

"It's very peaceful here," she commented as she opened the menu.

"It's one of my favorite places to come when I need to decompress from the day. Sometimes running a restaurant is hectic and crazy, especially lately. Our chef has been in a cranky mood. He misses my parents and is anxious for them to return."

She looked up from her menu. "How long have they been gone?"

"They're taking an extended honeymoon of sorts. They came back briefly for Zack's wedding, but they're about seven weeks into a three-month trip through Europe."

Their conversation was interrupted by the waitress who came to take their order. They decided to go with some traditional dishes to share–pad thai and chicken fried rice.

"It's your turn. What are you parents like?"

"Mmm," she said, scrunching her nose up for a second. "My maternal great-grandfather came here from Italy, although they all still think of themselves as Italians. My mother has the typical Italian mama persona down pat. Whenever we do something she doesn't like, she crosses herself and says Mama Mia!" She leaned in closer to confide. "The only thing is, our family isn't even Catholic."

His deep brown eyes danced with mirth. "She sounds fun."

She leaned back against her seat again. "Dramatic would be a much better choice. My dad, on the other hand, is rather quiet. He loves to build things. It doesn't matter what it is— a house, a car engine, a set for a school play—he does it all. After school, I would sit in the garage and do my homework, listening to the clank of tools. Sometimes we'd talk about different things happening with friends or at school." She smiled as she thought about her dad. "You know, my dad and brothers would have coronaries if they had any idea I was having dinner with the great DG."

Graydon put his forearms on the edge of the table and leaned toward her. "I remember you said they watch everything."

She leaned slightly forward, following Graydon's lead. "Bowling, curling, golf and huge variety of other sports I consider too boring. But they enjoy it and seem to find it entertaining from all the bantering I overhear."

"Sounds like the guys in my family when we all get together. How did you get into cooking?"

"Aside from my temper, that's probably the only other thing I inherited from my mom. We may not have been the quietest house on the block, but we definitely had the best smells wafting from the kitchen." She twirled the straw in her soda. "I guess food was my mother's way of saying she loved us, too. In high school, I took cooking classes and enjoyed it enough that I decided to attend culinary arts school, which eventually led to opening Sweet Confections."

They briefly paused their conversation when the food arrived. Once they added a bit of each entrée to their plates and sampled them, they began their conversation again in earnest. She told him about Kristen and how they came up with the idea to open Sweet Confections together and how they were outgrowing their current location. They talked more about her love for creating food, specifically desserts, and she discovered Graydon wasn't a fan of chocolate.

"How can you not like chocolate? I can't comprehend how that's humanly possible."

"There's something about it. I don't know—the aftertaste maybe?" He shrugged. "It's never been my favorite."

"Maybe you're not picking the right kind of chocolate." She thought for a moment. "I may need to try a few recipes to see if I can sway your opinion."

"You're welcome to try," he replied, lifting one shoulder, then letting it drop in a half shrug.

She put her elbow on the table and leaned her chin on her hand. "I just can't imagine going through life without the exquisite pleasure of chocolate treats. If you aren't a fan of chocolate, what do you like?"

"Well, cheesecake had been my weakness until just recently."

She dipped her head, her hair cascading down over the side of her face, embarrassed by his reference to the wedding reception. "I really am sorry about that. Sometimes my temper gets the best of me."

He reached across the table and rubbed a few strands of auburn hair between his fingers. "I remember thinking that I'd better tell you who I was before you figured it out if your red hair was any indication about how you'd take the news."

"I've had more than one moment when I wished I had taken a few minutes to think things through before acting."

"Don't worry about it. We'll just keep it in the 'things we'll laugh about later' category."

She wondered how many of those moments they would acquire. Eventually their plates were taken away and a Thai dessert was brought out for them to share. They lingered over it, not in a hurry to leave. She was vaguely aware of the light chatter of diners around them, but the overall mood in the restaurant remained peaceful.

"I know you probably need to get up early in the morning, but would you like to take a short walk through the arboretum? The gardens there are lit up at night."

"That sounds nice." He helped her out of her chair, then placed a hand on her lower back to guide her to the front of the restaurant.

"Graydon!" a feminine voice called. They turned toward a vaguely familiar beautiful Hispanic woman.

"Hi, Sheila." He changed their direction to meet up with his friend. "Rachel, this is Sheila Montoyez. She's the public relations manager for the DG Foundation. Sheila, this is Rachel Marconi. You might remember her from hockey camp."

Sheila seemed a bit flustered, but recovered quickly. "Of course. I think I interrupted a conversation between the two of you. It's nice to meet you, Rachel."

"It's nice to meet you, too, Sheila." They shook hands, although she barely felt Sheila's touch. Instead, she was distracted as Graydon's hand slipped from her back to around her waist. It came to rest on her hip, his thumb lightly brushed the curve of her waist.

"So, what are you up to tonight?" he asked. Sheila's gaze snapped from where his hand rested on Rachel's waist, up to his eyes.

"Oh, I'm just meeting some friends for dinner. I'm a little early."

"If I know you, then you're probably about fifteen minutes early. You've always been great about keeping me on time."

She smiled faintly. "Yes, it's not always an easy job, either. I didn't know you had plans tonight. It wasn't on your schedule."

"I don't keep everything on my work calendar," he replied.

There was an awkward pause as Rachel looked between the two co-workers. She wondered what their history was. Had they ever dated? Is that why Graydon put his hand around her waist like that? The warmth she felt dimmed and she edged away a bit.

"Well," he said, breaking the silence, "We should probably get going. I'll see you tomorrow morning."

"It was nice to meet you. I hope you have fun with your friends tonight," Rachel told Sheila.

"Yes, thanks. The same to you, too," she replied.

His hand left her waist as he led her out of the restaurant. The night air had cooled, but was still comfortable.

"Sheila seems nice. Have you worked together long?" Rachel asked while they drove to the gardens.

"We met about eight years ago when I started the DG foundation. She came highly recommended from one of my sisters. She's a PR genius, always coming up with new ideas for publicity and to help kids."

She hesitated, then asked, "Did you date?"

He turned in surprise, then laughed. "Me and Sheila?"

"Why is that funny?"

"I guess it shouldn't be. I've never thought of Sheila that way before. When we started working together, I was engaged. Sheila and I clicked business-wise and became good friends, but that's it. After my hockey retirement, she ganged up with my family to keep my butt in gear when all I wanted to do was hole up in a dark room and wallow in misery. I think of her more as another sister than anything else. Why do you ask?"

Graydon pulled into the arboretum parking lot. He turned off the lights, but left the truck running. He turned toward her. The lights in the parking lot kept half his face in the light and the other half in the shadows.

"She seemed surprised to see you with someone." *Me, specifically,* she thought.

"It's been quite a while since I've taken a woman out who wasn't a family member."

"How long is quite a while?" She immediately regretted asking. It wasn't any of her business how often he dated.

"About two years. I tried dating after things broke off with Carissa, but it just wasn't working. I didn't meet anyone I wanted to spend extra time with. Until you."

"Oh," she replied, at a loss for words. Carissa was obviously the woman he was engaged to, but what happened? She wanted to ask, but wasn't sure if she should at the fledging stages of their friendship.

Together they entered the gardens. A fairy exhibit recently started. Thousands of white twinkly lights were strung all over, draped from pole to pole creating a canopy between the trees. There were lanterns placed along the path and tiny fairy statues hidden among the plants and flowers. It was magical.

They started down one path when he took her hand and tucked it into the crook of his elbow. She looked down at where her hand rested, then up at him. His gaze was questioning and cautious.

"Is this okay?" he asked quietly.

Peace filled her heart. "Yes, it is," she answered. They strolled quietly for a few moments before she broke the silence.

"Tell me about your hockey camps. I know my nephew loved the one he attended. What made you think to start them?"

Graydon was quiet for a few seconds before answering. "I got to a point in my career that while I still loved to be on the ice, I wanted to do something more. Something that didn't involve talking trash and edging out the competition, but still involved my love of the sport. I talked with my parents about it one weekend during a family reunion. My mom suggested I start a camp for kids. I liked the idea and mulled it over for a few months. I mapped out some ideas, who I wanted to involve, then I started talking to my hockey buddies." He shrugged. "It took a lot of research and time to set it up the right way, but eventually it all came together. I hired on a small staff to work in our office, which is how I met Sheila. She also doubles as my assistant, keeping track of my appearances and meetings. My cousin Zack is our event co-ordinator. He puts together all the locations, equipment, etc."

"Do you have events that aren't in Kansas City?"

He nodded. "We host camps in New York and California. That way we hit each of the coasts, but Kansas City is our corporate headquarters. I have friends who are on hockey teams in the other states. They create a big draw for local attendees. We also host a hockey day camp for the metro area Special Olympics teams. Any athletes can sign up. We provide the housing, food, and all the equipment. They need to find their own transportation, but we're trying to figure out some contacts to help teams farther away get free busses to attend. It's by far my favorite camp."

"Why?"

He didn't reply right away. They turned onto another path that led them over a bridge that spanned a pond filled with floating flowers and candles. About halfway across, he paused and leaned against the railing. Their elbows rested beside each other. She looked up when he started speaking again.

"I guess the difference is most of the kids don't care who I am. But when they step out on the ice for the first time, it reminds me of my first hockey practice. The excitement in their eyes reminds me how much I wanted to learn how to make the stick and puck work together. It doesn't matter how many times they attend, each goal they make, each puck they hit, it's like they just won a gold medal and are the kings of the world." He finally lifted his head to meet her gaze. "It's incredible."

She was quiet for a few moments, contemplating what he had just shared. Her heart swelled, thinking of her little nephew with autism and how this guy standing in front of her would totally get him. Not only that, but he actually went out of his way to be a part of making the lives of others with special needs better. Something he most certainly didn't have to do. She thought that was probably one of the most attractive qualities she'd ever found in someone.

"Did Jordan tell you about his younger brother?"

"No, why?"

"He has autism. He's only five years old, but I think he's absolutely amazing. I'd never tell my nephews this, but he's my favorite of all the boys. After spending so much time with him at physical therapy and ABA therapy sessions, I can't help but feel a deeper connection with him."

"Special Olympics doesn't start until the kids are eight, but I would love to have your nephew come to the rink so I can teach him to skate. Every kid is different, but if he likes it, then it's one more accomplishment and skill he can work on and use as a reward for everything else he has to work so hard at."

"Really?" She looked at the pond below and blinked away the tears prickling in her eyes. He placed a finger under her chin and turned her face back toward him.

"Really," he said. His thumb rubbed against her cheek and trailed down over her chin before he dropped his hand, then straightened. "I should probably get you back home so I don't get any threatening phone calls from Kristen in the morning, telling me you overslept and it's all my fault."

She chuckled and tucked her hand back on his arm. They walked back the way they came, talking about their schedules during the coming week. The conversation was once again comfortable. She was sad to see the evening come to an end when they arrived back at her home. He walked her to the door, where she paused, not quite ready to say good night.

"I really enjoyed spending time with you." He took her hand in his. "I hope you'll consider getting together again."

"I—" She cleared her throat so she wouldn't stumble over her words. "I'd really like that."

"Great. I'll call you tomorrow." He raised her hand and kissed the inside of her palm. Tingles cascaded down her arm. She never felt anything so intimate from something so simple.

He waited to make sure she was safely inside before leaving. She locked the door, then leaned her back against it. The evening's events flickered through her thoughts, along with everything she learned about Graydon. He was definitely a different man than she originally imagined. Good and funny. She wondered if this was the real him or if it could be another illusion that would end with a hard bumpy landing. She clung to the seed of hope that was planted inside her heart.

Chapter TEN

*R*achel felt vibrant and ready to whip together some wonderful sugar confections. On the drive to work, she thought about adding some new cookies and cupcakes to the menu. She'd have to dig through her recipe files and look for something she hadn't made for a while. Something light and airy, to reflect her mood. Maybe some meringue tarts or sugar-dusted chocolate mousse flowers. She continued to brainstorm, enjoying how the sky changed from inky darkness to a faint navy blue tinged with a pinkish-orange. She pulled into the parking lot behind the bakery and found their custodian, Charles, hauling a big sudsy bucket outside.

She grabbed her purse, wondering what was going on. As she got closer, she realized what the bucket was for. Eggs shells and yellowish slime trailed down the back door and walls.

"Oh no! Who would do this?" She looked to see if there was any damage to the windows.

Charles, a retired school janitor, shrugged then muttered, "Probably some teenagers with too much time on their hands. They got the front, too." He bent down and grabbed the sponge in the bucket, but she stopped him.

"Let me call the police first. If it is teenagers, we may be the first round of businesses to get hit. We'd better report it so the police can be on the lookout."

She went inside and called the local police department. In the meantime, Charles started on some indoor clean-up while she sorted through her recipe files. She found a recipe for Strawberry Meringues and checked their ingredient inventory, determined not to let the vandals disrupt her good mood. When a firm knock sounded on the back door, she set the recipe aside. She opened the back door and greeted a stocky, blond officer.

"Hi, I'm Rachel Marconi, the owner."

"Officer Giles." After a handshake, they stepped outside to talk. He took pictures to document the egging. "Have you had any other trouble recently?"

She shook her head. "No, it's always been pretty peaceful here. I'm hoping this is just a one-time thing and not the beginning of a trend."

"I'll talk with the rest of the businesses in this area to let them know what happened. If you have any other problems, you can contact me at these numbers and email address." He handed her a business card.

"Thank you. I appreciate you coming out so quickly. Is this the beginning or end of your shift?"

"The end. I'll get this report written up then head home for bed." He handed her a clipboard to sign some paperwork. She scribbled her name on the highlighted line, then handed it back.

"I have some muffins inside. I haven't started my baking yet today, so they're a day old, but still yummy. I'd be happy to make a bag to send home with you."

He smiled and rubbed his flat stomach. "That sounds fantastic. Thank you."

She put together a bag with a variety of blueberry, chocolate chip, and cranberry bran muffins, then handed them to Officer Giles with another note of thanks.

Charles rambled back in. "Everything good for me to start cleaning up?"

"Yes. By the way, with all the craziness this morning, I didn't get a chance to ask how your grand-daughter is feeling."

"Good, now that she's back at school and her friends are signing her cast. She sure loved those cookies you sent over. Said you were better than those Keebler Elves."

The laughter shook off the morning's annoyance. "Kids say the cutest things. I love it! Be sure to let me know if she needs any other cheering up."

He nodded, then went back outside to start on the egg mess. Rachel went into the small office off the kitchen to put the officer's card in the desk's top middle drawer. Then she got to work. She started with vanilla cupcakes. When they went into the oven, she rolled out dough for the strawberry meringue tarts. She paused just long enough to put in a call to a local grocery store that provided business delivery and ordered some fresh raspberries, blueberries, and strawberries. As the cupcakes came out, she refilled the cups and popped more in to bake. Once the tarts were filled with dough, she baked them in another oven for a few minutes to set the crust, then pulled them out to cool while she waited for the berries. She had just started on M&M cookies when Kristen arrived.

"Well, someone's on quite the baking streak." She swapped her coat for the apron on the peg by the door. "What's Charles doing out front?"

"We got egged last night."

"What!" She pulled her apron strings tight and knotted them.

"Yeah, it wasn't too bad though. I already called the police. They came by, took some notes, and told me to call if there are any other problems. It was probably just some teenagers."

"Dang brats," Kristen muttered. She pulled out big metal bowls and ingredients to start on some birthday cakes they had in the queue for pick-up that afternoon. "So, how was your date? Details, please." She batted her eyelashes like a beauty queen. Rachel loved their silly banter and teasing.

"It was great. We talked a lot and none of it was stupid jock stuff. He's not at all how I thought he would be."

"See, good surprises come in interesting packages and with interesting timing, too," Kristen said. "Speaking of interesting timing, I ran into Victoria downtown and asked her about a new location for Sweet Confections. She said there are several properties we could look at, but she also mentioned a new development I thought would be really cool to be a part of."

Rachel continued scooping M&M cookie dough onto cookie sheets. "And?" she prompted.

"She and an investor are in the last stages of having a new shopping district approved downtown. You know that older neighborhood between City Hall and the elementary school, near the creek?" Kristen finished pulling the cake batter ingredients out and leaned against the counter.

"The one with all the brick homes that are empty?" She had always liked that area and wondered why the homes weren't filled with families.

Kristen nodded. "Apparently, an anonymous investor has been purchasing the homes as families moved away. Now they want to turn it into a shopping district targeted toward women."

Rachel paused, giving Kristen her full attention. "That sounds really cool!"

"I thought you would love it," Kristen bubbled with excitement. "Victoria couldn't give me very many details, but she did say the investor is willing to front a portion of the renovation fees for each business, if they sign on before each particular house is remodeled."

"I wonder how much the portion will be?" While they had diligently been saving a percentage of their income for upgrades and shop repairs, Rachel wondered if they would have enough set aside to take on a house remodel. Part of her really hoped so. The project was definitely intriguing.

"Victoria said they still have some details to iron out but she's hoping to have the official announcement and details at next month's meeting. January at the latest."

"Then we should both plan on attending. I'll check with Shawna and some of the temps to make sure the lunch shift is covered."

The two friends continued to chat, mix and bake the morning away. Rachel filled the pastry case and Shawna arrived just before eleven to open. Rachel and Kristen continued baking and decorating, going back and forth between the kitchen and the front of the shop to help Shawna depending on how busy it was. This was what she loved most about the bakery. Not only creating delightful pastries and cakes, but the flow of work and visiting with customers.

Later that afternoon, the bakery shop's phone rang. "Hello, Sweet Confections. This is Kristen." She paused. "Sure, she's right here. Just a moment." She put her hand over the phone's mouth piece and waggled her eyebrows. "It's for you."

Rachel had a pretty good idea who would be on the other end of the line, but still got butterflies in her midsection as she wiped off her floury hands. She took the phone from Kristen and used her normal greeting, doing her best to sound casual.

"Hi, Rachel. How's your day going?"

The sound of Graydon's voice made her want to giggle like a silly teenage girl. She barely suppressed the urge, although Kristen wasn't helping as she waltzed around the bakery humming the theme from Sleeping Beauty. "Well, other than a glitch this morning, it's been a really good day. We're baking up a storm, as usual." She turned her back, doing her best to ignore her friend's antics.

"I've been thinking about you a lot today. I know I said I was busy in the evenings for the rest of this week, but I wondered if we could meet for a late dinner tonight?"

"I planned to go home, order some take out and watch something on the DVR – probably a Food Network Challenge. I'd be willing to share if you don't mind a quiet night."

"Sounds perfect. But don't worry about take out. I'll bring either some pasta or barbecue from the restaurant. Is sometime between seven-thirty and eight okay for you? I can't get away any earlier than that."

"That works for me." After she hung up the phone, she turned around to find Kristen leaning against the counter with her arms folded.

"So . . ."

"Oh, it's nothing. Graydon is coming over to my place for

a late dinner and to watch some TV. No big deal." She tried to shrug it off, but couldn't keep the wide smile off her face.

"No big deal, my foot." Kristen sighed. "This is the part I miss the most about dating—the anticipation. I love Todd, but I miss those first dates when everything is all butterflies and excitement. You better spill the beans tomorrow. I want a full update."

"Yes, ma'am," she said, giving her best formal salute.

Chapter ELEVEN

*R*achel dashed around the living room, straightening pillows and magazines, putting shoes away in the closet, and doing a quick vacuum job. Then she went into the kitchen and put the dirty dishes in the dishwasher. She wouldn't actually run it because it took too long for a single person to fill it, but she found in times like this that the dishwasher made a great hiding spot for last-minute clean ups. And if anyone opened it, they wouldn't think anything about finding her dirty dishes there. Finished tidying, all she had left to do was wait for Graydon to arrive.

She pulled out her mail from the day before and started the process of sorting it out again. She came to the envelope from Italy, debated about whether to open it or not, then gave in and broke the seal. She bit her lip as she began to read.

My dearest Rachel,

It breaks my heart that after all the time we spent together and cared for each other, that you have not answered any of my phone calls or returned any of my emails. Please, if you ever cared for me at all, contact me. I need to talk with you so much. I miss you. I love you.

Yours always,
Nico

Her stomach knotted up. Didn't Nico understand why they couldn't be together? Today, she had deleted twelve messages from him. It was less than when they first broke up and continued to decrease. She felt bad ignoring him, but returning his calls would only lead him on. Still, it had been a month. Maybe one more conversation would end it all. Knots of uncertainty twisted inside her.

The doorbell announced Graydon's arrival. She shoved the mail in a kitchen drawer and pushed aside all thoughts of Nico. She walked across the room, opened the door and smiled. It was so good to see Graydon. And yes, Kristen was right. The butterflies were fantastic.

"Please, come in." He moved to pass by her, but paused briefly to drop a kiss onto her cheek. The butterflies swarmed happily. "I hope you don't mind sitting in the living room. I usually pull the coffee table out and use it as the table. I'm pretty casual after baking all day."

"No problem. I tend to grab a snack or microwave something, then watch TV while I exercise to relax from the day."

"Aside from the exercising, that's what I usually I do, too." She smoothed her hands over her hips. Well, her body was what it was. There wasn't a magical way for her to go from a curvaceous size ten to a skinny mini size four. Not that she wanted to kill herself on the treadmill to try either.

He pulled out to-go containers, filling the room with a

delicious aroma. She covered her stomach with her hand when it grumbled.

"That smells wonderful. Let me go grab some plates." She moved to the kitchen and started pulling plates out of a cupboard. She jumped when Graydon placed his hands on her waist. She turned around to face him. "Hi," she whispered, her heart thumping wildly against her chest. Thankfully she held two plates in her hands, so she couldn't give into temptation and run her hands up his arms. His strong, muscular, very capable arms.

"Hi," he said back, gently squeezing her waist, pulling her attention back to the present. "What can I do to help?" She directed him to where the utensils were stored, then turned to fill glasses with ice water. She briefly put her wrist under the cool water, but it didn't do much to help calm her before they returned to the living room. There was salad, shrimp linguine and sliced cheesy garlic bread. Once their plates were full, she pulled up the menu for her recorded Food Network Challenges.

"Let's see, I have Disney cakes, villain cakes, wedding cakes, mystery cakes, crazy cakes." She continued scrolling through the list. "Anything look interesting?"

"Wow. You have a lot of episodes recorded." He swirled some linguine on his fork, then put it in his mouth.

"My goal is to be a competitor on the show. The underdog. Kristen and I sent in our applications last year, but still haven't heard anything."

"How long does it usually take to hear back?"

She shrugged. "I don't really know. I guess it depends. You never know when you'll be selected. Sometimes a bakery gets in at the last minute because someone needed to cancel.

I just want a chance to get up there and show them what I can do in eight hours."

"Eight hours? Isn't that a lot of time for a cake?"

"Depends on the requirements. There's a good reason why they call it a challenge. I know an episode you'd probably like." She scrolled down and clicked on Extreme Cakes. "This one is fun and definitely appeals to the macho power tool side of cake decorating."

"Cool," he said, shifting into a relaxed position. "Power tools and cakes. It can't get better than that."

Soon the two were wrapped up in the competitors' introductions and the challenge requirements. During commercials, Graydon made guesses about who would win. She just smiled and came back with quips to make him second guess his opinions. During one of the breaks, he asked why she kept the episodes she already watched.

"They're like study guides. Each time I rewatch one, I learn something different about another baker's technique, how he stayed on task or what he did that totally threw him off time."

"Kind of like in hockey. We watched the recordings from the opposing team's previous games so we could study the people we would play against, create a game plan, how to press them into turning the puck over to us, or trick them in their own plays. In a way, that's what you're doing. Studying the competitors, and if one day you have a challenge against one of them, you'll know what tricks to pull out to top their best cakes."

Rachel tilted her head and studied Graydon. "I never thought of it that way before, but you're right. I guess preparing for a hockey game and a cake challenge have a few similarities."

His large hand covered hers, warmth sinking in. She was tempted to lean forward, just for a little kiss, but held back. She felt so comfortable with him, and after their conversations, it was like they had known each other for much longer than a couple of weeks. The commercials ended and pulled her attention back to the episode.

"Now, let's see if my guess is right about who's going to win the challenge." Fifteen minutes later, Graydon was miffed. "It's not fair. Duff's team had the best extreme elements. Their cake should have won."

It was hard to hold back her smile. "Well, it generally isn't a good idea for the cake to explode during the demo stage."

"Still, they had the best stuff. They can't help it if they planned a little too much on the pyrotechnics side."

She couldn't help but laugh. He was such a guy, which made it so funny to see him worked up about a cake. They picked up their dirty dishes and took them into the kitchen. As she finished rinsing the last plate, Graydon's arms circled around her waist. He leaned forward to rest his chin on her shoulder.

"Thanks for tonight. I enjoyed relaxing and spending time with you."

She leaned back against his chest and placed her hands over his. Together, they looked out the window over the sink at the stars in the sky.

"I enjoyed it, too," she said quietly.

"Can I ask you a question," he asked after a moment of silence. She nodded, so he continued. "After spending the last few weeks getting to know each other, how do you feel about dating now?"

She paused before responding. "After that night with

Nico, I told myself I just wanted a break, to not be attached to anyone or put myself out there to get hurt again."

"And now?" he prompted.

"Now I'm still wondering. Except I met this man who is so completely different than anyone I ever thought I'd be attracted to, a pro hockey player—

"Former pro hockey player," he broke in.

"Yes, but you are still involved with hockey, and even though you've got a former in front of the pro, you're still in the media spotlight. I'm not sure how I feel about that."

He conceded with a nod. "There is a but, right?"

She turned to face him. His eyes were warm, yet serious. "But on the other side, you're not anything like I expected. I can't imagine a celebrity sitting on my floor for dinner and watching reruns. You do some pretty great things for others, too."

"So, there's two conflicting sides?"

"Yes." She paused for another moment. "But I'm leaning toward spending more time with you on dates or whatever you'd like to call it."

He cupped her face with his hands, his fingers brushing the hair at the nape of her neck. "Good, because there's a whole lot more I want to learn about you, Rachel Marconi. I'm not like the tabloid stories you see at the grocery store. I don't date multiple people at the same time. Never have, never will. If you decide to go out on a date with someone else, I want you to tell me. I would do the same for you. Honesty is important to me. If dating doesn't work out between us, I hope we'll walk away with a good friendship."

How had he stayed single this long? She felt blessed to be where she was, with him, right now. "Honesty and friendship."

His thumb brushed across her cheek, sending tingles cascading through her. He placed a tender kiss on her forehead, then they leaned into each other. His chin rested on the top of her head, his hands lightly caressed her shoulders. "Could we do this again tomorrow night?"

She listened to his heartbeat, a spark of hope growing in her heart. She couldn't think of anything she'd like more. "I'd love to."

"Good. Then I'd better say goodnight before—well, before."

She nodded in understanding. It would be too easy to get carried away. As much as she would love to curl up and snuggle with this man, she also knew it wasn't the right thing. They needed to concentrate on getting to know each other. Too much intimacy too soon would overwhelm any friendship they might form. She walked with him to the front door. He pulled his keys from his pocket, then stood in the open doorway. He took her hand and leaned close to whisper, "I'll call you tomorrow."

He gave her one more quick kiss on the cheek before he jogged down the steps. Once he was in his truck, she closed the door, securing the locks. She floated to her room, where she hoped sweet dreams would fill the rest of her night.

Chapter TWELVE

*R*achel rushed through her room, dressing as fast as possible. She hated it when she overslept. She thought she hit snooze, but it must have been the off button instead. She checked her watch and groaned. She was a good twenty minutes behind. Thank goodness Kristen had called to find out where she was. It was Kristen's morning to be at the bakery early or else they would be in some serious doo doo. Everything was started, but with the weekend rush, they had a queue of cakes that needed to be decorated.

She twisted her hair up and clipped it out of the way, then quickly brushed her teeth. As she spit, a dribble of toothpaste ran down her Sweet Confections shirt. She wiped it off, but knew it would leave a smear when the toothpaste dried. Dang it all. She grabbed another shirt, shoved it in a plastic bag, figuring at this rate it would be safer if she changed when she actually got to the bakery. She shoved her feet into sneakers, yanked open the door, then screamed.

Nico stood on her doorstep. He was immaculate, as always, except that his clothes were rumpled as if he'd been there for a while. Waiting for her to open the door. Prickles skated down her arms and she gripped the doorknob until her knuckles turned white. When he reached out to out to steady her, she stepped behind the door, using it to partially block him from her.

"What—" she tried to catch her breath. "What are you doing here?"

"I didn't mean to scare you. I just needed to talk, Rachel. You haven't answered my phone calls. Did you get the letter I sent?"

She glanced out to the street, hoping one of her neighbors might be leaving for work or checking the mail, but only saw Nico's car parked at the curb. She stiffened her back, determined to end the conversation, as well as his obsession about their relationship. "I got your letter. And yes," she said, cutting off his next question, "I read it. Listen, the last time we talked, I made it clear I don't want any further contact. Nico, you're married. That's it."

"Can't we be friends?"

"Maybe if you'd been honest right from the start we'd still be friends because there never would've been anything romantic between us. We could have gotten to know each other and become friends with limits. Friendship and only friendship."

He leaned forward, his hands gripped the door frame. "So we could be friends. We can talk and stay in touch."

His eyes were frantic, yet pathetic. She felt a tug to say yes, but knew it would be a terrible decision. "There would always be a layer of feelings there. You would like me more than as a friend, and I—"

"Would feel that way, too."

"No, I would feel bad for you. I need to move on and you can't be a part of my future. This is the way it needs to be."

His expression fell into a sad, depressed frown. "Please, Rachel. You're the one person who understands me. Maybe we can try to talk in a few months."

She edged the door closed a bit more. This wasn't going

as smoothly as she'd like. "I won't change my mind. I hope things either work out with your wife or that you'll find the strength to start a new life without her, but I won't ever be a part of your future. You need to accept that."

Tears gleamed in his eyes. He looked away, back toward where his car was parked. He rocked back on his heels a few times before saying anything more. "I guess this is it. I tried, right?" He looked at her one more time, a brief glance, then turned and walked away.

She closed her door and twisted the lock. Then stumbled to the couch and let what just happened sink in. Were things really over with Nico? She could only hope so.

She peeked out the kitchen window and saw his car was no longer parked out front. She cautiously opened her door to check if he was truly gone. Still, she felt uncomfortable while she locked the house door and got into her car. She looked around again, but didn't see any sign of Nico. She took deep, even breaths to work through the leftover nervous energy jittering through her.

When she finally arrived at the bakery, Kristen was grumpy. "It certainly took you long enough to get here. Did you decide to take the long way or what?"

"I'm sorry. I was rushing and running out the door. I need to change my shirt. I have toothpaste all down the front of this one. Have we opened the front yet?" She hurried to the bathroom and started changing her shirt with the door only part-way closed so she could continue their conversation.

"I was leaving my house, but Nico was outside waiting for me." She heard a clatter of metallic bowls hitting the floor, then the bathroom door was shoved open, knocking into Rachel just as she pulled on her Sweet Confections shirt— the clean one. She stumbled back and yelped when her hip hit the sink. *Geez Louise,* she thought, as she shoved her arms and head through the appropriate shirt holes.

"What? He was at your house?"

She rubbed her hip, then edged past Kristen to open the store front while she explained what happened.

"Do you think he'll actually stop contacting you then?"

She shrugged. "I guess we'll find out." She hoped her nonchalant attitude worked. She didn't want Kristen to realize how freaked out she was. His actions were kind of, well, stalkerish, if she admitted the truth to herself. But that was stuff you read on tabloid covers. It didn't happen to girls like her. She went into the back, pulled out the trays filled with the fresh muffins and cookies Kristen made that morning. Together, they filled the pastry cases and prepared for customers to arrive.

"With all this talk about Nico, I almost forgot about your date last night. How did it go?"

Heat bloomed in her cheeks. "Oh, it went okay."

"Whoa, girlfriend," Kristen nabbed the back of Rachel's apron when she tried to scoot away. "What happened?" When her blush deepened, a sly grin appeared. "He kissed you! Ooh—I'm right aren't I?"

She pulled her apron out of Kristen's hands, then escaped into the kitchen to retrieve another tray.

"Come on, you know you want to tell me. He did, didn't he? Was it nice? Did your foot pop?"

"Did my what?" She paused on her way back to the front of the store.

"You know, in Princess Diaries when Anne Hathaway says she hopes her foot pops when she gets her first kiss. So, did it?" Kristen waggled her eyebrows.

"Well, I don't kiss and tell." She held up a finger, cutting off Kristen's squeal. "Not that I'm saying any kissing happened."

She stomped her foot. "Man, I always miss the good stuff."

"Sweetie, I think you've got the good stuff going on with your hubby already. Don't worry too much about my practically nonexistent love life."

"Yeah, but the beginning of young love is always the best. All those hormones. Man, it never gets any better than that."

Rachel patted Kristen's pouting face. "Thanks for the great point of view you just gave me about marriage. Now, let's finish getting this all set up before our customers arrive."

Twenty minutes later, the bakery was full of lunchtime customers stopping for a sweet treat. Kristen brought out more trays filled with their afternoon batches of decadent chocolate and caramel swirl muffins. The rush finally passed, giving them time to restock and Rachel went back to the kitchen to work on some cake decorating.

The bell over the door chimed. "Oh, Rachel, I believe you're wanted out front," Kristen said.

Rachel wiped her hands on a towel and brushed some flour off her apron as she walked into the store front. She almost tripped over her feet when she saw Graydon leaning against the counter, chatting with Kristen.

"Hey, beautiful," he said.

"Hey there, yourself." A huge grin reflected her happiness. She knew Kristen would be gloating later. "What are you doing in this part of town?"

"Just thought I'd stop in and see the two prettiest bakers in Crystal Creek."

"Oh, he's smooth," Kristen said, wiping off the counter.

As she walked past, she whispered loud enough for Graydon to hear, "He's got my vote." She winked, then went back into the kitchen.

"Hopefully she'll be productive and bake something, rather than stand out of sight and eavesdrop." Rachel approached Graydon until she was directly across the counter from him and put on a saucy grin. "Welcome to Sweet Confections. What's your pleasure today?" She walked behind the pastry case. "Chocolate or caramel? Oh wait, you don't like chocolate. How about something light and sweet like these peach crème éclairs." She removed one from a tray. The crust was light and flaky, the filling just sweet enough to pull the juicy tartness from the peaches. The combination of the two would burst on his tongue. "Try this."

Graydon reached out and clasped her hand. Instead of taking the éclair from her, he guided her hand and the treat to his mouth. He took a small bite, licking away the crème on the corner of his mouth. The act felt intimate, creating a rushing warmth to swirl from her head all the way down to her toes.

"Wow," he said, looking down at the éclair. He took the rest from her, dropped her hand, and took a bigger bite. "This really is good." He finished the rest of it, devouring the treat. As he licked the crumbs off his thumb, he looked up at her. "Can I get five more of those to go?"

So much for sensual. His attention certainly changed once he got a taste of some good food. Who was it that said the way to a man's heart is through his stomach? If that's the case, then she needed to dig out her best recipes—non-chocolate ones—and ply Graydon with them. The thought brightened her smile. She grabbed a pink and gray striped box and filled it with the éclairs. "Would you like to try anything else?"

"No, I think one treat today will be great. Gives me something to look forward to tomorrow."

Her eyebrow quirked into a high arch. "Are you planning to come back every day to try something new?"

"Would that be a problem?" he asked, leaning against the case next to the register.

"Certainly not for our business nor for our recipe books. We bring out new stuff every day. But I don't want you to think you have to be a regular customer for me to go out with you again."

"What if I just like to ogle the owner?"

"As long as it's not the married owner, then I think that would be fine." She handed over the bag, then rang him up on the register. After he paid, he leaned in a bit and curled his finger, motioning for her to come closer.

"Is something wrong?" she asked, knowing there wasn't.

He curled his finger again, so she leaned forward. He touched the hair pulled back at the side, then brought his face close enough to drop a soft kiss on her cheek, just a few millimeters from the corner of her lips. She inhaled sharply as he lingered there, hoping he might move a little closer to actually hit the target—her lips. Instead he drew back. She blinked to clear her dazed vision only to see the wicked gleam in his eyes.

"Now that's the best part of coming in. Are we still on for tonight?"

She nodded, then cleared her throat. "Yes, we are. My house? Seven-thirty?"

"It's a date. I'll see you then."

She stood there for a minute after he left before Kristen

broke her thoughts. "Yeah, you've got it bad. Even if Nico hadn't been married, he wouldn't have had a chance after you met Graydon. Poor guy."

She pondered her friend's statement and realized if the breakup hadn't happened, she and Graydon would not have met. A blessing in disguise and quite possibly the super glue to mend her broken heart.

Rachel was surprised to see Graydon's PR manager come into the shop just before closing.

"Hi, Rachel, I don't know if you remember me from the other night or not," the beautiful woman said.

"Sheila, right?" The two women shook hands again. "What can I do for you?"

"Well, Graydon brought some incredible éclairs to the office today and I just had to stop by to see if you had any left."

She walked along the case with Sheila following parallel to her. "We're actually out of those particular treats, but we have a few others to choose from. We don't have a very good selection right now, I'm afraid. We only bake enough to sell out so the pastries are fresh each day. Do you like chocolate?"

"Am I female?" Sheila asked, a sassy grin flashing across her beautiful face.

"We have some wonderful bon-bons, dark chocolate with whipped chocolate filling or white chocolate-citrus-filled ones. If you're into cookies, there are a few peanut butter white chocolate chunk cookies or cherry macadamia nut cookies left."

"What about these?" She pointed to two cupcakes off to the side.

"The white one is vanilla bean with a whipped cream cheese center topped with strawberry cream cheese icing. The pink one is a dark chocolate velvet cake topped with cherry buttercream."

"How does anyone ever choose?" Sheila asked, her eyes wide, taking in all the choices.

"You should see the customers who come in when we open. It's the adult version of kids in a candy store."

"I can honestly imagine that's true. Let's try the vanilla cupcake and one of each of the bon bons," she said, pointing to each treat before looking back up and meeting Rachel's eyes. "Cookies have never really been my favorite. Sorry."

"No problem. Everyone has something different that appeals to them."

They met back at the register after the treats were boxed up. Sheila reached over and lightly touched Rachel's hand. "By the way, I wanted to apologize if I seemed surprised when we ran into each other the other night. I had no idea Graydon was dating again. I think it's wonderful. He really needed to get past his ex-fiancée." She waved her hand in the air. "I'm getting off track again. What I meant to say is that I hope I didn't offend you and, if I did, I'm sorry. I hope we can become good friends."

Rachel felt more at ease, certain she must have mistaken Sheila's surprise as anything other than friendship. "That would be nice. By the way, I also put the chocolate cupcake in there as a little bonus. I saw you eyeing both of them and thought you might like an additional treat."

"Oh, my hips may never forgive me, but I can't wait to sample them all!"

Rachel finished ringing up the transaction, then accompanied Sheila to the door. She locked up, then went in the back and grabbed the broom. She swept up the crumb messes, mulling over Graydon's former engagement. Maybe she should ask him about it. Or she could do an internet search and find the information easily enough. No, she didn't feel right about that. Graydon would talk about it when he was ready. She could wait until then. Maybe.

She put the broom away, then began removing trays from the pastry cases. Charles would get the rest when he came in later. After stacking them on the kitchen counter, she filled the sink with hot, sudsy water. This was her least favorite part of owning the bakery and usually one of the teens did it, but tonight there was a big school activity. She didn't mind doing it occasionally, besides she could use the monotonous chore to think through all the changes in her life recently.

When she was a teenager, her dad once told her that trials and pitfalls were put in a person's life so they could grow into the person God wanted them to become. That teaching moment stuck with her and ever since, she tried to look at difficult situations to see how she reacted, how it affected her, and what she could learn.

The breakup with Nico left her wondering not just about men, but what her future might hold. What if she never married? Could she be content with her work and let being an awesome aunt replace her desire to be a mom? She asked herself a lot of hard questions while she scrubbed the trays.

She finished putting away the last item when Charles arrived. They chatted for a few minutes while he hung up his coat and she got her things together to leave. It was almost seven o'clock, so she had thirty minutes to get home to meet Graydon. She pushed the car remote to unlock the door, then paused when she noticed an X on the side of her door. She rubbed it, thinking maybe it was some dust, but the grooves confirmed her suspicions. Someone had keyed the door. The X wasn't very big, but still. Someone had purposefully damaged her car. She walked around the back to see if there was any other damage and found another X on the bumper. Then another on her passenger side door.

"Crap!" Annoyance rushed through her. She stomped back over to pound on the bakery door.

"What's wrong? Are you okay?" Charles peered past her to look for any trouble.

"Some idiot keyed my car!" She brushed past him, went to the phone and once again called the local police department. The dispatcher said an officer would arrive momentarily. She looked at her watch and realized there was no way she'd be able to meet Graydon, then pulled out her phone to call him.

"Hey, Rachel," he said. "I was just getting ready to leave. What's up?"

She heaved a deep sigh. "I'm sorry, tonight just isn't going to work."

"What's wrong? You sound upset."

She fought back frustrated tears and explained the situation.

"I didn't think your area had much vandalism," he said, surprise evident in his voice.

"It just started recently. This is the second time our

bakery has been targeted. Anyway, an officer is supposed to be here in a few minutes, then I'll need to call my insurance company." All the complications this added to her already-busy to-do list started to stack up and overwhelm her. Why did life have to rear up and bite her in the butt, just when things started to perk up?

"You still need to eat. How about if I bring dinner over for you? I won't stay if you don't want me to."

"I'd like that, but honestly, I'm too frustrated right now. I think I'd rather grab something from a drive through and be alone."

"I understand. How about we try again tomorrow night?"

She didn't need to look at the calendar to know the answer she didn't want to give. "I work late the next few nights, fulfilling our weekend orders."

"Weekends are busy at the restaurant and I need to be on hand."

"And we have a wedding reception Saturday."

"What about Sunday," he inquired.

"My family gets together every Sunday for dinner."

There was silence on the other end of the line. She wondered if he expected an invitation. Surely he couldn't. The chaos that would follow if she showed up with a pro hockey player would be enough for a week's worth of migraines.

"Uh, how about Monday." She grimaced, knowing it was almost a week away, but also sure she wasn't ready for family introductions.

Thankfully, Graydon agreed. "How about I make the plans? Can you get off work a little early, say, about four-thirty?"

"I'll check with Kristen and get back to you." There was a

knock on the bakery back door. "It looks like the officer is here. I'm really sorry about tonight. I was looking forward to seeing you."

"It's okay. Send me a text message to let me know you got home safely."

"I will. Thanks." She hung up, then opened the back door and found Officer Giles standing there.

"Good evening, Miss Marconi. I heard you had another incident. This time with your car?"

She greeted him, then led him to her car. They walked around it, while she pointed out each of the keyed marks. He made notes and took pictures, asking her more questions while he worked. "Did you see anyone lurking around?"

"No, we don't have any windows that face this direction, but Charles would have said something if anyone was hanging out. He's inside if you'd like to ask him any questions."

"Did you have any problems in the shop today?"

She shook her head. "It was a pretty normal day."

He nodded and made a few more notes. "I'll talk with him, then give you a copy of the report."

After talking with Charles, Officer Giles finished his report, then handed it to her. "It's most likely teenagers again. I'll recommend additional units patrol this area for the next week. Hopefully we'll find the kids who are doing this."

"Has anyone else had any problems?"

"Not that I know of, but I'll check on it and get back to you."

Once the officer left, she said good night to Charles and went back out to her car. As she started it up, she looked around the dark lot lit by two lamp posts. She felt antsy, like someone was watching. Which was impossible because if there was someone out there, the officer would have surely seen him. It couldn't be Nico, could it?

She bit her lip, then pulled the car out of the lot. On her way home, she stopped by a Taco Bell drive through. Her taste buds were sad as she thought of the yummy meal she missed out on with Graydon. It was even more depressing to think of the time she could have spent laughing with him rather than frustrated by teenagers.

When she finally got home, she sat down to eat and sort the mail. Her home felt lonely, so she pulled out her cell phone to send a text message to Graydon.

R: I MADE IT HOME. EATING TACO BELL. SORRY ABOUT TONIGHT.

She clicked send, then went back to eating her tacos, waiting for his reply.

Beep. Beep.

G: GLAD YOU'RE SAFE. I MISS YOU. MONDAY IS TOO FAR AWAY.

Her thumbs worked their magic on her phone's keyboard.

R: I AGREE. LIFE IS TOO BUSY.

His text came back much faster this time.

G: MAYBE I'LL HAVE TO THINK OF SOME WAY TO SQUEEZE IN A VISIT.

The prospect of seeing him, even just for five minutes, filled her with excitement.

R: I'D LIKE THAT. I BETTER FINISH THESE TACOS. I'M SUPER TIRED. READY TO END THE DAY.

G: LOOK FORWARD TO A BETTER, BRIGHTER DAY TOMORROW. SLEEP WELL. GOOD NIGHT.

R: GOOD NIGHT.

She continued to refresh the screen. Just seeing his name made her feel better. She eventually went to bed, wondering when they'd see each other again.

The diner waitress filled the two coffee cups. "What can I get for you tonight?"

"This will be all," Tom replied, pulling his hat off his balding head. The waitress sniffed, clearly miffed about not getting a bigger order, but said to let her know if they needed anything before she moved a few booths away to check on another customer. He sighed. It was all a part of business, but still he sympathized with the woman, knowing how many hours his own wife stood on her feet doing the exact same thing.

He turned his attention back to his client, Mr. Giambiasi. He pulled a plain manila envelope out of his dark jacket pocket, then slid it across the table. His client picked it up, flicking through the photos, pausing now and then to assess details.

Being a private detective wasn't as glamorous as Tom thought it would be. Every once in a while he landed an exciting case—like the ones Mr. Giambiasi brought—but mostly he ended up following cheating loved ones. It sucked all the goodness out of life. He was thankful for his own wonderful wife, who continually restored his faith in humankind.

His client placed the photos back in the envelope and tucked them into a briefcase. "Good work. Keep it up and add this person to your surveillance as well."

Tom lifted the photo his client offered and was captured by the target's green eyes and long auburn hair. He glanced up at his client, wondering how they were connected, but that wasn't any of his business. Tracking and reporting were his job. He flipped the photo over to find the typical background info written there.

"Consider it done," he said, tucking the new target's photo into his shirt pocket.

Mr. Giambiasi pulled out his phone, tapped in some information, then tucked it back into his coat pocket. "The transfer is complete. I look forward to hearing from you soon."

Tom nodded, then watched his client leave the diner. He looked over at the untouched cup of coffee left behind and sighed, dug out some cash and left it on the table for the waitress, hoping the tip would cheer her up. Then he too left, excited about beginning a new pursuit.

Chapter THIRTEEN

*L*ater that week, Graydon couldn't stop thinking about Rachel. Her face and laugh popped into his thoughts throughout the morning, sometimes at the oddest times. Like when Chef Mike smacked him over the head for grinning like an idiot and staring off into space when he was supposed to be going over the menu and specials.

Waiting a week to see her was torture. Even though his schedule overflowed on the weekends, the rebellious side of him wanted to play hookie. To drive over and spend the evening with her, even if she was decorating cakes. He wondered what it would be like to watch her in action, starting with just cake and building up from there, creating a masterpiece. Would it be like watching a sculptor create something from nothing? The list of things he wanted to know about and experience with her was getting longer and longer. Which he considered a good sign. If the list ever ran out, well, he'd probably want to brainstorm a new one with her. He didn't think it was possible to feel so strongly about someone after such a short period of time.

It hadn't been like this with Carissa. Their relationship had been exciting, always in the media. Their schedules full of charity events, hockey games, places to go and be seen. But after the accident, Carissa easily walked away, on to look for the next guy who would keep her in the limelight. It crushed him when she walked out. And again six months later when she died in a car crash.

Now he wanted what his parents had. A serious relationship, where both people were willing to stand up and support each other, no matter what life brought. Hopefully there would be a lot of laughter and blessings, but life always brought bumps and bruises too. He wanted someone to hold onto during those rough patches. His gut told him Rachel might be that person.

Time will tell, he thought. *Just be patient.*

But patience wasn't his best trait. Which is why he ended the meeting with Chef Mike early, canceling a meeting with Sheila, and was out getting sandwiches, fruits, chips, and sodas for an impromptu lunch with Rachel and Kristen. He made one last stop at a florist shop to pick up a simple arrangement of fall flowers.

He parked in front of Sweet Confections and waited until some customers left, then went inside. Kristen looked up from behind the counter where she was wiping down the glass on the pastry case.

"Hey, stranger! I'm glad you're back. I think someone's missing you today." She winked. "And if those flowers are for her, you're going to melt her little frustrated heart."

"Is she having a rough day?" He set the lunch bags on a nearby table.

"Insurance company woes. They finally got the deductible worked out, but they mixed up her current contract with an outdated one. Now she just needs to get the car into the repair shop. I'll go back and grab her for you."

"Be sure to come back. I have stuff here for you, too." He motioned to the bag filled with food. Kristen disappeared through the swinging doors. When she returned, she had a frazzled-looking Rachel in tow.

"Graydon, I didn't expect to see you today, but I'm so glad you came," she said, as he pulled her into his arms for a hug.

"I brought these for you." He stepped back and handed her the flowers.

She brought the bouquet of yellows, oranges, and green close to her face and breathed in deeply. When she lifted her head, her shoulders were a bit more relaxed. Her face was smooth with less worry crinkles lining her forehead. "Thank you."

"Let me take those and get them in a vase and water." Kristen took the bundle of flowers and disappeared back into the kitchen.

Rachel wrapped her arms around him and buried her face in his neck. Wisps of her breath touched his skin, sending light goose bumps down his neck. Graydon ran his hands up and down her back, finding the tight muscles and massaging them until they relaxed.

"That feels amazing," she moaned.

Her warmth seeped through his shirt as her body relaxed against his. With one hand on her lower back, the other moved over her shoulders, then up to caress her neck. Another moan rumbled through her as his fingers moved in circular motions at the base of her skull. While his massage was relaxing for Rachel, it had the opposite effect on him.

Awareness thrummed through his veins, sending his hormones on a happy rush. He took a deep breath in an attempt to calm things down, but instead was surrounded by the heady blend of vanilla and Rachel's warm skin. His lips brushed her temple, her cheek. He felt Rachel's breath hitch as the kisses traveled closer to her lips. Before he could reach that tantalizing destination, Kristen loudly cleared her throat, announcing her return.

There was something about being caught making out by a girl's best friend that induced the immediate effects of a cold shower. Graydon reluctantly loosened his hold on Rachel and stepped back. Her eyes fluttered, then opened to reveal that she wasn't just feeling relaxed. At least he knew they were on the same page when it came to their reactions to each other.

"We probably have about ten more minutes of peace, if we're lucky," Kristen said, bringing them both back to the present. "So let's eat while we can." The trio pulled out the sandwiches, fruit, and chips. Kristen had predicted correctly when a customer soon came in. She hopped up to assist the client, then came back to sit with them.

"Kristen, tell me more about your family," Graydon said. "All I know is that you're married and have a little one."

Kristen motioned for Rachel to hand her a bottle of water. "Todd and I have been married for five years and we have a two-year-old daughter named Daphne. We live not too far from Rachel's house, in a more family-oriented neighborhood."

"How did you two meet?" He piled chips on his sandwich, then squished them together between the bun, making a satisfying crunch.

Kristen cringed. "That is so not right, but my hubby does the exact same thing. I just don't get it."

He laughed, then picked up his sandwich. "It gives it a crunchy, but salty taste. You should try it sometime."

"No thanks." She took another bite of her fruit and saluted him with her water bottle. "Healthy foods help me fit into my jeans. I'll stick with the fruit and water. Thanks though."

"Next time I'll make sure to bring a chef salad, if you prefer."

Kristen nodded, then got up to help another customer, giving them a few more minutes to visit.

"You may have to wait for your story about Kristen and Todd."

"We should go out on a double date with them sometime." He decided to test out something. "I'd like to meet the rest of your family, too."

Just like the other night, she became quiet. He didn't know why, but he knew she was avoiding the subject of her family. "Why do you do that?"

"Do what?" she asked, folding her sandwich wrapper.

"Get quiet when I bring up your family. Is there some reason you don't want them to meet me?"

"It's not them meeting you. Well, that's not true. It is that a little." She paused again, then leaned forward. "Here's the thing. I'm afraid they'll scare you off."

He couldn't stop the laughter that rumbled up. She never ceased to surprise him. "Scare me off? Have you seen the kind of guys I faced down on the rink?" She glared at him. "Well, I guess not since you don't like hockey. Believe me, your family couldn't be nearly as scary as them. I'm a pretty tough guy, you know."

She tapped her fingers on the table. "Let me ask you a question. Are you ready to get married?"

He jolted in surprise. That wasn't exactly a topic he was ready to jump into.

"And that's exactly why you shouldn't meet my family yet," she continued. "My mom is all about marrying off her only daughter, who, to her dismay, is over the age of twenty-five and still single." When he laughed again, she folded her arms across her chest. "I'm not kidding."

"Nope, she's not," Kristen said, rejoining them. "Her mom has one single focus, to get Rachel into a white dress, hear her say 'I do,' and be sure she makes the official name change the next day. My theory is her mom thinks she hasn't fulfilled her job until each of her kids is married and has at least one munchkin of their own. It's like her gold medal of sorts."

He shifted his gaze between the two of them. "You're serious. You're not just trying to pull one over on me?"

"Buddy, I'm as serious as a heart attack," Kristen said, then took a few more bites of her fruit salad.

"Anyway," Rachel said, interrupting the direction the conversation had gone. "I'm not subjecting you to them any sooner than necessary."

He was now the silent one, mulling over this new revelation. He was definitely serious about wanting a future with Rachel, but how fast did he want things to move? One thing he knew for sure, she was certain he couldn't handle her family. And he wanted to prove to her that he could. "I think your family sounds intriguing. I also think you should take me with you. This Sunday."

"Ha! You really have had too many knocks to the head if you think that's a good idea. Trust me, let's wait a while. Actually go on a few more dates first."

He let it slide—this time. But he planned to bring it up again. He was curious how long they needed to date before she took the plunge. He helped her clean up lunch. "We'll wait and see what happens."

She eyed him warily. He could imagine the wheels turning in her head, wondering what he was up to. It's a good thing she wasn't the only one who could put on a poker face. "Well, I better let you two ladies get back to work."

"Thanks for bringing lunch, Graydon." Kristen disappeared into the kitchen to give them one last moment of privacy before he left.

"It really was great to see you," Rachel said. "I like having you pop in during the day. It gives me an extra boost of energy."

"I'll have to see if I can fit in a few more. This weekend will be hard though. How about we call each other or even text. Sometimes the restaurant is too loud for phone calls, but I can squeeze in some texts."

"Sounds like a plan." She leaned into him. He wrapped his arms around her waist, enjoying the feel of her tucked against him. He rested his chin on her head, closed his eyes, and just stayed like that for a minute. "I hate it, but I have to go get back to work, too."

"Thanks again for lunch and the flowers."

He dropped a quick kiss on her nose, loving the impish grin that appeared on her face. He headed back toward Brisket and Noodles, devising a plan to see that grin again soon.

Chapter FOURTEEN

*W*hen Monday finally arrived, Graydon's single focus was to clear as much from his to-do list as he could before his date. Anything not completed was pushed off to Tuesday.

After picking up Rachel, they crossed town and pulled up to the gated entrance to his neighborhood, then rolled down the window. The cool fall air rushed into the vehicle. The weather in Crystal Creek was fickle, but thankfully had taken on a deep chill—perfect for his plans for their evening. Graydon reached over and took her hand in his, as the security guard left his station and came over to the truck.

"Hey, Stan," he greeted the older security guard. "How are you tonight?"

"Doing good, Mr. Green. It's been a pretty quiet evening."

"Stan, I'd like you to meet Rachel Marconi."

The guard tipped his hat to her. "It's nice to meet you, ma'am."

She smiled warmly. "It's nice to meet you, too."

"Rachel may be visiting often. I'd like to add her to my VIP guest list," Graydon said.

"Of course, Mr. Green. Let me get that paperwork for you."

While Stan went to retrieve the paperwork, Graydon took a moment to tell Rachel more about the community.

"Normally when someone comes to the gate, they ask for I.D. and if you're on my list, they'll let you through. If not, they call up to the house to ask for permission. It can sometimes be a pain, but it's a good measure of protection for all the residents."

"It makes sense. I'm sure you don't want just anyone to show up at your door. I can only imagine how chaotic that could become."

Stan returned with the paperwork. Rachel gave him her driver's license to photocopy while Graydon filled out the forms. Then they both signed the paperwork and returned it.

"Thank you, Stan, and please tell Gloria I said hello."

"Thank you, sir." He nodded then returned to the office. Graydon pushed a button installed in his truck which opened the gates and they drove through.

"Who's Gloria?" she asked.

"Stan's wife. She's a sweetheart. Most of the residents consider Stan an extended part of their families." He turned down Arapaho Drive and wondered what she thought as they passed a variety of large homes—the smallest just under seven thousand square feet.

She laughed when he pulled into his driveway. "You're a Charlie Brown fan, I see."

"Best comic strip ever," he replied. Together, they walked over to the fountain that captured her attention. It featured Charlie Brown decked out in hockey gear, complete with ice skates and hockey stick. The actual fountain was drained, but now filled with twinkle lights and a solid plastic cover that made it look like the ice glowed.

"I love it," Rachel said, enthusiasm bubbling from her voice. "What prompted it?"

"I was a huge Peanuts fan when I was young and never

grew out of it. When I had this house built, my family gave me the fountain as a housewarming gift. I also have wooden Peanuts scenes for all the seasons."

"Your family is very thoughtful," she said, turning to him.

He took her hand and kissed the top of it. "I hope you'll get to meet them soon. They aren't nearly as scary as you think your family is."

She playfully bumped into his side. "Few families are."

He unlocked the door and entered the security code on the other side in the entry way. There were only two people who had keys to his house—his parents for emergencies and Sheila because sometimes she needed to come to the house to get files or an emergency change of clothes for a last-minute interview. There were very few people he trusted with his private space. He glanced at Rachel as she looked around the foyer. He hoped to make that three in the near future.

"Would you like a tour?" he asked. She agreed and he took her hand, then led her through an open archway into the living room. The house was mostly decorated in comfortable contemporary themes. Large over-stuffed chairs and couches, tables with simple lines.

"Did you have a decorator?"

"My mother, actually. She had a blast furnishing the house, adding all the artwork and family pictures." He led her from the living room into the formal dining room where a long mahogany table surrounded by ten chairs filled the room. "We hold most of our family holiday dinners here since I have the biggest table. It expands so we can add six more chairs."

Large windows helped lessen the formality of the room. The natural light made it feel comfortable rather than stifling. A white lace runner graced the center of the table with a large bouquet of silk flowers in the center. On either side were bowls filled with glass balls.

"I love Ansel Adams," she said, walking over to admire the black and white framed prints that lined one of the walls. "He had such an incredible eye for light, shadows, and textures."

"Have you ever read his biography? He would wait for days until the perfect combination came together." *Kind of like us,* he thought.

"I didn't know that. Do you own the book?"

He nodded. "You can borrow it sometime, if you'd like." He led her into what he hoped would be one of her favorite rooms, the kitchen. He paused just inside the doorway to watch the expression on her face.

Interest, then absolute delight filled her countenance. She left his side to explore the space. The kitchen was a heaven for someone who loved to cook. Since there were so many cooks in his family, he wanted it to be a place they could work together. Glass fronted mahogany cabinets lined one wall above the kitchen sink and work area. There was a large island that curved in an L-shape through the center of the room with plenty of space to move around without bumping into each other.

The walls were painted a warm green with lime accents and white trim. Modern but comfortable and inviting. It was easily one of his favorite rooms.

Rachel ran her hand along the counters, opening drawers here and there, checking out the double ovens and the Dutch oven. "This is absolutely incredible. I feel like I died and discovered heaven." She slowly spun in a circle, taking it all in.

"I take it you approve?"

"Oh yeah. A great big one hundred and fifty percent yes. Oh, look, you have a breakfast nook tucked over here by the bay windows."

He followed her, enjoying how her hands ran over the back of a few chairs as she walked around the space. "It's much less intimidating. I hate eating in the dining room unless I have a group of people over."

"I would probably feel the same way." She wandered over to the French doors that led to the back deck. He flicked the switch to turn on the backyard lights so she could see more than just black emptiness.

The picture of her standing there framed by the doors, so comfortable and part of his home, hit him hard. He couldn't believe he was in this position. It used to be he was the one being chased. It was interesting to be on the other side—the fully committed one. Somehow he knew it would be worth it.

"I'm going to grab the steaks." He turned toward the refrigerator.

"What can I do to help?" she asked.

"Why don't you set the table?" He told her where the plates and utensils were stored. Once they gathered what they needed, he started the grill. When the table was set, she got the green salad, dressings, and potato salad. Once finished, she pulled on her coat and returned to Graydon's side while he tended the grill on the back deck. They both leaned against the deck rails, looking over the backyard.

"The yard's much bigger than I thought it would be and kid-friendly, too," she said, referring to the huge wooden play set area.

He shrugged. "Kids love that kind of stuff. It keeps my nieces, nephews, and friends' kids busy."

"I'm sure it does. My nephews would love it," she said.

"I've met Jordan, tell me about the rest of them," Graydon said, moving back to the grill to flip the steaks.

"I have four nephews. Jordan, Malone, Stockton and Emery."

"I'm seeing a theme here." Graydon chuckled. "So, who belongs to who and what's the story behind their names?"

"Jordan, Malone and Stockton belong to my brother Adam and his wife, Eva." Rachel put her hand up and interrupted before he could come back with a joke. "I already know. We've heard all the jokes a million times. Ha ha – Adam and Eva." Graydon sealed his lips together and smirked. So Rachel went on. "Anyway, they're both huge basketball fans. My other brother and sister-in-law, Christopher and Faith, have a little boy, Emery." She sighed. "Faith was my one hope to get away from the sports themed names."

"Why is that?" He lowered the grill lid and resumed his place next to her at the railing, putting his arm around her and pulling her close to keep her warm in the chilly air. Her nose was starting to turn pink, so he leaned down and kissed the tip of it. She giggled then tucked her head against his chest before continuing the name saga.

"Faith is a literature major. She's all about the greats— Shakespeare, Bronte, Dickens. So far, she's convinced Christopher that it's much cooler to name your kids after classic authors than athletes. Which brings us to Emery, who's five months old."

"Themed names are a thing in my family, too. Our names all start with Gr, like my parents - Graham and Gretchen."

"Really? I would think it'd be hard to find very many names."

He brought up his hand to tick off his siblings and names. "I have two sisters - Grace and Greer, and one brother, Grant."

"I'm seriously impressed," Rachel said. "Aside from knowing Adam's kids are named after athletes, I don't know anything about who the kids are named after. I just know the guys watch a variety of whatever sports are on. I don't keep track of any of it."

He waggled his eyebrows. "Oddly enough, I find that extremely sexy."

Rachel perked up, looking up to meet his gaze. "Really? You don't think I'm a twit because I have no idea who plays for who or what season certain sports are?"

Graydon pulled her closer. "Not at all. I've met tons of women who could spurt of stats like guys in the locker room. I used to think that was the kind of woman I should be with—someone who knows all the ins and outs like me. But, honestly, I really love that instead of seeing me as a statistic, you see me as Graydon Green. Just me." He reached his hand up, cupping her face. "I really love that about you."

Graydon leaned in and gently, but firmly sealed his lips to hers. He nibbled and teased, then deepened the kiss. Rachel clung to his shoulders, while his fingers sunk into her rich red hair, the silky strands sliding between his fingers. He moved one hand down to her neck. His thumbs gently caressing the underside of her chin, loving the glide of her soft skin beneath his fingers. When she pulled back, Graydon placed a few soft, brief kisses on her lips, then eased back even more.

"I think I could kiss you forever and never grow tired of it," he whispered. He smiled as heat filled her cheeks. The back of his knuckles trailed over her cheek, then he stepped back. "The steaks should be done by now."

After the steaks were plated, they went back inside to enjoy the warmth of the kitchen and their meal. Once they were settled in, Graydon picked up the conversation where they left off. "So, I take it you don't want to name your kids after sports icons?"

Rachel jerked, quickly looking up at him, her pretty green eyes wide. "Um," she paused for a moment. "Well, since I'm really not into sports, probably not. Sometimes I wish my family wasn't quite so sports-centered." She looked back up at Graydon. "I hope that doesn't offend you."

"No. My family is a lot like yours. It didn't bother me, since I loved sports, but my oldest sister, Grace, resented it. She was into music and art. I remember one night, finding her crying in her room because Dad had missed one of her concerts. I sat with her on the floor while she told me how much she hated it that Dad went to all my games, and even most of my hockey practices, but that she had to practically drag him, whine and moan and cry, just to get him to attend one of her concerts." He paused for a moment, lost in thought. "I was stunned. I honestly hadn't thought about it. I mean, I just figured Mom went to her stuff, Dad came to my stuff. I didn't think my sister cared one way or another. But I was wrong."

He looked at Rachel. The expression on her face intent and empathetic. She reached out and took his hand.

"I talked with my coach and after that, I never missed one of her concerts until I went off to college. Even then, I came home on whatever weekends I could to hear her play. And you know what, she's pretty amazing. I always thought she should have majored in music."

"What did she decide to do instead?"

He smiled, irony filling his voice. "She's a computer programmer and designs video games. Her very first project for Sony was a hockey competition game." Rachel laughed and he continued the story. "She got a bunch of my teammates and I to be the voices for some of the players and coaches. It's a really awesome game. I'll have to show it to you sometime."

"That's probably the only sports video game I'd actually be interested in seeing."

"So, no sports icon names. What kind of names do you like?"

"I haven't thought about names very much. If I had to choose now, I'd want my kids to be named after something meaningful. Not an icon or some celebrity, but someone we knew and admired, that the kids would interact with and could look up to as an example."

He tilted Rachel's head up to meet his gaze. "You're one amazing woman, do you know that?" He placed a quick kiss on her lips, then turned the conversation to her nephew, Malone's upcoming birthday, and Lego-themed birthday cake ideas. Legos was something he could totally get behind, being a huge fan as a kid himself and still enjoying them with his nieces and nephews now. Together, they discussed possible themes, then settled on an astronaut design with Commander Malone on the vest to personalize it.

"You're just a big kid deep down inside, aren't you?" She tipped her face up to meet his gaze.

"I don't think you have to search very deep to find my inner-kid," he replied. After dinner was cleaned up, Graydon took Rachel's hand. "I have a surprise for you."

"Did I ever tell you I truly hate surprises?" She folded her arms and leaned back against the kitchen counter.

He hesitated, assessing her expression. "Really?"

She tilted her head, holding his gaze. Then she winked and smiled.

"Oh no. You fibbed. You know what that means," he asked, stepping close, bringing his hands to her hips.

Sparkles lit up Rachel's eyes as she leaned toward him. "Mmm, what?"

His hands gently squeezed her hips, then slid up to her waist and up a little farther until they rested on the lower portion of her rib cage. He brought his lips to her ear, nibbled on the lobe as she tilted her head to give him more access to her throat. He placed a kiss just below her ear, then whispered, "Tickles."

He proceeded to gently dig his fingers into her ribs as she squealed and tried to squirm away, but he pulled her closer and continued until she begged for mercy. His hands cupped her face and he gave her a loud smacking kiss. "Are you ready for your surprise now?"

Still laughing, Rachel nodded her head. They bundled up and he led her outside. This time he took her to the back corner of the house lot, where a large fence surrounded a basketball court.

"Are we going to shoot some hoops?" Rachel asked. "'Cause I should warn you, I'm the air ball queen."

Graydon chuckled. "Air ball queen?"

"Hey, someone has to claim the royal title." Rachel shrugged.

He loved the teasing glint in her eyes and wanted to see it there more often. He pulled the court gate open and stepped aside. Rachel peered in and gasped.

"It's covered in ice!" She looked up at him. "How does it work?"

"In the winter, I have it filled with water and a freezer system helps the natural weather to keep it chilled enough for skating. It's not as smooth as ice at a rink—no Zamboni. But it's fun and convenient, too." He bent and opened one of the long storage boxes situated next to a bench. Inside were several sets of ice skates in a variety of sizes. Together, they found a set for Rachel and they laced up their skates.

Graydon took her hand and led her onto the ice. He steadied her as she wobbled and found her footing. Then he turned backwards and took both her hands to lead her around the court.

"You're doing a great job. Just lean forward a bit more, that's it," he encouraged her.

She looked up, excitement in her eyes. "It's like roller skating," she said.

He rolled his eyes. It was nothing like roller skating, but he wasn't going to argue the point.

"I think I'm good now," she said, pulling her hands back. He let go, but stayed nearby for when she undoubtedly would need to be caught. She pushed ahead a little, then a little more.

"You're doing good, but be careful. I don't want you to get hurt."

She looked over her shoulder at him, then surprised him by turning in a full circle, then bursting forward, gaining speed. His eyes widened and his heart just about stopped beating. She was going to get hurt. Before he could call out a warning, she prepped, jumped and landed a single axle.

What the heck?

She glided over the ice and back to circle around him

before stopping precisely in front of him. "I said I didn't like hockey, not that I couldn't skate," she mocked with a wide grin on her face. Then she took his hand and together they took off, playing chase, showing off for each other, and laughing. Lots of laughing.

He wasn't sure how long they played before she started to get tired and he suggested they head back inside to warm up. They switched into their regular shoes and held hands back to the house.

"Now that I know you can actually skate, you should consider coming with me to the California hockey camp." He glanced down at her, noticing the rosy hue on the tip of her nose and her cheeks. Rather than making her look red all over, it gave her a happy, carefree look.

"Only because I can skate, huh?" she countered, surprising him.

"Well, that and your magic food skills. I could put you to work charming, I mean, organizing the caterers."

Rachel's laugh echoed in the dark night as they climbed the back steps. "It's a tempting offer. I'll consider it."

Graydon paused just outside the door, squeezing her hand gently. "I really would like to have you there, to experience what I love about the camps."

"I'd love to come. Let me check into the timing and talk with Kristen."

Once inside, they set their coats on the table in the kitchen nook. Rachel shivered and rubbed her hands together. Graydon placed her hands between his and chafed them together.

"I'll make some hot chocolate to warm us up," he suggested.

"I know something else that would do the trick," Rachel

said, as she edged closer, then she raised her lips to his. The kiss started out tentative, but then she opened her lips and rubbed her tongue against his, sending heat cascading through him. Her hands left his and moved up his chest. Even with his sweater as a barrier, her hands against him felt wonderful. His own moved to her hips, his thumbs brushing against the edge where her jeans met soft skin.

He led her a few steps back until she was supported by a wall, never breaking contact with her mouth, feeding her hot, open-mouthed kisses. A groan ripped from deep within him. His hands slid up over her back. She felt silky, soft, and oh, so sweet.

He broke his lips away, panting against her neck, still caressing her with his hands. "I'm definitely feeling warmer." He gently kissed her neck, then pulled back. It killed him to put distance between them, her wide eyes filled with desire where she stood limp against the wall.

Holy wow. He took another step back and sucked in a deep breath. Patience, he told himself. "I should probably get the hot chocolate." She nodded, still a bit dazed from their kisses. All he wanted to do was dive back in. "On second thought," he said. "Maybe we should call it a night."

Her beautiful green eyes were once again clear and she nodded in agreement. "Too much, too soon. No matter how much I enjoyed it," she said, with a devilish grin.

He took her hand, kissed the back of it, then they gathered their things and started back to her house.

His preparations had paid off. It felt good to share their family stories and a blast to see Rachel on the ice. It was amusing to bring out his sweet baker girl's competitiveness. Memories from the evening made him chuckle again.

"What's so funny?" She turned to face him from her seat in the truck.

"You, cutting me off when we were racing to the other side of the court. You have some sneaky moves."

She smacked his arm. "Well, you were deliberately picking on me, the pro hockey player racing a poor ice skating amateur. It wasn't good sportsmanship."

He laughed some more while she pouted. "Just a side note, I know you don't like violent sports, but woman, you play like a linebacker getting ready to tackle the opposing team."

"I never said I wasn't competitive," she replied, defending herself.

It had been a fun and a life-changing evening. His heart was still turning in circles and pounding like he just won the Stanley Cup. Who knew love could be like this?

Did he just think the L word without keeling over into a six foot hole? He considered it for a moment. Yes, he did and it felt good, too. He pulled up outside of Rachel's town house. They continued to banter back and forth as they walked up the front sidewalk. He was so focused on their conversation, he almost ran her over when she stopped abruptly.

"Hey, are you okay?" Color had drained from her face and she looked white under the street lamps. He grasped her arm, afraid she might faint.

"Nico," she whispered.

He looked up, surprised to see the man from the restaurant coming down the stairs. His strides ate up the ground between Rachel's front porch and where they stood. As he neared, Graydon could see Nico looked on edge. Graydon pulled Rachel closer to him and wrapped his arm around her waist, trying to let her know she was safe. Graydon's protective instincts kicked in, adrenaline surging through him. He tried to rein it in; he didn't want to beat the poor guy to a pulp. Yet.

"Rachel," Nico began. "I need to talk to you. Right away."

She shivered beneath his hand. "What are you doing here? I thought you understood things were really over."

"There's something going on. We need to talk." He glanced briefly at Graydon. "Without him here."

"Well you can bet that isn't going to happen," Graydon said, joining the conversation.

Nico turned to face him. His eyes turned from anxious to furious. When he raised his clenched fists, Graydon tucked Rachel behind him. *This guy is nuts,* he thought.

"You're the one who's screwing everything up. It's all your fault. If you would just go away, everything would be fine." Nico's fists clenched, the veins bulging on the back of his hands. Then he lunged, his fist flying wild.

Graydon knocked him to the side, making Nico stumble and fall onto the grass. Then Graydon turned so Rachel was closest to the town house door. "Get inside, lock the door and call 911."

Instead, she pushed past him. "This is ridiculous. Nico," she pleaded. Graydon caught her and pulled her further away, terrified Nico would grab for her. "Please, stop it. Go home or to your hotel or wherever you're staying. Don't make this worse."

Surprisingly, Nico paused and looked down the street. Graydon had no idea what he was looking for, but he seemed calmer. Still, he stayed alert, just in case it was a trick.

Nico returned his attention back to Rachel. "We *will* talk.

Soon." Then he jogged down the street in the opposite direction.

They remained still, then heard a car door slam, an engine roar, and fade off. Graydon turned to Rachel. Her face was still pale and her eyes showed a mixture of worry and fear.

He cupped her face with his hands. "Are you okay?" She shook her head in the affirmative, but he could see the shine of tears gathering in her eyes. His heart clenched, hating to see her hurt. She gasped when he lifted her in his arms.

"Graydon, I can walk," she protested, but he ignored her until he set her down at the front door. Once they were in her townhouse and the door was locked, he led her to the couch and sat with her across his lap. He stroked her hair and encouraged her to talk. And she did. Everything came tumbling out—Nico's betrayal, the real reason behind their breakup and his continued attempts to mend the relationship since. Slowly, her chatter came to a halt and they sat curled up together on the couch. He ran his fingers through her hair. It seemed to help, so he continued the motion. He had no idea how much time passed before her breathing slowed and he knew she had fallen asleep. Still, he stayed where he was.

He listened to the night sounds outside. Dissecting them, wondering if Nico would try to come back. The clock on the DVD player indicated it was after midnight. Everything seemed calm outside. Gradually, he shifted Rachel so she was lying on the couch. He stretched his arms and legs, then checked the house, making sure the windows were locked. Once he was certain everything was secure, he returned to the couch and lifted her in his arms. She stirred and snuggled into him as he carried her into the bedroom, where he had already pulled the covers down. He carefully placed her on the bed, removed her shoes, then tucked the covers around her.

"Rachel," he whispered. He repeated her name again, until her eyelids fluttered open. "Hey, how are you feeling?"

She closed her eyes, then reopened them, more aware of where she was. "I'm okay." Her voice was a bit wobbly and cracked. "What time is it?"

"Just after midnight."

Her eyes widened, then she pushed herself up onto elbows, realizing where she was. "You put me to bed?"

He sat on the edge, sinking into the soft mattress. "You were out cold," he replied, smoothing some hair and tucking it behind an ear.

"Look at your shirt." She reached out, putting her hand on his chest. "There's mascara all over it. It's probably ruined." She looked at him, her eyes luminous. "I'm so sorry."

He placed his hand over hers, giving it a gentle squeeze. "It's fine. Don't worry about something as insignificant as a shirt." He kissed her hand. "Listen, do you want me to call Kristen? She would come over and stay with you."

She closed her eyes and shook her head. "I just want to sleep."

When she opened her eyes again, he could see the remnants of fear lurking in their depths. He studied her for a moment. Finally, he nodded. "I already checked the house. All the doors and windows are locked."

She put her hand against his cheek. He loved the feel of her soft skin against his. "Thank you."

"Do you mind if I camp out on the couch?"

"Y-you want to stay?" She stammered, a blush spreading over her cheeks.

"You shouldn't be alone tonight. If you don't want to call Kristen, I'll fit just fine on the couch."

She chewed on her lower lip, pulling the comforter into a knot in her hands. Then she looked up at him. "Okay, but could you sleep here?" A deep blush covered her cheeks. "I don't mean sleep with me, well, I do, but not, you know . . ." She dropped back onto the pillows and pulled the comforter over her head.

Graydon chuckled, then pried the cover out of her hands until her face reappeared. "If you're offering to let me sleep on your very comfortable bed, rather than a short couch, I accept. Rachel," He tipped her face up until she met his gaze. "I can sleep beside you and not, well, you know," he said, imitating her earlier stumble. She swatted his hand away and they both laughed, releasing some of the night's anxiety.

He kicked off his shoes, then climbed onto the bed, lying on top of the covers. He looked over and found Rachel holding the comforter to her chest with a death grip. He pulled her to his side, where she nestled her head into his shoulder and finally relaxed. He kept his arm wrapped around her, while his other hand held hers on top of his chest.

"Could I ask for just one more favor?"

"Anything," he replied, rubbing his thumb across the back of her hand.

"Would you stay just until I fall asleep? There's a spare key hanging on the key rack in the kitchen. You can use it to lock up."

He looked down at her, confused. "May I ask why?"

"You'll think it's silly," she said.

"Try me."

She nibbled on her lower lip again. This time, instead of

notching up his worry, it made him want to kiss her instead. Nope, no thinking about kissing. Finally, she sighed and replied, "I'm just not ready for the morning after thing. I have horrible morning breath and ran out of mouth wash yesterday." Once again, her face bloomed with a blush, this time a light pink dusting her freckled cheeks.

"I love it when you blush." He looked down at where she tried to hide her face. "Bad morning breath, huh?" She nodded against his shoulder. He chuckled. "Okay, no worries. I'll stay until you're back in dreamland and lock the door behind me when I leave."

Graydon pulled her into a tight hug, just holding her, feeling her melt into him. He brought his lips down close to her ear. "I love you, Rachel Marconi. Don't you forget that."

He felt her smile against his cheek, where she placed a soft kiss. "I love you, too," she replied softly.

He turned his face so their lips just barely touched in a light caress, clinging and sweet. Man, the feelings that burst through him. Not lust or need, but protectiveness and the urge to comfort. To keep her safe. To love.

He tucked her head back to his shoulder and rested his cheek against the top of her head, while he stroked her long length of auburn hair. He continued holding her like that until long after her breathing evened out, signaling that a deep sleep claimed her. He listened to the sound of a cat meowing nearby, something about it comforting. Everything sounded fine, like nothing out of the ordinary had happened that night.

But he knew better. He'd be keeping a much closer eye on Rachel from now on. Because no one—and he meant no one —was going to intimidate or hurt the woman he loved.

Chapter FIFTEEN

ing, ring, ring.

Rachel woke abruptly as her cell phone continued to go off. She looked at her bedside clock. 5:24 am. Who in the world would call at this hour?

She grabbed the phone. "Hello?" she croaked.

"This is the Crystal Creek Police Department. We're trying to reach Rachel Marconi, owner of Sweet Confections."

Fear trickled like icy water through her arms and chest. "This is she."

"Ma'am, there's been a break-in. We have officers at the store now. Could you please meet them?"

"What happened?" She scrambled out of bed and hurried to her dresser, where she pulled out some socks, jeans and a sweatshirt.

"We can't give details over the phone. The officers on location will answer your questions."

"Okay. Thank you, I'm on my way." She threw the phone on the bed, quickly took off her pajamas, then yanked on her clothes. She needed to call Kristen, but first shoved her feet into sneakers and grabbed her purse. Paper fluttered to the floor and she quickly snatched it up, then turned it over.

R—

I hope you got some rest. I'll call you later today.

Love —G.

PS - Don't forget to add mouthwash to your shopping list.

A hysterical giggle bubbled up before Rachel stamped it back down and rushed out of her townhouse, wishing she had not asked Graydon to leave. How she craved his solid calmness at this moment. She fumbled, trying to get the key into the car door, so worried she didn't think to use the remote. She finally got into the car and sped out of the parking lot. Thankfully, work traffic was still pretty light, but in another thirty minutes, she knew it would fill up with drivers on their daily work commute into downtown Crystal Creek and further into Kansas City.

She pulled her phone out and speed dialed Kristen. Her husband answered within the first few rings.

"Todd, you need to get Kristen down to the store right away. The police called to say there was a break-in."

"Did they say anything else?" She could hear him shaking a sleepy Kristen awake.

"No, but I'm on my way. They said we'd find out more when we got there. I'm only a few blocks away now."

"Okay, we'll be right behind you."

She turned the last corner. Just ahead was Sweet Confections. Three police cars with flashing lights were parked at the curb, blocking the front entrance. She pulled to a stop behind the last cruiser, then rushed up the sidewalk. They were already stringing yellow crime scene tape around the perimeter of the store. An officer stopped her before she could get any closer.

"Can I help you, ma'am?" asked the female officer.

"I'm Rachel Marconi, one of the owners. I received a call telling me there was a break-in."

The officer extended her hand. "I'm Officer Seddon. Let me take you back to Officer Giles. He was the first responder and will lead the investigation."

She gasped when she caught the first glimpse of the store front. The windows were broken with a chair hanging halfway out of the frame. Officer Seddon guided her around the debris outside and the officers who were sorting through the glass shards for evidence. Inside was even worse. The pastry case was smashed, tables and chairs were thrown around. Paint had been haphazardly sprayed on the walls. Back in the kitchen, pans, trays, and utensils were all over the floor. Finally, she spotted Officer Giles.

"This is the owner, Rachel Marconi," Officer Seddon said by way of introduction.

Officer Giles held out his hand. "We need to stop meeting like this," he replied as they shook hands.

She swallowed the lump in her throat. "Do you have any idea who did this?"

"Rachel! Where are you?" Another officer blocked Kristen and her husband.

"It's okay. This is my business partner."

Todd wrapped his arms around both the women, comforting them. "It's going to be okay. We'll get through this," he murmured.

"Sorry," Rachel said, wiping the tears off her cheeks.

"It's perfectly normal. Break-ins and vandalism are a shock."

Officer Giles went over the details found so far. Much of it was what Rachel had already seen on her way to the kitchen. The officers needed to do a thorough search before the women would be allowed back in. Then their job would be to catalog missing and damaged items for both the police report and their insurance company. He also suggested that they hire a professional cleaning crew to come in rather than trying to take care of it all themselves. He recommended a few companies that worked with the department.

"Did you keep any money on site?" Officer Giles asked.

"Not much," Kristen replied. "Each night we do a bank deposit. We only keep about one hundred and fifty dollars at the store overnight for change the next day."

He nodded, writing the details in his notepad. "Do you know of anyone who would want to target you this way?"

Rachel, still numb, shook her head. Kristen did the same.

Officer Giles eyed both women. "I have something else to show you." He led them to the pastry refrigerator, where someone was taking pictures. When he moved aside, she saw everything was just as they left it—except for a huge knife sticking out of a wedding cake. Stuck to the shelf was a piece of torn paper. She edged closer to read the writing on the note.

I saw you. Stay away.

Her vision became fuzzy and the room started to spin. She felt hands grabbing her and voices echoing like she was in a tunnel.

"Nico," she whispered, just before everything went black.

Rachel blinked and squinted against the bright light. She moved her head to the side, but a dull ache settled in. She was lying on something cold and hard. After a moment, she realized it was the floor. Her vision cleared and she saw Todd off to the side talking to Officer Giles.

"Hey, you're awake. You scared me." She turned her head and found Kristen sitting beside her, holding her hand. She tried to sit up, but was pushed back down. "Be still for a minute. The officer called for an ambulance. That note shocked you enough that you passed out."

The note, knife and cake. It all came rushing back. Rachel closed her eyes, wishing the nightmare would go away.

"Do you really think Nico destroyed the bakery?" Kristen asked.

"I don't know. Maybe. He showed up last night at the end of my date with Graydon. He was scary, Kristen. He kept saying we had to talk and that everything was Graydon's fault. I thought things were finally finished, but then last night . . . and now this? I just don't know." She pushed herself up to her elbows, then slowly sat up.

"How did he know about your date? Do you think he's following you?"

The thought of being spied on made her feel icky and disgusting. She pulled her knees to her chest and wrapped her arms around them, seeking comfort when really she was terrified. How had everything spun out of control?

Officer Giles returned with two ambulance workers in tow. A tall black EMT with a friendly smile knelt beside her. "Hello, ma'am. My name is Bill. I was told you fainted. I see you're sitting up, are you feeling better?"

"I think so. I was just a little overwhelmed."

"I understand. I'd like to do a quick check to make sure you're alright. Is that okay with you?"

She nodded her approval, then Kristen stood and moved a few steps back to give them some room. Rachel answered the EMT's questions about the morning, if she was sick, if she had eaten, etc. while he took her blood pressure, pricked her finger to test her blood sugar, and attached a glowy thing to her finger which somehow gave a reading on her oxygen levels. The tests and questions didn't take long.

"Everything looks good, although your blood sugar is a little low. I recommend coming to the hospital for a few more tests. You can ride with me or have someone bring you."

Rachel shook her head. "No, I'm okay. Thanks."

Kristen stepped closer. "Are you sure? You passed out. Maybe—"

"It was just the shock of everything." Rachel looked at Bill. "Really, I'm feeling much better now. I don't need to go to the hospital, but thank you for coming. I appreciate your help."

"You're welcome. I suggest getting some good food into your system soon." Bill's silent partner handed him some paperwork. He looked it over, then handed a pen and the papers to Rachel. "I just need you to sign these before we can go. If you start to feel lightheaded again, you should call us back or go to a hospital, okay?"

"Thanks." Once everything was taken care of and the ambulance was gone, Officer Giles and Todd rejoined Rachel and Kristen. "I'd like to get up now," she said and Todd reached over to help her stand. She swayed slightly, then regained her balance. "I'm okay," she reassured an anxious-looking Kristen.

Officer Giles pulled out his notebook and turned the conversation back to the break-in. "Mr. Fields told me about your former boyfriend and the subsequent break-up. I would like to get access to any phone messages you may have."

"I deleted them, but I have the phone records of when he called and how often. I can download them and print them off for you," she offered.

"Actually, after you download them, you can email them directly to me." He gave her his card again. "If it is your ex-boyfriend, then you should consider obtaining a restraining order. People in this frame of mind can be dangerous."

A shudder rippled through her. After seeing the extreme damage done to the shop, she agreed that whoever did it was not in a good frame of mind.

"I need to get some more information, then you can go. I'll call when you can start cataloging the damages."

After giving him Nico's full name and contact information, she promised to email the phone records and anything else she could think of later that morning. She took one last look at the debris and damage, then joined Kristen and Todd out front.

Kristen was on the phone with the insurance company, but Todd told her what they had found out so far. Kristen clicked the cell phone shut, then looked at the time display. "It's not even 8 am and I'm exhausted. We need food and to talk."

The trio went to a nearby pancake house. Rachel sank into the booth, then put her head in her hands. She just couldn't get over what happened at Sweet Confections. What had pushed Nico so far over the edge that he would do something like that?

Once the waitress took their drink orders, Kristen began the inquisition. "What in the heck happened last night?"

Her shoulders felt like two tons of bricks were sitting on them. She drew in a deep breath, then recounted the previous evening's events.

"And you didn't call me? Me, Rachel? I'm your best friend! I can't believe you let something like that happen without picking up the phone and asking me to come over. I would have stayed with you or brought you back to our house."

Todd coughed into his hand. "Honey, maybe you should ask if she was alone last night." He glanced meaningfully at Rachel.

"Well, of course she was—" Kristen broke off when she saw the blush rise on Rachel's face. "You *were* alone, weren't you?"

"Well, um, I guess the answer would be yes and no."

The waitress arrived with their drinks so Kristen had to hold back her questions. As soon as the waitress turned, Rachel raised her hand to ward of Kristen's questions.

"Just a minute, okay. I'll finish explaining, but let me get it out a bit at a time." Then a thought popped into her head. "Where's Daphne?"

"We called a neighbor and she came over to stay with her. She's fine, don't worry." Kristen grabbed her hand. "But thanks for thinking of her. And, Rach, I'm not trying to be pushy and bratty. I'm just worried about you."

Rachel squeezed her best friend's hand, thankful to know they were in this together. "Like I said, I wasn't alone last night. Graydon stayed most of the night to make sure Nico didn't come back."

"But what if he had? What would you have done, Rachel? You shouldn't have been alone. Especially after what we saw this morning."

"I agree with you now. But last night—" She paused to swallow past the lump in her throat. "I'm not going to lie. I was scared. I just wanted to pretend it was a fluke, that it wasn't as terrible as I thought." She paused for a moment. "Now I'm officially freaked out."

"Well," Todd said, "I suggest we start by calling a lawyer friend of mine and beginning the paperwork for a temporary restraining order. If Nico violates it, then we can get a permanent one and take further steps if necessary."

Rachel nodded her agreement. Todd was right. She needed to take some kind of legal action.

"And," he continued, "I think you should move in with us for a while."

"Oh no," she balked. "I don't think that's necessary."

"I think Todd's right," Kristen said. "You need to be with someone else until we know you're safe. So your choices are us or your parents."

"Just pull out the big guns, why don't you?"

Kristen just smirked. "I knew you'd see it my way."

Rachel grimaced, knowing when her friend had her beat.

The waitress came back with their orders. She placed the biggest stack of pancakes they offered and a side of scrambled eggs in front of Rachel. The adrenaline from that morning was wearing off. She needed some food in her stomach before she got too shaky. She picked up her cranberry juice and gulped down about half the glass. The clink of utensils against plates replaced their conversation while they each devoured their breakfasts. The details of the morning's wreckage continued making her gut twist into knots.

"We need to pull our files together and figure out what to do about our clients' orders," Kristen said. "Once we're allowed back in, we can check which orders are intact and which need to be redone. In the meantime, we'll want to call anyone who has pick ups for today and let them know about the break in so they don't show up and freak out."

"I have most of the orders on my phone," Rachel said. "I usually put in our client's phone numbers, too. I guess the anal side of me is paying off now."

The girls shared a brief, slightly forced chuckle. She fought off another round of tears. "I wonder how long it's going to take to get the bakery back in full working order." She looked up at her best friend. "I'm so sorry. This is all my fault."

Kristen slid from her side of the booth, around the table to sit next to her. "It is not in any way, shape, or form your fault. Nico makes his own choices and he'll pay the consequences for them, too."

"I bet it won't take long to get everything together," Todd said. "Once the insurance person does his stuff and the cleaning crew gets in and depending on when the front window can get replaced, you guys should be back into the bakery in a few weeks."

"Let's go back to my place so we can start a list." Kristen slid out of the booth. She waited for Rachel to join her while Todd paid the bill. "It's going to be fine. On the bright side, I think I see Chocolate Lava Sundaes on our lunch menu."

Rachel couldn't help but laugh as she put her arm around her best friend's waist. "Chocolate and girl power. Who can beat that?"

Chapter SIXTEEN

*G*raydon leaned back in his leather office chair at the DG Foundation and scanned the papers for the upcoming Los Angeles hockey camp. He and Sheila were thirty minutes into their morning meeting, which so far focused on contract details.

"This all looks good. Tell Zack to finalize everything with the rink in L.A." He set the paperwork down and turned his attention to his assistant.

Sheila made some notes in her planner. "That should work. He's going to be out there in two weeks. We also need to get bids from a new caterer. The people we used last time messed up the orders and the delivery time frame, as well."

"Actually, let's hold off on that."

Sheila looked up at him, a quizzical expression in her dark brown eyes. "Can I ask why? It's going to take a lot of time making contacts, getting bids and narrowing down the choices."

"I asked Rachel to join me for the camp. I think being in charge of the food would be a natural place for her to contribute."

Surprise flickered across Sheila's face. "Oh! Well, if she can make it, then you're right, the catering would be a good choice for her, considering her expertise. It would also lighten my to-do list a bit."

Graydon nodded, glad Sheila was on the same page, and flipped through a few pages in the L.A. hockey camp binder. "Have we started on the break out schedules?"

"Zack and Carson were working on it yesterday. They're brainstorming some new stuff to try. Carson also mentioned more L.A. pro players are interested in volunteering this year."

"Excellent. The more we have to come in for special sessions, the better. The kids love that." He looked up sharply when the office door slammed open and Zack hurried into the room.

"Graydon, you have to see this." He grabbed the TV remote and turned on the news channel.

"What is it?" Sheila asked as they joined Zack in front of the TV, where he was intently listening to the reporter who was being filmed live.

"Paul, can you tell us if the police have any leads on the vandals?" asked the news station anchorman.

"Right now, they are only reporting the damages, but this type of violent vandalism hasn't been seen in this neighborhood before. Nearby businesses are antsy and quiet. In fact, when I talked with Claudia Jessop, owner of Just Shirts Laundry Care, she told me she was shocked when she arrived at work this morning and saw all the police vehicles outside Sweet Confections."

Graydon felt like everything around him froze as he zeroed in on those two words. Sweet Confections. The reporter continued talking, but he turned to Zack. "What happened?"

"I don't know exactly. There was a break in with a lot of damage. I came in to tell you right away. I wasn't sure if Rachel had called yet."

Graydon strode back to his desk and dug through his briefcase until he located his cell phone. He clenched the phone, his heart beat thumping hard, the veins in his hand jumping. No missed calls. Was Rachel okay? Had she been at the shop when the vandals struck? He hit speed dial, listening to the phone ring as well as staying half tuned to the reporter.

The camera man moved the focus from the reporter to the bakery. Graydon swore when he saw the busted out windows and debris covering the sidewalks.

Zack swore under his breath. "That's one serious mess."

Sheila covered her mouth with her hand and shook her head from side to side.

"Hello, Sweet Confections. This is Rachel."

He looked away from the TV, relieved to hear her voice. "It's Graydon. I just saw the news. Are you okay? What's going on? Where are you?" He shot out question after question.

"Graydon. I'm sorry. I wanted to call you, but I've been swamped with calls from clients and family. I—" there was a brief moment when Rachel cut out. "Hang on a second. That's my brother."

"Okay," He barely got the word out before he heard the phone click over to the other line. He paced back and forth in front of his desk, waiting for her to come back on the line and listening for news updates. There wasn't much more to report though. No one was hurt. The bakery was broken into during the night while it was closed. *Thank you, God*, he thought with a short prayer.

"I'm back. Sorry about that. My brother was calling to offer us his kitchen to use until the bakery is back up and running, but I had to explain that it was illegal to run a bakery out of a house. You know, food safety laws and all that. Anyway, I'm glad you called. And yes, aside from being extremely stressed out, I'm okay. Physically anyway."

"Where are you?" His fingers felt numb from the tight grip around the phone.

"We came back to Kristen's to start putting to—" Another brief cut out. He heard her sigh. "Hang on another second. It's a client."

The phone clicked again before he could reply.

"Sheila, find me the address for Todd and Kristen Fields. Zack, call Brisket and Noodles and get Chef Mike on the phone. Tell him it's urgent."

He went into action. It was obvious that talking on the phone wasn't going to get him very far. He couldn't just stay here and wonder if she really was okay. She said she was fine physically, but he needed to see her. Touch her.

"Graydon, chef's on line one." Zack handed him the phone receiver.

He kept the cell phone to one ear and put the office line to the other. After a quick conversation, he had a few ideas of how he could help until Rachel's bakery was in order. While he was on the phone, Sheila slipped him an address written on a torn piece of paper from her planner. He nodded to her, got off the phone with the chef, and heard Rachel's end of the line click.

"I'm back," she said, sounding drained. "Today is going to totally suck. In fact, it's most definitely hit the #1 slot of suckiest day of my life. Crap! I can't even say more than two sentences and my phone is beeping again."

There was a brief pause. "It's my mother. I'm sorry Graydon but I'm going to have to take this."

"I understand. Is it okay if I hold?"

"Are you sure? Okay, hang on." Click.

He grabbed his briefcase, gave Sheila and Zack a few instructions to follow up with Brisket and Noodles, then took off. He was out the door and in his car in record time. He looked at the address Sheila gave him. He weaved in and out of traffic as he made his way over to the family neighborhood Kristen had described.

Rachel's line clicked again. "Oh my gosh. Someone shoot me already. My mother is on the war path!"

"What's up?"

"She's been on the internet all morning, looking up security systems and calling me every twenty minutes with updates on what she found and her opinion of what we should install. I'm about ready to pull my hair out!"

"While I agree with your mom that a security system would be a good idea, I can see how her timing isn't the best. It sounds like you've been bombarded with phone calls this morning," he said, maneuvering through traffic.

"It got worse when it hit the morning news. Several clients called to check on their orders, wanting to know if we'll be able to fulfill them."

He made a few last turns, then pulled up to the curb outside a nice two-story house. He double checked the house number, then got out of his truck and strode up the sidewalk to the front door, listening to her vent all along the way. He pressed the doorbell.

"Holy mackerel! Now someone's at the door. Kristen's upstairs with Daphne and I am going to explode. I just can't take this anymore. Hang on a sec."

The front door swung open and he came face-to-face with an extremely frazzled Rachel on the other side. Her hair was a mess and her cheeks were flushed.

"I thought we might be able to talk with fewer interruptions if I just came over." He pulled his phone away from his ear and hit the off key. He barely had enough time to catch Rachel when she launched herself at him.

"It's more than okay, I needed you so much." She buried her face in the curve of his neck.

He held her tight, finally at peace, knowing she was truly safe. He breathed deep, her familiar vanilla scent comforting him. "Why didn't you call?"

"At first it was just the urgency. I needed to get to the bakery. Then I was in shock after seeing the note, dealing with the police and insurance, then clients." She paused to take a deep breath, then just sighed.

"What note?"

She pulled back. The look on her face did not comfort him one bit. In fact, it did the exact opposite. "Let's go inside and I'll explain."

When Kristen returned with her daughter, Rachel handed the phone over so she and Graydon could talk uninterrupted. She went over the morning in detail, from the moment she got the phone call until he showed up at her door. He never felt such a conflicting set of emotions before—deep fear for her safety, as well as a boiling anger. He wanted to get his hands on that Nico guy and squeeze until he was no longer a problem.

"Now, we're trying to figure out when the bakery will be back together. We need to make phone calls to find other bakeries to fill our clients' orders."

He reached across the table and took her hand. "You know, I happen to have a restaurant with a rather large kitchen." He held up his hand before she could say anything. "I already talked to our chef. If you can bake early in the mornings, he said you can have full use of his kitchen until 9 am. At which time he needs at least half of the kitchen to begin lunch preparations. They need the full kitchen around eleven for the lunch rush, but he's willing to help out. I set aside a room off the kitchen for decorating, too. For today, though, he said he's willing to set aside a small portion of the kitchen so you can get your clients' orders done. What do you think?"

Her green eyes were wide and held an expression of disbelief. Silence filled the room, making him second guess his actions. Maybe he should have waited and talked to her first. Maybe she wouldn't like that he jumped in. What if she thought he was interfering? The twisty knot in his stomach was replaced by determination. Well, they needed help and the restaurant could fill their needs. He was going to help however he could. They'd just have to get used to it. Before he could open his mouth to say something he might regret, she broke the silence.

"You are most definitely a knight in shining armor." She reached over and took his hand. "Thank you." Her voice cracked on the last word.

He pulled her close. "You're welcome," he whispered, then tipped her head back to place a light kiss on her lips. He wanted to linger, but knew time was of the essence for these two women who had become an important part of his life. He pulled back and brushed his thumb over her cheek. "Are you ready to get back to work?"

A slightly crooked smile appeared. "Lead the way."

While Graydon and Todd spent the rest of the morning contacting clients, Rachel and Kristen went to Brisket and Noodles. She was nervous about meeting the head chef. The chefs she knew were excessively possessive about their kitchens. She couldn't fathom any of them willing to let strangers take over a portion of their sacred work environment.

"I am Chef Mike," the stout man said with a thick Bronx accent. His squinty eyes looked them over. "Which one of you is Graydon's girlfriend?"

Holy mackerel, she thought. *Girlfriend.* "That would be me." She met his gaze, steady and serious. She couldn't let him see her tremble in her boots. She was a professional. If she squirmed, he would most likely tear her to shreds.

After a moment, in which she was sure she sweat through her deodorant, he grunted. "Graydon is a good man. His family has helped mine many times. If a friend of his needs help, I'm happy to give it. Let me show you the workstations you can use."

She sent Kristen a relieved glance as they followed the chef to a side corner of the kitchen. There were some ovens back there so they wouldn't interrupt the rest of the workers.

"I had my staff bring out extra baking pans. There's a variety of rectangle, square, and round. If there's something you need that isn't here, just let me know."

She looked at the mixing utensils, bowls, and baking items. Bags of flour and sugar as well as other baking ingredients sat on a counter nearby.

"For today, you are welcome to use our supplies. We will talk about reimbursement after your bakery is sorted out."

"Thank you," Kristen reached out and shook his hand. "We appreciate your generosity."

Chef Mike nodded. "I'll let you get to work and will check back later."

Once they were alone, they sorted through everything, then made a plan. Kristen started mixing up batters, while Rachel created their signature buttercreams and fillings. The majority of the clients were willing to change their orders to vanilla or chocolate cakes with a simpler filling and buttercream icings. A few chose to cancel their orders altogether. As Rachel mixed, she went over the individual orders, devising ways to adapt each one but still bring out the unique design the client requested.

Once the icings and fillings were stored in the refrigerator, she sketched out her thoughts and made notes in the margins. When everything was ready, they divided up the orders, moved to the side room so Chef Mike could have his kitchen back and continued their work.

They were vaguely aware of Graydon and Chef Mike stopping in a few times to check on them. They worked straight through until early evening when the last cake was picked up. The clients were kind and gracious. Of course, it helped that Kristen and Rachel discounted the cakes for all the trouble and changes the clients were willing to make. When the last client left, Rachel met up with Kristen.

"It's been quite a day, girlfriend. Way to hustle." Rachel stretched her arms above her head, then leaned to each side.

It felt so good to stretch out the tight muscles before leaning against the wall.

Kristen took the spot next to her. "Ditto. Right back at you."

They took a moment to rest before diving into the to-do list. Rachel looked down the long list. "We need to go back to the bakery and do inventory. That's going to be a blast."

"I suggest we order pizzas. I'm starving." Kristen placed a hand over stomach, which chose that moment to grumble.

"Did I just hear someone say she wanted to order pizza rather than something from our restaurant?"

Rachel looked up to see both Chef Mike and Graydon standing in the doorway. Both had scowling eyebrows and grumpy expressions. "We were just brainstorming. We haven't actually decided—" She was cut short when the chef waved his hand through the air like a karate chop.

"Pizza, schmizza. You will have a decent dinner. You work hard, you make sure you eat good. I will put something together to take with you. No arguments."

"Holy mackerel," Rachel whispered to Kristen. "He's as bad as my mother."

Chef Mike laughed. "I'll take that as a compliment. I think I'd like to meet your mother, if she can be compared to me."

Graydon interrupted their banter. "I propose that both of you take a one-hour break. You need a chance to unwind before you tackle the inventory. Kristen, go home and visit with your family. Rachel, if you want to go back to your place, I'll go with you to be sure you're safe."

"I always keep a few changes of clothes at Kristen's. I think I'll just go with her, take a shower and maybe a short nap."

He nodded. "Good. Then I'll meet you both at the bakery

around five-thirty with dinner for us all. Todd already made arrangements for Daphne so we can work together."

They gathered their things and he escorted them to Kristen's car. Before she got inside, Graydon pulled her into a hug and rubbed her back.

"Oh," she moaned. The pressure of his hands rubbing up and down her back felt like heaven. She wanted to melt into him and let him continue the massage. Instead, his hands came up her back and rested on her shoulders.

"Go take a hot bath and a nap. I'll see you in a bit." He dropped a kiss onto her forehead, then opened the car door.

She watched his image fade in the side view mirror as they drove away. It reminded her of the first time they met and riding away in the cab. Kristen broke into her thoughts. "That's one fine man, you've got there, Rachel."

She couldn't agree more.

Chapter SEVENTEEN

Rachel picked up the Sweet Confections open sign. She brushed off the dirt, but broken glass had dug deep scratches into it and one corner was bent. She tried unsuccessfully to fix it before setting it aside.

She looked from the sign to the plywood that temporarily covered the front windows and door. The glass had been swept away by Victoria and Charlee—both from the Women in Business club. Victoria was also putting together a crew from the club to do some deep cleaning after everything was cleared out. Charlee, a renovation expert, had offered to help repair the walls and anything else construction related. Meanwhile, Zack, Graydon and Todd had stacked the damaged tables and chairs on one side of the room.

She surveyed the disaster again. Perhaps this would be a good time for her to talk with Kristen and really consider how much they wanted to put into repairing the current bakery versus transitioning to the new shopping district Victoria was organizing.

Rachel wandered to the front counter and ran her hand over the bent pastry case frames, rubbing one finger over a particularly deep dent. "I wonder if they'll be able to straighten this and replace the glass or if we'll need to order a new case?" She shivered and tucked her fingers into her sweatshirt. The windows were boarded up as best they could be, but cool air streamed through the holes and cracks, leaving the bakery chilly.

Graydon joined her at her side, where he'd been throughout most of the day. Maybe not physically, but she knew he'd spent the majority of his day helping Todd get things arranged for clean up and contacting clients. He'd done so much more than he needed to. He could have looked at everything, decided her life was too complicated and walked away. She wouldn't have blamed him. Sure, she would have been devastated, but she could understand wanting to escape a bad situation. Instead he stepped up and jumped into the fray with her.

He inspected the case. "It looks like the metal is flexible enough. They might be able to pound out the dents. The suppliers are sending reps to check out the equipment tomorrow."

She stared at him, wondering how she got so lucky to have him in her life. "How many times today have you stepped in to make things right for us?"

He smiled and took her hand. "Not just for anyone. For you, Rachel. As far as I'm concerned, you're a part of my life now. I'd like to keep you there." He squeezed her hand. "Let's get out the notebooks and start a list."

She pulled out one of the many notebooks Sheila had kindly supplied for the clean-up. She also thought ahead and picked up pens and a case of water. Rachel was deeply grateful for Graydon's friends, who she now considered her good friends as well.

"Why don't you do the inspecting and I'll write everything down." He took the notebook, then settled into a slightly bent chair.

"Sounds like a plan." She proceeded to go through the

stuff that was normally in the front of the shop, starting with the biggest most obvious items—the tables and chairs, pastry cases, counter and cash register. Then she dug into the other supplies; to-go boxes, pastry wrappers, order forms, pens, and other items.

"Hey, Rachel? Are you out here?"

Rachel cracked her head on the counter when she quickly stood. She was trying to decide if it was the stars circling around her or if her sisters-in-law were really standing in the kitchen doorway. She shook her head to clear it.

"Oh crap," she said. "Please, please, please tell me you're alone."

Faith and Eva looked at her strangely. "It's just us," Faith replied. "Why?"

She sighed in relief, then nodded toward Graydon. "He's why."

Both women turned and saw who was behind them. "Oh. My." Eva fanned herself. "Is that really DG? And what's he doing in your bakery?"

She listened to Faith and Eva talk about Graydon as if he wasn't even in the room. He got up from the bent chair and walked over to greet the two women.

"Hello, ladies. We haven't met yet. I'm Graydon Green." He shook their hands.

"May I repeat, what are you doing here?" Eva turned to Rachel, who walked over to stand next to him. He put his arm around her waist and looked down at her with a wide grin on his face.

"Oh my gosh! You're dating!" Faith exclaimed.

"No way!" Eva looked between the two, continuing to shake her head "No wonder you asked if the guys were with us. They would have gone totally ballistic if they knew he was here." She looked at Graydon apologetically. "I mean, if they knew you were here."

"No problem. I'm kind of used to that reaction."

"Well, it looks like the gig is up," Rachel told Graydon, who seemed relaxed and rather pleased with the turn of events. "We're going to have to introduce you to the family now. Do you think you can handle it?"

"Are you kidding? I'm going to enjoy every minute of it." He squeezed her hand, but she just shook her head. The poor fool had no idea what he was in for.

Faith laughed. "You haven't met Rachel's mom yet, have you?"

"Why does everyone keep saying that? She can't be that bad. After all, she raised Rachel," he replied.

"Yeah," Faith said slowly. "Rachel's a lot like her Dad. But you'll see for yourself soon enough."

"I don't think you guys give the lady enough credit, but like you said, I'll meet her soon enough. Like, maybe, for Malone's birthday on Sunday?"

"Oh yes!" Eva said. "Malone would love that!"

Rachel just shook her head in resignation. "I guess that's as good a time as any. Just when I hoped life wouldn't get any crazier."

"Don't worry, we'll be there to protect you from the deluge of wedding magazines your mom will be throwing your way," Eva said. "And who knows? When you spring Graydon on everyone, we may just end up in the ER with a bunch of hyper-ventilating guys."

"What are you doing here anyway?" Rachel asked, hoping to veer the subject away from weddings.

"We came to lend some girl power and we brought chocolate." Faith waggled her eyebrows.

"Ooh, where is it?" Rachel slipped her arm through Graydon's.

"In the kitchen with Kristen and the rest of your clean-up crew," Faith replied.

"Well, let's take a break and snag some before they eat it all," Rachel said. They turned and walked back toward the kitchen. She let Eva and Faith go ahead, then pulled Graydon closer. "Now that you have a glimpse of what you've gotten yourself into, are you ready to run away?"

"No way. I think your sisters-in-law are fun. I look forward to meeting the rest of your family, no matter what you guys say about your mom."

"You poor, pitiful man. Well, it's your funeral." She shrugged, but couldn't keep the teasing smile off her face.

"It's not too late to back out yet," Rachel reminded Graydon as she pulled into her parents' driveway Sunday night. "In fact, I can put the car in reverse right now—"

"Park the car, Rachel. O ye of little faith." They had teased each other back and forth on the way to her parent's home. "You did tell them you're bringing someone, didn't you?"

"Are you kidding? Then they'd be peering out the windows like I was still in high school, trying to get the first look at my date." She shivered with repressed memories.

"You didn't have a very happy dating life, did you?"

She shot him an icy glare. "You have no idea, and no, I'm not sharing any details. Let's go, buster." Rather than go through the front doors and kill the male members of her family instantaneously, she took him through the gate leading to the back yard.

"Chicken. Bwuck, bwuck, bwuck," he chanted.

"I prefer to think of it as being health conscious," she jabbed back. She took the birthday cake from his hands. "I'd better protect the goods before all heck breaks loose."

"What about me? Aren't I considered goods?"

"Sweetie, if after all those years of hockey, you can't protect yourself, then it's a good thing you retired." She gave a sassy wink, then opened the door before he could reply. "Mom, I brought a friend to dinner with me."

"What? And you didn't call? Eva, go set another place at the table."

She glanced at Eva, who tried to hide a huge grin while she got out the extra place setting. Natalie bustled over to meet her daughter's guest.

"Ooh," she said, looking him up and down. "Is this your, um, friend, dear?"

"No, I just saw him off the freeway entrance holding a sign and thought he could use a hot meal."

Eva gasped from across the room and dropped the silverware.

"Rachel," her mother whispered harshly. "I taught you better manners than that."

She straightened up. "You're right. Sorry. Graydon, this is my mom, Natalie Marconi. Mom, this is Graydon Green, my, um, friend."

He took her mom's hand in both of his, then bent and

gave her a kiss on each cheek. "I'm her boyfriend. She's just too shy to admit it."

"Oh!" Natalie blushed and fluttered.

"I see Rachel inherited her pretty blush from you, Mrs. Marconi."

Rachel leaned closer to Graydon and whispered. "Now you've done it."

"Well, come in, come in. We're so excited to have you here." Natalie guided him further into the cozy warmth of the kitchen. "Tell me how you met Rachel, what you do, where you went to school, are you from here –"

"Mom, he can only answer one question at a time." Rachel put the birthday cake on the counter.

"Well, ma'am—"

"Oh, you must call me Natalie. Please. After all, we're practically family."

Rachel rolled her eyes as her mother laid it on pretty thick. But then, she watched Graydon as he chatted with her mom and realized he was laying it on just as thick. The suck up.

"He seems to be holding his own," Eva said, leaning against the counter beside her. Faith joined them on Rachel's other side.

"How long do you think the peace will last?" Faith asked.

"No long enough," Rachel answered. Sure enough, her brother Christopher swung the kitchen door open.

"Hey, is there any more—" He stopped abruptly when he spotted Graydon. His gaze went from first Graydon to his mom, then quickly back to Graydon.

"Christopher, come meet Graydon," Natalie said.

Instead of moving forward, he got a deer in the headlights look on his face and very slowly backed out of the kitchen.

"Well, that was odd," Natalie said, turning back to her new best friend. "I assure you, my son doesn't normally act like that."

"Brace yourselves," Rachel said to the girls. Graydon flicked his gaze over to her, but she just shrugged. Like he didn't know what was coming next. Come on. The guy was a pro hockey player. He got stampeded all the time. Right?

Suddenly, the kitchen door burst open. All the boys, young and old, clambered to get over and past each other. They froze just inside the kitchen doorway, staring at Graydon like he was a pile of a million dollars.

"Star struck and dumb," snickered Eva.

Faith and Rachel both stifled laughs, waiting to see what the guys did next. The kitchen door swung open again and Jordan walked in. He continued past the guys, right on over to Graydon as if it was no big deal the hockey superstar was in his grandmother's kitchen.

"Hey, DG. Whatcha been up to?" he asked, giving him a fist bump.

"Jordan, dude. It's good to see you. I'm doing good. Just hanging out with your Aunt Rachel. She invited me to dinner."

As one, the sea of heads attached to the guys swiveled to stare at her, as if they couldn't believe what had come out of the great DG's mouth. Her youngest brother was just about bug eyed.

"Have you been keeping up with your hockey practice?" Graydon asked Jordan. "You were working on that back spin trick, right?"

When the guys returned their attention to Graydon, Rachel leaned over to Eva. "Did you set that up?"

She didn't say anything, just smiled and winked. Now

how cool is that? Jordan got to one up his brothers, grandpa, dad, and uncle.

"What's the matter with all of you?" Natalie asked, her hands on her hips. "I swear, the men in this family have no manners. Get over here and meet Rachel's boyfriend."

The kids went right over. Christopher started to join them only to trip into Adam. "Boyfriend?" His voice cracked.

Rachel ignored her brothers, focusing instead on Graydon while he interacted with Malone and Stockton. Malone had a hold of Stockton's arm, trying to hold him in place, but poor Stockton didn't look very comfortable. She knelt beside him, letting Malone go to shake Graydon's hand.

"Hi, Stockton," she said and her little nephew turned to her.

"Auntie Rachel!" He wrapped his arms around her and she gave him a special bear hug.

"How's my favorite little guy," she asked. He looked up at Graydon, concern wrinkling his brows. "That's my friend, Graydon. He's a nice guy."

Graydon stepped over and knelt down beside them.

"Gordon," Stockton said, pointing at him.

"No sweetie, his name is Graydon," she corrected.

"No, no, Auntie Rachel. He's huge! Just like Gordon the Big Engine! He's Gordon."

She looked to the man in question. "I think your name has officially been changed."

"That's fine. I like Thomas the Tank Engine, too. You know who my favorites were?" he asked Stockton, who shook his head. "Donald and Douglas."

"The twins!" Stockton burst out, bubbling with excitement.

"That's right. I used to wish I had a twin brother so I could be just like them."

Stockton giggled, then he wrapped his arms around Graydon's neck. "Bear hug," he requested. Graydon sent a questioning glance to Rachel.

"Just wrap your arms around him and give him a big squeeze until he gasps for breath."

He looked unsure, but did as she explained. He started the hug gentle, then slowly increased the pressure until Stockton gasped. He immediately lessened his grip, while still holding the little boy in his arms.

Stockton rested his head on his shoulder. "Gordon is good," he said.

Her heart melted right then and there. Her most special guy in the world just declared her boyfriend to be a good guy. There could be no higher recommendation in the world. Stockton stepped back and patted the big man's shoulder. "Bye bye, Gordon. See you later!" Then he ran off to play in the living room.

Rachel leaned over and gave Graydon a quick kiss on the cheek. The poor guy looked like he was still processing the encounter.

When they stood up, Eva gave Graydon a big hug. "He's definitely a keeper." She cleared her throat. "All right boys, get over here and say hello 'cause it's almost time for dinner. Move it!"

The rest of the men descended, asking all sorts of questions about hockey, his career, and what he was up to now. The questions went on and on, but Graydon took it all in stride. Answering back, then following up each answer with a question about one of them.

"Let's go in the living room and catch a game on TV,"

Adam suggested. "I'd love to hear Graydon's point of view on the action."

"Actually, I don't watch sports on Sundays." The guys, even Rachel, was surprised by his announcement.

"Why ever not?" Adam asked.

"When I was playing pro, I was constantly surrounded by sports. It was my life and controlled almost everything I did. But my mom raised me to respect Sundays. So I try to keep sports to a minimum. When I was playing pro, it was difficult to do, but now that I'm retired, I prefer to take the day off to remember what's really important."

"Oh." Adam seemed at a loss of what to say.

"Well, Graydon," Rachel's dad said, giving him a manly pat on the back. "Let's head into the living room. We can keep the TV off and find something else to talk about."

Graydon winked as he walked past Rachel and the girls, then disappeared through the kitchen door with her dad and brothers.

"Huh," Faith said. "How refreshing to meet a guy who has his priorities straight."

Rachel had never asked Graydon about church, other than what he had told her about growing up. She didn't think to ask about his beliefs and convictions as an adult. Apparently that was a conversation they should have in the near future.

Natalie cornered Rachel near the table. "So, what makes your brothers and dad so interested in this Graydon guy?"

"Well, he used to be into sports," she hedged.

"How into sports?" she countered, arms crossed and ready to pry as much information out as possible.

Rachel coughed into her hand. "He was a pro hockey player."

Her mother's eyebrows shot up. "Really? And you're

actually dating him? Not that I think he shouldn't be interested in you—don't take that the wrong way. It's just that you've been rather vocal about some of the more physical sports."

"He's a good guy, Mom. You just have to get to know him."

"I can already tell he's special, especially after the way our little Stockton took to him." Her mother looked away, her eyes suspiciously moist.

"We haven't been dating long, Mom."

She waved the comment away. "I'm not going to ask. Let's just get to know him."

Rachel was shocked. She wanted to wave her hand in front of her mother's face and check her temperature. "Okay," she said slowly.

Natalie smoothed the wrinkles from the tablecloth. "Let's get the guys in here."

Rachel went into the living room to tell them it was time for dinner. She almost laughed when she found them with their cell phones out, talking about the different features and applications. She sat on the arm of the couch next to Graydon. "What are you guys doing?"

He wrapped his arm around her waist and showed her his phone. "Christopher just helped me install a new application. It can track where your cell phone is. Hey, where's yours? We should put it on both our phones and test it out. It could be fun." He waggled his eyebrows.

"You are such a goof ball." She pulled her phone out of her back pocket and handed it over. He messed around with it, pulling up the application to download.

"Why don't you get it installed, then tell me how it works later. Dinner is ready, guys."

He clicked on a few more things, then handed it back. "It's downloading now. We'll let it do its thing while we eat dinner."

Then the chaos began. There was lots of hustle and bustle as the younger kids raced to see who would get to sit next to Graydon.

"Sorry, little dudes. I brought him, so I get to sit next to him."

"And I promised your Grandma I'd sit next to her, too," Graydon added. "But next time, I'll save a seat and we'll draw straws. Deal?"

The kids groaned a little, but moved around the table to sit in their normal spots. Dinner continued with everyone talking about their week. As a family, they talked about the break in at Sweet Confections. Rachel avoided saying anything about the police or Nico. Graydon took her cue and didn't mention it either.

"Thankfully nothing in the kitchen was destroyed. The ovens and coolers would have absolutely killed us to replace. As it is, the biggest expense will be replacing the pastry case. Insurance is covering part of it, but we need to come up with the money for the remainder of the cost."

"We can help you with that," her dad said. "We have money put away."

She was already shaking her head. "No, Dad. Kristen and I will figure it out. We've already started looking into loans."

"Why go to a bank when we can loan you the money?" he countered. "If it makes you feel better, we'll charge you interest."

She smiled. Interest indeed. "I appreciate your offer, I honestly truly do, but I don't want to mix family with business. We have some great contacts and it'll get figured out." Her dad was quiet, not responding. "Don't be mad, okay?"

"You remind me of myself. Wanting to do it all on my own, support our family." He reached over and took her hand. "I'm proud of you. Don't forget that."

She felt a lump lodge in her throat. "Thanks, Dad." She squeezed his hand back. He knew the thank you meant I love you, too. They didn't say the actual three words very often, but she knew it underlined everything they said to each other.

Ding dong.

"That's odd," Natalie said, putting her napkin down. "We don't usually get visitors on Sundays."

Rachel waved her mother back to her seat. "Sit, I'll get it. It's probably one of the neighbors short on sugar or something. You know how Mrs. Morris next door is always missing something from one of her recipes."

She opened the door, expecting to see a neighbor. Instead someone grabbed her arm and yanked her outside.

"What the—" She was cut off short, the front door closing behind her, then pulled around the corner of the porch. It was so fast, she didn't even get a look at who had a hold of her arm. She could only see a black jacket and hat. She dug her feet in and yelled.

The man turned and clamped his hand over her mouth. "Shh!" he said.

Nico! She struggled in earnest while he tried to keep her mouth covered to muffle her cries for help.

"I need you to listen to me, Rachel," he panted. "It wasn't me who broke into your bakery. I'd never do that to you."

She heard the front door open and footsteps on the porch.

"Rachel?" Graydon called. She tried to respond, yell for

help, but Nico was dragging her off the side steps of the porch.

"Please, be quiet and listen. I couldn't go back to Italy. I stayed to watch over you."

She felt sick as tingles went up her arms and legs. What was he saying? Did he just admit to stalking her? She dug her feet into the ground to keep him from dragging her away. She thrashed against his hold, desperate to break free. Fight, Rachel. Don't let him win.

"Rachel!"

She heard the shout, then felt nothing but air beneath her feet. She was once again yanked around, this time away from a scuffle of arms and legs. More feet pounded and she was pulled into her dad's arms, where she couldn't see anything beyond his shoulder.

"Stay here. Your mother is calling the police. It looks like the boys have things under control."

She heard grunts and voices, but all she could do was shiver. Not because she was cold, though. She just couldn't stop shaking. Her father kept his arms wrapped around her. She got a glimpse of Nico pinned to the ground, blood on his face while her brothers and Graydon held him down.

The blare of sirens grew until the cars stopped at the curb. The rest became a repeated blur of events, with questions from the police. The women kept curious kids from the windows, while family members tried to figure out what happened. This time though, handcuffs were brought out and Nico was taken away.

Rachel's mind swirled. Someone wrapped her in a blanket and she looked up to find Graydon standing behind her with his arms wrapped around her waist, alternately rubbing his hands up and down her arms. When the questioning came to a close, she leaned her weary head back against his chest. "I'm so tired."

"Let's go inside. You can lie down on the couch and I'll get you some hot chocolate."

She continued to lean back against him, exhaustion from the adrenaline let-down making her arms and legs heavy. Graydon's arm slipped to her waist and he led her inside the house.

"Tell me what you need." He brushed the hair from her face, as she got settled in the living room.

"Advil. My head is killing me." He left her on the couch to get the much-needed medicine while her nephews gathered close. Stockton scooted onto the couch. She adjusted her position so he could lay against her with his head resting on her shoulder. It felt so good to have him snuggled up to her. The other boys piled onto the couch around them.

"Love my Auntie Rachel," Stockton said. "Lots of loud, bad noises, Auntie Rachel."

"Yes, there were, but they're gone now. It's all nice and quiet."

Graydon returned with the Advil and a glass of water. After downing the tablets, she settled back, finding comfort from her nephews and the soft murmuring voices around her. Slowly, her eyes drifted shut and she rested. Lowered voices and conversation flowed around her. She heard Graydon talking with her family. Probably sharing more details than she wanted them to know. Her eyes stung, knowing her mother would become even more protective, but worse than that, knowing how deeply her father would worry.

Too late now, she thought. Nico had once again invaded her life and shook things up. Would it ever stop?

Chapter EIGHTEEN

*M*onday morning dawned bright and clear, but Rachel had to drag herself out of bed and into the bathroom. *Oh my,* she thought. *You don't look like you got much beauty rest, girlfriend.*

She splashed cold water on her face and started her morning routine, grateful to be in her own home. Her mother pushed hard for her to stay at their house. It took a lot of fancy foot work and convincing before her mother finally let her leave.

Well, if anything good came of last night, her family now totally loved Graydon. Not because of his former career, but because of how he had defended her. He was a permanent fixture on their Christmas card list. Now, she wondered, what was his status in her life?

He seemed interested in a serious relationship, but what would it evolve into? She tried to imagine married life with Graydon. Some was easy to picture, but other parts she just couldn't envision.

All with time, my dear. Don't stress about it, she told herself.

She finished her morning routine and headed to the bakery. She and Kristen needed to fill out loan papers for the new pastry cases later today. She worried about the dent it would put in their financial plan, especially now that they were almost positive about wanting to move to the new shopping district.

She pushed the worry aside as she pulled out supplies to take to Brisket and Noodles for today's set of cakes. When she finished stacking them on the counter, she grabbed the mail to do a quick sort. There were bills to pay and a flier about advertising in the local newspaper. She considered running an ad for a grand reopening, a promo to kick off a good start after the tragedy. Maybe the paper could run a story and save them the expense. She paused when she came to an envelope with the Food Network logo emblazoned on the return address. What's this? She carefully slit the top open and pulled out the letter inside.

Dear Sweet Confections,

We invite you to participate in our upcoming fairy cake challenge as a last-minute participant. Please respond by calling the number below by November 20th. If you're interested, we will send contracts to sign. Enclosed is a list of requirements, as well as the location and other pertinent information.

Sincerely,

The Food Network Challenge

Food Network Channel

She sat on the cold bakery floor and reread the letter, making sure she didn't misunderstand anything. She laughed, a gamut of emotions poured through her as she speed dialed Kristen. Soon they both babbled over each other, making plans to review the documents together and respond right away. She couldn't believe it. Her dream was coming true. And if they could win that $10,000 prize, it would pay off the bank loan and put the bakery back on track.

Hope finally dawned on her very bleak horizon.

Over the next few weeks, Rachel felt like she was on a treadmill with no stop button. Additional people were hired to work in the shop due to the overwhelming community support of their reopening—which worked out great because they needed people to take care of the shop during the challenge.

Only two weeks away, she thought as her stomach fluttered. She and Kristen worked late every night, going over sketches, creating details, practicing techniques, timing themselves. They were going into the challenge as the under dogs, but were determined to do their best. And they were definitely focused on winning the grand prize. It was awesome to be a part of the challenge, but to win the prize—wow. It would provide incredible exposure for their shop and be a boost to their business.

The challenge was in Phoenix, which meant a completely different weather environment than they were used to dealing with. Originally, they talked about making the fairies out of pulled sugar, but she remembered a challenge episode where the competitors had a lot of difficulty because of the unfamiliar humidity conditions. So they decided make gum paste fairies with pulled sugar details for the wings. If it didn't work, then they could roll gum paste flat and shape it into delicate wings for the fairies and hand paint them. Kristen designed a variety of fairies for the cake. They were going to take a lot of her time during the challenge, which left Rachel to prepare and set up the cakes.

By the end of each day, Rachel's arms, back, and legs ached. She barely made it home to drop into bed, fall into an exhausted sleep, then get up to do it all over the next day. Between the bakery and the challenge, she literally had no time to think about anything else.

Thank goodness Graydon took the initiative to stop in throughout the day, bringing treats, flowers or just to say hi and give her a kiss. She looked forward to his little distractions, keeping her fresh and focused without burning out.

Unfortunately, Sheila was annoyed with his constant changing schedule. Rachel encouraged him to stay focused on his work, but he assured her everything was in good hands. Still, she was sad to see her tentative friendship with Sheila diminish. She had become a regular, dropping in for treats and to chat. Rachel hoped that they could repair their friendship after the challenge.

"Hey, Rachel, did you get to the store to pick up more butter?" Kristen asked as she prepared to frost a batch of Cherry Limeade cupcakes.

"Nuts. I totally forgot." Rachel looked up from the batch of cookies she was organizing on a tray to take out front. A pink piece of paper was stuck to the metal freezer door, a visual to remind her about various items that needed to be taken care of. Apparently she stuck it there, then completely forgot about it. Again. "Let me get these cookies out front, then I'll run to the store while you keep working."

At the store, Rachel zipped down the aisle, grabbed twelve pounds of butter and a few other necessities. She stood in the checkout line, thinking through the remainder of the day when a pair of arms wrapped around her waist. She jumped and gasped, briefly attracting the attention of the woman putting her groceries on the checkout belt.

"Hey there, gorgeous," Graydon said.

Her heart thudded hard inside her chest, as she turned to face him. "What are you doing here?"

"I was on my way to see you, but Kristen said you ran to the store. So I pulled out the handy dandy Google tracker your brother installed and popped in to surprise you. That's quite a lot of butter, my dear," he teased.

"I know. I forgot to order more from our supplier and so we were short. Then I forgot to pick it up this morning before work. Do you see a theme here? I can't seem to keep anything in my head where it belongs." They moved forward in line and she placed the items on the conveyor belt.

"Don't worry. It will all come together. You've both been working hard; it's only natural to forget things here and there."

She snorted. "It's been a lot more than a little bit here and there though." The checkout woman rang up the purchases and Rachel swiped the business card, signed the receipt then Graydon grabbed the bags. Together, they walked out into the parking lot. "Where are you parked?"

"By your car. I scouted out the lot before parking. I was hoping to take advantage of however many minutes I could steal from your schedule."

She unlocked the door and placed the bags inside, then

turned to wrap her arms around his neck. He slid his arms around her waist and pulled her in close.

She leaned back and looked up into his eyes. "While you're here, there's something I need to tell you about. I got a call from Officer Giles. Nico had his alibi confirmed and was released this morning." Graydon's shoulders tensed beneath her hands. "But," she rushed on. "He agreed to return to Italy and when he is in the United States on business, to keep his distance from me."

Graydon's hand wrapped around the back of her neck, his fingers sinking into the back of her upswept hair. "If he even comes near you—"

"Officer Giles assured me that he won't." Graydon's eyes were hard and serious, so she quickly went up on her toes and placed a quick kiss on his lips. "It really is going to be okay."

His thumb brushed the side of her cheek. "Okay, I'll trust the officer. But if I see Nico again, I won't promise to be nice."

"I wouldn't expect you to." She smiled and snuggled her head against his chest.

"What would it take to convince you to take a night off, say maybe this Friday?" he asked, changing the subject.

"Mmm, that's a tempting offer. What were you thinking?"

"I have a dinner thing to attend. No big deal, but I would love to take you with me."

"I'll talk with Kristen. I'm sure her family would like a night with her, too. I'll text you, okay?"

"Sounds good." He placed soft kisses on her lips while one hand rubbed the nape of her neck. "I've missed that, too." He gazed into her pretty green eyes. "I just miss you, Rachel."

She nodded, then touched her forehead to his. "Me, too."

"You miss you, too?" he teased.

She laughed and thumped her fist against his chest. "You know what I mean. Silly boy." The rumble of his laugh vibrated against her hand. She wanted to grab a hunk of his sweatshirt and not let go. Not let him go. She craved being with him like a woman craves chocolate when she has PMS. The only difference was those chocolate cravings went away after a day or two. Her desire to be with Graydon, to just have him nearby to share the ups and downs of the day with . . . Well, that yearning continued to grow.

She just wasn't sure if she trusted her relationship instincts. But, oh, how she wanted to.

He pulled her close for a tight hug, then groaned as he released her. "Okay. Go, work hard. Stay focused, at least for the next few hours, then let me know about Friday." He smiled and dropped one last kiss on her lips before he opened the door for her.

Back at the bakery, Rachel talked to Kristen who was more than happy to schedule a break.

"Let's hand the shop over to the girls early that day, then make a night of it. I really miss Todd and Daphne. I'm afraid my daughter may not remember who Mommy is."

Rachel agreed, then texted Graydon. She looked at the clock. With freedom looming ahead, the two days until Friday arrived seemed much too far away. She couldn't wait to see Graydon and do something, anything, that wasn't related to cakes and sugar frostings.

Chapter NINETEEN

hen Friday's lunch rush was over, Rachel and Kristen untied their aprons and prepared to leave for the day. Rachel couldn't wait to go home and soak in a nice hot bath, unwind, and prepare for her date with Graydon. As she hung up her apron, Shawna came into the kitchen with a large white box tied with a gauzy turquoise bow.

"This just came for you, Rachel," Shawna said, sliding the tempting box onto the stainless-steel counter while the women gathered around it.

"What could it be?" Rachel asked, turning the box around in a circle to view it on all sides.

"It's definitely not flowers," Kristen said, referring to its large size.

"Just open it," Shawna urged, bouncing on her toes.

Rachel tugged on the end of the gauzy ribbon and pulled the bow free. When she lifted the lid, a small note card was nestled on top of thick turquoise tissue paper. She picked it up and opened it.

R.

A little something for tonight. More to come.

Love - G.

"Ooh . . . What are you doing tonight," Kristen asked.

Rachel shrugged. "Just going out for dinner." But when she pushed the tissue paper aside, she gasped.

A gorgeous navy gown was tucked inside. She gingerly picked it up and pulled it out of the box. The material was soft and silky with tiny sparkles that shimmered as she turned it this way and that. The top had a graceful curving neckline and sheer lacy sleeves that reached to her elbow. The material gathered around the bust line, then fell in layers to reach her toes. It was incredible. Amazing.

"Oh my, look at these shoes," Shawna pulled out a beautiful pair of navy satin-covered heels encrusted with rhinestones around the edges. While Kristen drooled over the shoes, Rachel's cell phone rang. Shawna pulled it out of Rachel's purse and handed it to her. She saw Graydon's name on the screen.

"You would not believe the delivery I just received," she said instead of her usual greeting.

"I hope you like it," he said.

She could hear the excitement in his voice, which made her smile all the more. "I love it, but it seems a little fancy for dinner, don't you think?"

"Well, I never said where we were eating. Actually, it's a charity event."

"Oh my gosh! Do you mean the Crystal Creek Children's Hospital benefit?" Beside her, Kristen and Shawna squealed.

The children's hospital benefit was The Event of the holiday season put on by Crystal Creek's founding families - the Belliston's, the Taylor's, and the Westhoff's. All sorts of incredible musicians, celebrities and Kansas City's rich of the rich attended.

Holy mackerel. That was Graydon's crowd, Rachel realized, terror shooting through her. This was a step into his celebrity world. Her hands trembled as she tucked the gown back into the box.

"Rachel, are you still there?" Graydon asked, his voice breaking up the thoughts tumbling around in her mind.

"Yes, of course," she said.

"I said I thought you might enjoy a fancy night out after all the hard work you've been caught up in, but if you're too tired, we can skip it."

"No, it's okay. I was just surprised." She hoped she sounded convincing because deep inside, she was nervous about what the night would bring. They decided on a time for Graydon to pick her up, then got off the phone. Kristen and Shawna asked all sorts of questions, then grabbed her stuff and ushered her out to the car to prepare for the evening ahead.

Unfortunately, the relaxing hot bath and pampering was spoiled by the anxious knot growing tighter in her stomach. What if she did something embarrassing? What if people treated her like a nobody? What if . . . And what if . . . And what—

Rachel shook her head, trying to clear the negativity away. Thankfully, Graydon arrived to save her from herself. When she opened the door, he swept her into his arms and twirled her in a circle. Laughter bubbled up and poured out.

When he finally stopped, her arms were wrapped around his neck and she melted against him, enjoying the happiness in his chocolate brown eyes. He lowered his head and captured her lips for an achingly sweet kiss. Her hands sank into his short dark hair and she felt her pulse beat rapidly against his fingers where they caressed her neck. When he pulled back, her eyelids fluttered, then met his gaze.

"You're beautiful," he said softly.

A smile tugged at her lips. "You haven't even seen me in the gown yet."

"It's not the dress that makes you beautiful, Rachel. It's everything that makes up you," he said, giving her a light squeeze. "But since you mentioned it . . ." He took her hand and spun her out, as if they were dancing. The skirts swirled around her, swishing back and forth before settling into place around her ankles. "You look mighty fetching, my dear," Graydon said, a mischievous gleam in his eyes.

"My, what big eyes you have, Grandma," she replied, then clapped her hand over her mouth while Graydon threw back his head and laughed. She really needed to think before blurting things out. "Ahem, what I meant to say is you look dashing in your tux, sir."

He tugged her close again. "You know I love it when you blush." He gave her a quick kiss before stepping back. "Shall we go?"

Outside, a gleaming black limo was parked at the curb. A young man opened the back door for them and Rachel slid in, then Graydon followed her. He took her hand in his and all too soon they were in downtown Kansas City, pulling up to the Kauffman Grand Ballroom. Lights blazed through the darkness, illuminating the sidewalks and red-carpeted entry crowded with men in tuxes and women in glittering gowns, diamonds, pearls, and all sorts of gems dripping from their necks, ears, fingers and wrists. The anxious knot returned.

Graydon took her hand and turned her to face him. "You are gorgeous, just as you are." His hand caressed her cheek.

She closed her eyes, wanting to soak in the comfort of his warmth. He tipped her chin up, so that their eyes met once more. "But, just so you feel brave enough to face everyone tonight . . ." He leaned over, opened a small drawer and pulled out a slim black box. He lifted the lid and Rachel was sure her eyes popped wide open.

A gorgeous set of diamond and deep blue sapphire jewelry were displayed against creamy black velvet. Her fingers lightly touched the classic lines of alternating gems on the necklace, then down to the bracelet and earrings. Graydon removed the bracelet and clasped it around her wrist. Once she was draped with the necklace and put on the earring studs, she turned to face Graydon again. "They're incredible."

He shook his head. "No, it's the person under the jewelry that makes them shine." He placed a tender kiss on the inside of her wrist, just above the sparkling bracelet. "Remember that tonight is about fun. Just be the wonderful Rachel I love and everything will be perfect. Oh, and smile."

He motioned for the driver to open their door. He exited the limo first, then helped her step out and into the camera flashes as fans lined the streets, hoping to get glimpses of their favorite celebrities. Graydon wrapped an arm around her waist, smiled and waved to the crowds as he led her across the red carpet. The camera flashes were blinding, but she did her best to smile and not squint. How did celebrities do this? Someone needed to invent contact lenses to filter out the crazy stimulation.

Finally, they were inside the building, away from the crowds but not necessarily the cameras.

"Mr. Green, who is your lovely companion? Smile!"

Rachel's head swirled with confusion as questions came

from all different directions. Graydon smoothly answered the reporters all while guiding her through the foyer, pausing here and there for certain magazines and newspapers until they entered the main ballroom. She blinked rapidly, readjusting to the dim lighting.

The ballroom was gorgeous. Twinkling lights were wrapped around marble columns and also entwined among the garland swags along the balcony. A live band played back up as local Kansas City singer, David Cook, belted out his latest best-selling single. Rachel took a deep breath, trying to relax as she took in the hundreds of guests socializing and surveying the themed Christmas trees they came to bid on.

"You did great," Graydon whispered into her ear. She smiled, wishing she could pull him into a quiet corner for just a few minutes, but they were already getting bombarded by Graydon's acquaintances. Graydon handed her a flute of champagne as he introduced her to a variety of people. Thankfully, there were a few she knew from past catering jobs and was able to ask about their family members from weddings, baby showers, and other special occasions. Overall, she felt like she was doing pretty well. With some practice, she could get used to this—maybe even enjoy it, too.

"Hey, I finally see some friends," Graydon said, redirecting her toward a Christmas tree decorated in Kansas City Chiefs memorabilia, season passes, and more where a small group was chatting. "Hey, Amelio, good to see you buddy," Graydon said as he embraced the dark, curly haired man she remembered from hockey camp. They thumped each other on the back.

What was it with men and back pats? Couldn't they just hug without beating on each other, Rachel wondered.

Amelio turned to greet her, grinning. "This must be the famous Rachel. Zack and I have talked about you at the office. Ever since Graydon met you, he's been like mush in our hands. We could plan anything we wanted for LA hockey camp and he'd just look at a picture of you on his phone and agree."

Rachel felt heat infuse her cheeks as they shook hands. "It's good to know I'm not the only one distracted at work."

Amelio laughed, then turned to introduce her to their other friend, Reece Stone. Reece's disheveled curly blond hair lent him a lazy beach boy look, but his piercing green eyes gave away his intelligence and sense of control. He nodded politely and shook her hand. "We've met before, I believe."

Rachel was surprised he remembered. "Yes, my bakery catered the dessert bar at your sister's wedding."

"My mother and her friends raved about your crème brûlée cake for weeks afterward. It makes an impression, even on a thick-headed guy." His eyes crinkled when he smiled, giving her just a peek at the nice guy he might be underneath his business-like demeanor.

Their conversation was broken up when a delightful red-headed young woman wearing a knee-length emerald green dress grabbed Reece's arm. "Guess what I just did? I convinced old lady Westhoff to donate all the plants and vegetable seeds!"

Reece's smile widened into a full-blown smile. "I'm sure Cecilia Westhoff worked her wiles and tried to get you to sweet talk her into the donation."

"Oh, I sweet talked her into *three years* of donations. I may have led her to believe she came up with the idea of a walkway filled with stepping stones with the donor's names on them. One of which will have her name on it, naturally."

The red-head batted her eyelashes as if the accomplishment were easy. Rachel knew Cecilia Westhoff, and while the old lady was a sweetheart, she was a successful business woman from an era when women were meant to stay at home and raise babies. After years of businessmen trying to take advantage of her, she really knew how to drive a hard bargain —and at the end of the negotiations, she got exactly what she wanted. It was impressive to meet someone who actually pulled a sly negotiation on Mrs. Westhoff.

Reece turned back to the group. "Have you met my partner in crime, Piper Daniels?"

"From Crystal Creek?" Rachel asked.

"Yes," Piper drew out. "Wait, you're Rachel, right? You were a few years ahead of me in high school."

"We had the same study hall one year and spent most of it hiding in the library. I never told you, but I was so grateful to have someone else hiding out with me, even if we were across the room from each other," Rachel replied, thankful to see someone here she actually knew. Well, maybe not well, but still, more familiar to her the majority of the people in attendance.

"I remember that! What are you up to now?"

"I own a bakery in Crystal Creek. Sweet Confections."

"That's your place? Dr. Dansie brings in treats for the staff each week. They're incredible and the sole reason I walk to work most of the time."

"I've teased him several times about serving cookies to his clients to get more business. I love that he's a dentist with a sweet tooth."

A reporter joined them, asking for an interview with Graydon and Amelio. They excused themselves and went to stand by the Christmas tree Graydon's former hockey team had donated, leaving Rachel with Reece and Piper.

"So, tell me more about the donation from Mrs. Westhoff," Rachel said. "It sounds like you're planning something fun."

Piper's eyes sparkled as she explained her idea for Crystal Creek's community garden, how it would help the youth and senior citizens, and bring not just fresh food to people in the community who need it, but also build unity, too. Reece had already donated an empty lot downtown and tonight she was here with him, drumming up donations for it.

"The gardens are an excellent idea! You should come to Crystal Creek's Women in Business meeting next month. We do a lot of community work and the ladies there have a lot of contacts. Bring some brochures and I'm sure we can get you five minutes to tell us about the project."

"That would be fantastic!" Piper and Rachel pulled their cell phones out of their beaded bags and swapped contact information. When they finished, Rachel looked over to where Graydon was still being interviewed. She wondered how much longer he would be.

Piper cleared her throat. "I, um, need to go check my makeup. Would you excuse me?"

Her cheeks turned pink and Rachel felt empathetic. "Would you mind if I followed you? I haven't figured out a good way to escape all these people and now seems to be the best time without a reporter to make note of me asking to use the restroom."

Reece and Piper both laughed. "I felt the same way," Piper confided. After Reece agreed to wait for Graydon to return, the two women navigated their way through the glamorously clad people, discreetly asked a waiter for directions, then finally found their destination.

The bathroom was broken into two sections. First was a sitting room filled with luxurious chairs, benches and mirrors for touching up makeup, then a small archway led to the actual bathroom portion. The two split up, then met back at the sinks. While they washed their hands, a group of women entered the sitting room, laughing and talking about the event.

"Did you see what Clarice Taylor was wearing? That Vera Wang was so last season," one woman said.

Rachel slid a glance at Piper and just shrugged. They were stuck listening to the gossip queens.

"Oh, and Stella Wixom's lips! The augmentation that was supposed to make them sumptuously plump turned out to look like a big old bee sting," another woman said.

"More like a hive of yellow jackets had attacked it," a third woman said.

Piper rolled her eyes. "What a bunch of hypocrites. I bet every one of them has had some type of work done," she whispered.

Rachel nodded and dried her hands, grateful to be done and get out of earshot of the nasty women in the next room.

"Worst of all, that poor Graydon Green."

Rachel froze half a step short of revealing herself in the doorway. Graydon? What bad thing could they possibly think to say about him?

"Oh, dear Lord. Did you see that cow he brought?"

Not Graydon. No, he's perfect. *She* was the one they were discussing now. Rachel flattened her back against the wall and squeezed her eyes shut tight.

One of the women snickered. "How many more slices of

cake do you think she could eat before she explodes out of that dress? I mean, really, some women have no self-respect for their bodies."

Rachel's hand gripped the loose material at her waist and prayed for them to leave. Just let them leave, before she broke down, before they discovered her cowering against the wall.

"Well, look who we have here. Tweedle Dumb, Tweedle Dumber, and Tweedle Dipstick."

Rachel's eyes flew open to see Piper sauntering into the other room with the women. What was she doing?

"And you are . . ." One of the women asked, letting the question dangle, unfinished.

"Apparently the only woman in this room who knows how to exercise her brain," Piper continued.

"I recommend that you hold your tongue, young lady. You have no idea who you're talking to." This came from a platinum blonde who had to be pushing sixty and wore a dress that probably cost more than the new display cases in Rachel's shop.

"You're the ones who should be holding your tongues. Don't you have anything better to talk about than gossiping and ripping apart other women? Because if all you're good for is to be a useless ornament on some guy's arm and to rip other people apart, well, that's just a waste of the brains God gave you. That's assuming you're capable of doing something useful with your time."

"Why, you—"

"What I suggest, ladies," she said the word mockingly. "Is that you grow up and learn how to say something nice . . . or just shut up. Period."

Rachel heard someone gasp, then the clomp of feet as the

women left the sitting room and went back to the ballroom. She brought her hands up to cover her eyes. What had Piper done?

"Are you okay?" Piper asked, placing her hand on Rachel's arm.

"What were you thinking? Why would you do something like that?"

"Those stupid women—"

Rachel cut her off, removed her hand from her eyes and stared angrily at Piper. "Are probably out in the ballroom, telling all their friends about the crazy woman in the bathroom and they're all waiting to see who comes out. When they see us, it will just be more taunting."

Piper's cheeks went from pink to red. "You're worried about them teasing you more? Aren't you disgusted by what they said about you?"

Rachel looked away. "It's not any different than high school or college."

Piper grabbed Rachel's arm. "This is the real world. We're adults who don't have to take anyone else's crap."

Rachel twisted her arm out of Piper's grasp. "Because what? I'm going to march out there and say my size ten body is just as sexy as their skinny minnie ones? Compared to them, I *am* a cow."

Piper stepped back. "You believe them? They are just ignorant, spoiled brats who have no happiness or joy in life, so they put other people down. You, on the other hand, are so much more than them. They waste their time with their brunches and their tennis lessons while you make something wonderful with your sweat and blood. And you're gorgeous. But I can't make you see that. You have to see it for yourself."

Piper picked up her handbag. "I'm going back out to join Reece. Are you coming?"

Rachel closed her eyes and fought to control the sting of tears.

A moment passed before Piper grabbed her hand. "Come on. I'll take you back to Graydon."

Though they moved through the crowd, Rachel couldn't focus on anyone. Even though everything Piper said was true, and she wanted to really believe it, only one thing continued to echo in her head.

Fat cow.

Chapter TWENTY

On Monday morning, Graydon clicked through web pages, instant messaging his mom links while they talked on the phone.

"This one is my favorite," he said, sending another newspaper link with pictures from the charity event. The photo captured Rachel laughing at something he said while they danced.

"She's beautiful, sweetheart. I can't wait to meet her," his mother said.

"I'm looking forward to that, too. I invited her to spend Christmas with us," he confessed.

"You're pretty serious, then, if you want her to meet everyone."

Yes, he was serious. Rachel was everything he had been looking for, yearning for. He hoped that in a few weeks, he'd get to slip a sparkling ring on her finger.

If only he could get rid of the niggling tug that something was wrong. Rachel seemed off after his interview at the charity event. She said she was just overwhelmed and tired, which he completely understood. But still, he wondered if it was something more. Now that she was buried in prep for the cake challenge, it was difficult to find a block of time to allow for a decent conversation.

"Graydon?"

He turned his focus back to his mother. "Sorry, I was just scrolling through some more pictures." He pushed on the scroll wheel on his mouse to eliminate the guilt he felt whenever he fibbed to his mom. He thought that would go away when he became an adult, but it didn't.

"I said I'm glad you found someone special. I worried about you, especially after you and Carissa broke up, then how she died in that car accident six months later. I wasn't sure if you would ever fully recover."

"I'm doing fine. No worrying needed." He looked up when Sheila knocked on his office door for their morning meeting and waved her in. "Mom, I have to go. Rachel and I will see you at Christmas." He paused, listening to his mom end with a few details and to tell Rachel she said hello. "I'll be sure to tell her. I love you."

Once he hung up the phone, he turned his attention to Sheila.

"Good morning," she greet him. "Making holiday plans with your family?"

"Yeah, they're all flying in a few days before Christmas." Before they could get off track, he pulled up his spreadsheets and documents for the California hockey camp and started on the to-do list. When they got to the food section, he asked for the paperwork to pass off to Rachel.

"Are you sure you want to do that?" she questioned. "She's never been a part of the camp and doesn't know how they run."

"I'm confident she'll do a great job. Besides she can ask questions if needed."

"Maybe it would be better if she helped with the next camp. She could come and see how it all works this time around."

"I'm sure she can figure it out. She is a caterer herself. It's not as if we're asking her to put together the class schedule," Graydon said, frustration slipping through the calm professional tone he normally tried to keep. It wasn't often he and Sheila butted heads on work projects, but lately she had been extra touchy about Rachel. Sheila slid the catering folder across the desk. She looked annoyed, but changed the subject and continued the meeting. Once they finished reviewing camp items, Sheila pulled out the PR schedule.

"I've been approached by some local charities who are organizing events over the next few weeks. I have a variety of places for you to consider attending."

He looked over the list she handed him. "If you can prepare some cards, I'll send donations instead."

She paused taking notes. "Why? You usually attend the radio auction and participate as a guest auctioneer."

"I'm going to Phoenix for the Food Network Challenge, then my parents are returning from Italy. I want to spend the week with them and Rachel."

Sheila set down her schedule folder. "You just started dating. You can't possibly be that serious already."

"I am. If everything goes well over the holidays, I hope she'll agree to become a permanent part of my life."

"As in marriage?" She choked out the last word. "That's ridiculous."

Her strong reaction surprised him. Didn't he see how close he and Rachel had become? He wanted her to understand how he felt, how Rachel filled a part of him that had been empty. But he didn't know how to say it the right way. "She makes me happy, Sheila. I can't imagine anyone else making me feel this complete again."

She sputtered, then stood. "You can't do this. You're going to ruin everything!"

"Sheila—" Graydon rose out of his chair, but he didn't get to finish.

She grabbed her things and left the room. He sank back into his chair and dropped his head into his hands, wondering what had gone wrong. He didn't want to lose a friend he valued so much, but he also couldn't keep his feelings for Rachel hidden away either. And what did she mean about ruining everything? With Rachel in his life, he only saw things becoming better. He brought his fist down and thumped it off the desktop.

"Whoa, cuz." Zack came in and plopped into the seat Sheila had vacated a few minutes ago. "I just saw Sheila fly out of here like a bat out of hell and now here you are, pounding on your desk. What's up?"

He leaned back into his office chair. "Sheila's not very happy about my relationship with Rachel."

"Yeah, getting burned in love really sucks."

"What? " he asked incredulously.

"Quite honestly, I never figured out how you didn't know. I mean, the woman's whole schedule revolves around you."

"No, it revolves around the DG Foundation which is her job. Not me." He tried to emphasize the difference between the two.

"You really don't see it, do you?" Zack shook his head. "Dude, she would do *anything* for you. I think she's just been waiting for you to wake up and see she's been there all this time."

This was not good. At all. "Let me ask you a question and give it to me straight. Did I ever do anything to lead her to think I liked her as more than a friend?"

Zack leaned back in the chair, contemplating the question. "I don't think so. Anytime I've been around, you treated her like a friend, a co-worker you enjoyed working with."

He sighed in relief. At least he didn't need to feel guilty in that regard. Now he just had to figure out how to fix things. In the meantime, he finished a few things at the DG Foundation, then headed over to Brisket and Noodles.

He and Chef Mike worked together setting up the specials for the week, talked about special promotions for over the holidays, and the new dishes Chef Mike wanted to add to the next year's menu—which needed to be sent to the printer soon. He was going over supplier invoices when Rachel surprised him with a visit.

She knocked on the door frame. "Hey there, are you busy?"

A happy smile spread over Graydon's face as he stepped away from his desk, pulled her into his arms for a quick hug and nudged the door closed, not wanting any interruptions for the few minutes she may have to spend with him. "How did you escape the bakery?"

Rachel chuckled. "I promised Kristen I'd return with lunch. I put in a to-go order out front before sneaking back here."

They sat close to each other on the black leather couch. "I remember you sitting here the night we met. We've come a long way since then, haven't we?"

Rachel tucked her hair behind her ear and nodded. "It seems like a lifetime ago sometimes." She reached over and grabbed his hand. "Listen, I actually came because there's something on my mind that I just can't get out and I need to talk to you about it."

She was rambling. This couldn't be good. He rubbed his thumb over the back of her hand, hoping it would comfort her. It definitely helped him as the niggling worry from the charity event became a full-fledged knot in his gut. "Okay, let's talk."

She squeezed her eyes shut as she blurted, "I'm just not sure I can handle your world."

When she looked at him again, he saw conflict and fear twisting within her green eyes. She continued, dumping everything out at once.

"I just, I love you, but all the cameras, the media, all the attention—I haven't dealt with that before. And it makes me think—what if some day we have a family? What would raising a family in that environment be like? Would we be able to play at the park or go on play dates without the media hounding us?"

"Sweetheart, shh," he said, picking her hand up and kissing the back of it. "We've spent a lot of time together over the last few months and the only time we've been in the public spotlight was at the charity event. The only time anyone wants my picture anymore is if I'm helping with a charity event or putting on the hockey camps. But if it worries you, we can go through event invites together and decide what we can cut down on. I'm sure there are some who would be just as happy receiving a donation check in lieu of me attending their event."

Rather than seeing her fears eased, Rachel turned her head away, not meeting his eyes. His gut twisted even tighter. Something more than just the reporters was bothering her, but what wasn't she telling him?

"What happened while I was being interviewed at the gala?" When she didn't answer him, he persisted. "I know something must have happened because even though an event like that can be an overwhelming first-time experience, you were doing great until I left you with Reece and Piper. I need you to be honest and talk to me."

He tried to turn her face back toward him again, but she shook her head, lowering it to hide her face. When a tear streaked down her face, it was all he could do not to grab her close and promise everything would be okay. He couldn't make it better unless she trusted him enough to talk about whatever happened. But man, he was mentally kicking himself over and over for leaving her alone. Even if he had trusted Reece and Piper, he should have taken her with him for the interview, kept her by his side.

How could he have been so stupid? Would Reece say something, or let someone else do something to hurt her?

"Piper and I overheard some women talking in the bathroom," she finally began. "About you."

Graydon closed his eyes. What did they say about him? Was it something stupid from his past? Or, more likely, making up groupie stories about them together? He had run into that before. Some women tried to one up another by making up stories about stuff she did with other celebrities.

Would Rachel believe him when he told her the truth? Fear cascaded through him. He couldn't lose her to a bunch of lies. Just the thought of losing her left a gaping, hollow pit inside him.

"It wasn't about you, really," Rachel finally continued. "They were talking about your date. About me."

Graydon's eyebrows scrunched together. What could they possibly have to say about her?

"I just don't fit in," Rachel said.

Graydon lifted her head so their eyes met again. The

anguish he saw there matched how he felt inside. "Don't fit in how?"

"All of me," she replied, her hands fluttered in the air, around herself. He must have looked as confused as he felt, because she finally burst out what was really bothering her. "Don't you get it? You are perfect and gorgeous and amazing. And I'm me—awkward and fat and—"

Graydon cut her off before she could go any further. "Don't you ever say that again."

He pulled her close, one arm wrapped around her waist while the other sunk deep into the hair at the back of her head, keeping their eye contact. "You're absolutely perfect to me. For me. You're generous and funny. You're my best friend."

She tried to break into the conversation, but he wouldn't let her. He wouldn't let some stupid women who most likely said hurtful things to try to make themselves feel more powerful rip away the most amazing person he'd ever met.

"I don't want a skinny witch more interested in her celebrity ranking than about being happy with me. I did, once, with Carissa. Back then, the spotlight and hockey were all I thought about. But I thank God that my life changed. My accident was a blessing in disguise. My life holds more meaning now than it ever did then. And all I want is to share that with you. Just you, Rachel."

"But what if you change your mind? What if you decide I'm not what you really want? I'm chubby and I'm sure I'll just get chubbier if I have babies and what if you think my body is repulsive?"

He captured her lips with his, pulling her into a tender kiss that gradually built into a passionate exchange. He gradually readjusted his position, sinking backwards until he was laying back on the couch with Rachel draped across him, their hands sunk into each other's hair.

When he broke the kiss, they were both breathing hard. "We can put your fears to rest tonight, if you want."

Rachel's cheeks flushed from just-thoroughly-kissed pink to a deep rosy color. "That's not what I meant," she said.

He grinned. He knew it wasn't and so far, he had been very careful about not mixing the powerful but confusing emotions of an intimate relationship with their dating relationship. But now he was secure in his feelings, knowing he wouldn't confuse lust for love.

Still, if there was one thing he learned from his failed relationship with Carissa, it was to not be in a hurry to add anything that might mislead your true feelings for someone else. But he wasn't going to let Rachel leave his office doubting his attraction to her either.

He wrapped one of his legs around hers, pulling her even closer, then lowered his voice. "You are absolutely, completely sexy. Everything about you. I love your red hair." He drew his hand through her hair, loving the feel of the silky strands running through his fingers. "How soft your skin is." He moved his hand to her face, lightly running his knuckles down her cheek, her neck, and over her shoulder. "I love every one of your curves."

His hand pressed into her back, feeling her muscles shiver through the cotton, then down over her denim-covered backside. He gently squeezed her tush and she let out a little squeak. His hand trailed back up and just under the bottom of her top to rest on the soft skin at her waist.

"I love you, Rachel. The complete package." He looked into her clear green eyes, keeping his gaze steady so she could see the sincerity of his next words. "I want to spend the rest of my life with you. To someday wake up in bed next to you, not just one morning, but every morning. To fill our home with our kids, a dog and lots of noise and laughter. I want all of that with you. Only you." He wiped away tears from Rachel's cheek.

"But what if—" she began.

He put his finger over her lips and shook his head. "No more what-ifs. Do you love me?" he asked, desperately wanting her to say yes. Knowing that if she didn't, he would crumble into nothing.

She nodded.

"Do you trust me," he continued. She nodded again. "Then as long as we're together, we can figure everything else out. It will take some work and compromise, but it will all fall into place." He placed a kiss on her forehead, then let out a heavy sigh when Rachel laid her head on his chest. They stayed just like that, in their own little cocoon, as he held the person he loved most in this world close to him.

Chapter TWENTY-ONE

he crew at Sweet Confections worked furiously to fulfill holiday orders while Rachel and Kristen packed the challenge supplies. They decided to drive rather than risk shipping items. There was still a chance the cakes could be damaged, but they felt better about taking it themselves.

Rachel carefully wrapped, stacked and crated up the cakes. Kristen put their notes, time lines and sketches into an expanding file folder. One by one, everything got checked off on the to-do list and packed into the van. When the last item was loaded, they parked the van in Kristen's garage for the night.

The next morning, Rachel slid into the driver's seat while Kristen, Todd and Graydon buckled up to start their two-day trek to Phoenix. After the previous four weeks of preparing like crazy for the challenge, the actual road trip was a relief. Once she hit the freeway, she slid a CD into the stereo.

Todd groaned. "You've got to be kidding me! Chick music? Let's play something good. How about some Aerosmith or Guns N Roses?"

Rachel glanced up and met his eyes in the rear view mirror. "When you drive, you get to pick the music. I'm driving and I vote for Taylor Swift."

He slumped in his seat, but it wasn't long before he

sang along with her, albeit in a mocking tone. Every three hours, they stopped for a bathroom break and to switch drivers. To Todd's relief, everyone else brought music he liked.

Finally, when she thought the drive would never end, they pulled into their hotel parking lot in Logan, New Mexico.

"Thank goodness," Kristen said. "I think my butt is permanently numb."

"Don't worry," Rachel replied. "All the feeling will come back tonight, just in time for you to lose it again tomorrow."

Kristen stuck her tongue out, then Graydon opened the door for Rachel to jump out. She stretched her arms high into the air, then bent from side to side. "Man, long trips are brutal," she said.

"Let's grab our overnight bags and check in. Then I'm thinking a trip to the pool and hot tub are in order," he suggested.

Todd handed out their bags, then they checked the hotel.

"See you at the pool," Graydon said, patting Todd on the tush.

"Hey buddy. Keep those hands to yourself." Todd shoulder checked Graydon into the wall and the two started a shoving match while the girls rolled their eyes and went into their respective rooms.

Rachel and Kristen changed and beat the boys down to the pool. They were settled into the hot tub when the guys arrived and cannon balled into the deep end.

"They're as bad as a bunch of ten-year-olds," Kristen said.

"I don't know if I'd give them credit for a ten-year-old's maturity level." Rachel sighed and sunk deeper into the hot water. "Oh yeah. This is heavenly." She leaned her head back against the side. "I don't want to get out for at least thirty minutes. Even then, you may have to pry my poor body away."

The water around them sloshed as the guys joined them. "You're not getting in the pool first?" Graydon questioned as he settled next to Rachel.

"Nah, why bother with the appetizer when you go can for the main course?"

"Is everything food to you?" Todd asked.

Rachel cracked her eyes open and peered at Todd. "When you breathe recipes day and night, there are a lot of food analogies to be learned along the way."

"Kind of like how your vanilla bean pound cake was more interesting than the guys in college?" Kristen asked, quirking her eyebrow.

"Really? Vanilla bean?" Graydon playfully splashed some water at her.

"Aren't you glad it wasn't chocolate?" She took his hand to prevent any more water attacks. With her luck, it would end up in her nose. The group relaxed and chatted for the next thirty minutes until they finally decided they were pruny enough and should get out. She shivered when the cool air hit her, then wrapped herself in her towel. They walked back to their rooms and said their good nights.

By the end of the next day, everyone was excited to see the bright lights of Phoenix on the horizon. They once again pulled their van in and checked into their hotel. Kristen's stomach was acting up, so she decided to go to bed early. Todd stayed with her while Rachel and Graydon went to the pool together.

"Are you nervous?" Graydon asked after they settled into the hot tub.

"Nervous and excited, all mixed together. Part of me can't

wait and the other part wants to hide out in the bathroom and puke. I can't decide which is winning the battle. I just hope I don't throw up in front of everyone on national television. That would be the ultimate humiliation."

Graydon lifted her hand and kissed her palm, then twined their fingers together. "You'll do great. I know you will. Todd and I will be there the whole time, cheering you on."

Rachel turned and straddled his lap, wrapping her arms around his shoulders. "Have I told you lately how much it means to me that you came to the challenge?"

His hands settled on her thighs and he placed a quick kiss on her lips. "You're most welcome. Tomorrow is set up day, right?"

She nodded. "We have some training meetings to go over the rules and how everything will work, then we can set up our kitchen. It's hard to believe that in forty-eight hours this will all be over." She tilted her head to the side. "I hope we at least come in as runner-up."

"Don't think like that. Keep focused on the gold medal."

They lapsed into silence. She closed her eyes and let her body relax against his as the hot water and jets worked their magic. His thumb brushed over the side of her thigh and she focused on that gentle sweep back and forth. After a while, Rachel lifted her hand out of the water. "I look like one of those wrinkly dogs."

"A Char-Pei? Aren't they just the cutest little things," he said in a mocking girly voice.

Rachel laughed. "Ha ha. Let's go, buddy."

He helped her out of the hot tub and handed her a towel. When they were outside her door, he pulled her up against his wet chest, then leaned his head down, so his lips were next to her ear. "I love you."

She smiled against his neck and gave it a kiss. "I love you, too." With one final hug, they parted for the evening.

"Mr. Giambiasi, Miss Marconi is headed to Phoenix for the challenge," Tom reported over the phone to his client.

"Excellent. No problems, then?" his boss asked.

"No, sir. No one has been following Miss Marconi and her group left safely." He paused, not sure if he should mention the next item. But something nagged him that it was important, and over the years, he learned not to ignore that feeling. "Except there's this one thing . . ." He went on to fill his client in about some new information he'd discovered.

After the training meetings, Rachel and Kristen were outfitted with Food Network Challenge chef uniforms. She was proud of herself for not drooling or stumbling like an idiot when she met the show's host, Keegan, and her favorite judge, Kerry. But most of all, she was worried about Kristen.

She looked pale all morning. When Rachel asked if she was okay, Kristen insisted she was fine. But as the day went on, it was obvious she was struggling. After Rachel had to redirect Kristen three times about where some items needed to be stored, she pulled her aside.

"Okay. Spill the beans and tell me how you're feeling. Do you want to go back to the hotel and rest? Cause I'd rather have you rest today and be here tomorrow, than have you work hard today and not be able to do a thing for the competition."

Kristen sighed, then laid her head on Rachel's shoulder. "I'm not sick. Not how you think. I have morning sickness."

"You're pregnant?" She hugged her friend to her.

"I wasn't sure until just a few days ago. I was hoping I could ignore it until after the competition, but it looks like the nausea is starting to set in." Kristen pulled back. "But I promise, I am in this one hundred percent. I won't let you down."

"Kristen, you couldn't possibly let me down. It will all work out. But I want you to go back to the hotel and rest. With Daphne, didn't you feel better after a late morning nap?"

"But how is that going to help tomorrow? I can't just say, hey, prego woman here wants to pause the countdown clock for a thirty-minute snooze."

Rachel wasn't sure how it would work either, but she couldn't let Kristen see her doubt. "We'll figure it out. Maybe if you get enough rest today, you'll be able to work a bit longer before you need to rest tomorrow."

After a quick hug, she sent Kristen away. As she set up, the judges came over to ask why she was alone. She explained the situation and inquired if it was possible to have a cot set up in their break room in case Kristen needed to take a brief rest during the challenge. They consulted the rules and other contestants, who were fine with the suggestion.

During set up, she designated one section of the kitchen for Kristen to make the fairies and other cake props. She got the gum paste, baking sheets, paints, cutters, and everything else she would need set up. Then she worked to put together the rest of the kitchen in a manner that would be efficient for her work. The cakes were stacked and put into the refrigerator. Only one cake had cracked, for which she was grateful. Since they brought extra cakes, they should be fine.

When she transferred the buttercream and fondant from the carts to the shelves, one of the fondant lids popped off.

"That's not right. These should all be new and unopened," she mumbled. She pried off the lid and found that instead of the pre-colored pale blue fondant they ordered, there was a 70's puke green color in its place.

"What the heck?" She went to the trolley cart and pulled off two more fondant buckets. Both of the lid seals were broken.

"No. Please no." She crossed her fingers and hoped for a miracle, but opened the buckets and found a funky orange color and lemon yellow. "This can't be happening,"

"Is there a problem?" one of the judges asked.

"My fondant has been tampered with. These were all new buckets and marked as pale blue for our water fairy cake. But when I was setting up, I saw the seals were broken. These are not our colors."

Kerry came into the kitchen and called the other judges over to talk about options. Rachel looked up names of local restaurant supply stores. She couldn't find anyone who carried the blue she needed. She wanted to bury her head and cry.

How could this be happening? They had been so careful. Someone tampered with their supplies, there was no getting around it. But who? And why? As much as she hated it, she wondered if it could have been one of the other competitors.

The only way the blue fondant could be replicated was to get plain white fondant and color it herself. The task was daunting. It exhausted her just thinking of the sheer physical effort it required. The other option was to change the cake design. Armed with the information from the supply stores and their options, she went back to the hotel. She hoped Kristen felt up to a stressful conversation.

"How did it go?" Graydon asked, when she joined the other three in Kristen's room.

"Not as expected." She dropped into a chair beside Kristen's side of the bed. "Someone got into our fondant and switched the colors. Instead of pale blue, we have some nasty shades of green, orange, and yellow. Think 70's."

"What? How could that happen?" Kristen sat up and leaned against the headboard. "They were locked in the van the whole time."

"Which brings me to my next question. Todd and Graydon, could you go check the van and see if there's any signs of a break in?"

"No problem," Todd said. He grabbed the keys and both guys left the room.

"Now what are we going to do? We can't do a cake in those colors," Kristen said.

She pulled out her notepad and went on to explain what she had found out and detailed the two options. "If we want to stick with the original plan, then I'll get back to the kitchens and start mixing the fondant."

Kristen shook her head before she finished talking. "You'd be absolutely exhausted tomorrow. With me sick, I don't think that's a good idea."

They put their heads together and planned out a new cake that used similar design elements, hoping they wouldn't throw off their timed schedule too much. They stopped plotting when Todd and Graydon returned to the room.

"You were right. There are scrape marks on the side of the back door. They're small enough that we didn't notice, but when you're looking for tampering, you can tell they're there."

"Who do you think it could be? Nico?" Kristen looked to see what her reaction would be.

She shook her head. "I don't think it's him. And besides, he hasn't called or bothered me since the restraining order was put into place."

"How do you know? He could have come to get revenge. The Arizona police wouldn't be looking out for him like they were in Kansas City," Todd said.

Graydon walked over and stood behind her. He placed his hands on her shoulders and began working on the knots there. "I think we should report the vandalism. That way if anything else happens, it will be documented."

She nodded her agreement. Over the next hour, they answered questions and filled out police reports. Once that was taken care of and they finished the cake design, Graydon took Rachel's hand and led her out to the hotel's courtyard.

"You need a few minutes to relax." He led her to a bench and pulled her down to sit beside him. She leaned back and sighed.

"I'm terrified about tomorrow," she said, voicing her fears.

"What are you afraid of?" He absently ran his hand through her hair, twisting small sections around his finger.

"That everything will fall apart. That other things will be wrong, with the equipment or cake supplies, and we'll completely fail. And to top it off, it would all be documented on national TV for all my friends and family to see. Over and over again."

"You've watched enough challenges to know every competitor encounters problems. Hopefully, the fondant and new cake design will be the only bumps you'll have, but if it's not, you'll handle it."

"But what if I can't?" Her voice wavered.

"You will because you are filled with strength and faith. If there's a problem, then you'll figure it out together. Just be patient and think things through before making a decision." He pulled her hair over her shoulder and leaned close to her ear. "This is your opportunity to fulfill one of your dreams. So take any challenge thrown your way, grab it by the horns and conquer it. When the day is done, you'll be proud of how hard you worked and what you created. You can do it. I know you can."

He tucked a finger under her chin and tipped her head up so he could look into her eyes. "I believe in you."

He lowered his lips to hers, creating a warm tingle. The tingling moved from her lips, down her arms and into her fingers. She placed her hands on his upper arms to brace herself from completely melting into him. The kiss lingered, then deepened. She felt light and caught up in the sensations. It was beautiful and filled her heart until it felt like bursting.

When they pulled away, he held her in his arms, her head nestled just under his chin. They stayed like that for several minutes, each lost in their own thoughts and feelings. Finally, he stood and pulled her to her feet. "I would love to stay out here with you, but you need to get some sleep tonight."

She groaned. "I'm so nervous, I don't know if I'll be able to sleep at all."

"I felt the same way before a game. So the night before, I would plug in my iPod and listen to music to distract me from my thoughts. Eventually I'd fall asleep. I brought it for you, hoping it helps you, too."

Back in her room, Rachel prepared for bed. Hoping Graydon's idea would work, she put the ear buds in and hit play on the playlist he created. She smiled as the song Every Little Thing She Does is Magic began. She thought about Graydon and the magic that had come into her life since they started dating. Soon her thoughts wandered to their future and not long after, her eyes fluttered closed and sleep came.

Chapter TWENTY-TWO

"Contestants, in your places, please. We will begin in fifteen minutes."

A jumble of nerves shot through Rachel as she wiped down her workstation one last time and double-checked that the supplies were in place.

"Are you ready, girlfriend?" Kristen asked, putting her arm around her partner.

"No. Do you think they'd postpone the start long enough for me to go in the back to throw up?"

Kristen laughed. "That's my job, remember?"

"Oh yeah. Well, if you do go back there, puke a little for me too, okay?"

"You've got a deal. Now, let's get ready to kick some cake butt."

She looked out at the audience. Her parents had flown in that morning and sat with Todd, Graydon and Kristen's parents. People she loved, who counted in her life, were right there. Supporting her. *I hope I don't let them down,* she thought.

"Thirty seconds," the announcer said. They counted down and the filming began. There were introductions made, the rules were reviewed, and the competition's theme described. The competitors' introductions had been filmed the day before, to be added after the competition when the film went to the video editor. Finally the part came that they were waiting for. The audience counted down. Every number made Rachel's heartbeat kick up a notch.

"Go!" Keegan shouted and hit the timer's button to begin the eight-hour challenge.

Rachel spun around, pulled the first set of cakes out of the fridge and got to work. She sculpted the cakes to form a tree at the base of what would become a forest. She and Kristen had figured out a way to turn the original waterfall design into a forest scene with a focus tree that had a full leafy top made of green tinted cotton candy. She glanced behind her and saw Kristen molding the fairy bodies, then refocused on the task ahead of her. The sculpting had to be precise for there to be enough base to keep the rest of the tree steady. Once the base was completed, she stacked on a few more cakes to build the trunk of the tree. Four feet of cake. What an impressive sight.

After sculpting, she finally came to the frosting stage. She pulled out the buttercream and opened the lid. Then groaned. Not again.

"What's up?" Kristen asked.

"The buttercream is purple." They stared at the bright blob.

"What's happening over here?" John, one of the judges, asked.

"Someone tinted our buttercream," she said. "At least, I assume it's still buttercream." She dipped her finger inside and tasted it, then nodded.

The judges made notes about the tampered items. Keegan sent someone from the studio crew to talk to security. No one should have been able to get into the kitchens after everything was set up yesterday.

"Well, I guess it's on the inside. Hopefully it's the right

consistency to hold the fondant and not show through." Kristen patted Rachel's shoulder before moving back to her station.

Rachel dipped the spatula into the buttercream and began frosting the cakes. She heard some tittering from the audience when they realized the frosting had such an unusual color. Heat flooded her face and she glanced into the audience in search of Graydon. He nodded and gave her a thumbs up.

Keep going. Be patient and keep working. Achieve your dream.

The thoughts rolled through her mind, helping her stay focused. They were about ten minutes behind schedule, but were making good progress. Kristen finished the fairy bodies and began to heat the sugar for the wings. While she worked on that, Rachel kneaded the fondant which thankfully was still the new colors she'd picked up from the restaurant supply store yesterday.

"Rachel," Kristen called. Rachel left the fondant and went to her best friend. "I'm starting to feel sick. I need to rest for a little bit and get a snack. Can you make the wings?"

"Yes, let me put away the fondant so it doesn't harden." She quickly put the fondant away, then took over so Kristen could rest. She kept stirring the sugar, watching the temperature as it needed to be just right. Too hot and it would crack. If it wasn't hot enough, it wouldn't harden. Working with sugar was definitely Kristen's specialty, which made Rachel nervous.

"Where did your partner go?" One of the judges came up behind her.

"She needed to rest."

"How far behind will that put you?" The judge made notations on his chart.

Rachel chewed on her lower lip, then replied, "I'm not sure. But we'll work it out."

He consulted her written schedule, then left the kitchen. She looked around at the other competitors and saw how much they were accomplishing while she stirred sugar. She was tempted to turn up the heat to speed up the process, but knew it would ruin the results.

Patience, Rachel, she thought. *These wings are going to be incredible. It's worth the time it takes to get them done right the first time.*

Finally the sugar was ready to be poured into the wing molds. She swirled different colors of food coloring in to create a fantastical appearance. She set them aside to harden and went back to kneading the fondant. It felt good to put some physical force into the kneading and get back to what she was good at.

She draped the deep green fondant over the hilly portions of the base. Then smoothed and smoothed and smoothed, making sure there were no cracks or air bubbles. The smoothing was the most important part. If it wasn't done properly, then bumps from air bubbles would appear and if it wasn't warm enough, cracks would form around the edges where they were stressed.

"How are you feeling?" she asked when Kristen reappeared.

"I think I'll survive for a few more hours. What's going on?"

Rachel updated her, then Kristen consulted the time chart and jumped back in. They were behind, but in her gut, she also knew that what she told the judge was true. They would pull it all together. Somehow.

Once the hills were done, she grabbed the buckets of

brown and tan fondants and pulled out a big chunk of each. She rolled them into long round logs, then twisted the brown and tan shades together. After they were twisted, she rolled them flat again. The twisted colors created a cool-looking tree bark with depth.

Over the next hour and a half, Rachel got the tree draped, then used a sculpting tool to add texture to the tree. She even carved a heart with the name Daphne inside. She also sculpted the hill so it looked grassy. She was happy with how it turned out.

She turned her attention to molding the other items to make the cake come alive. She created mushrooms in bright colors. Two fairies would sit on them, talking and waving their wands. Small flowers would grow around the tree where another fairy would stand to make them bloom. A small blue bird was next. A friend for the fairy sitting on the hill to visit with.

She checked on Kristen, who was once again slowing down. She knew the stress would upset Kristen's stomach more than normal. "The fairy faces look incredible, Kristen."

"How much time is left?"

"A little more than ninety minutes." She handed Kristen a bottle of water and took a sip of her own.

"Crunch time," she replied, setting her face to keep working.

"You should go back and take a fifteen-minute break."

"We don't have fifteen minutes to spare."

"No, we don't. But we don't want to have you puking on the cake either. Just go sit, eat some crackers and practice your Lamaze or something. When you come back, you'll be ready to work again. Go." She shooed her friend out of the kitchen.

She started the cotton candy machine. Thankfully, the candy formed fluffy and full of poof. She pulled out the sugar glue spray to secure it to the tree "branches" which were curved clear plastic dowels. Draped through the dowels were tiny white Christmas lights with a battery-powered pack. Hopefully, the top of the tree would look twinkly and magical with the lights shining through the cotton candy.

Kristen returned, refreshed and ready to put the final touches on the fairies, their wings and wands. Once the top of the tree was finished, the girls placed the fairies on the cake. The fairy making the flowers bloom had a funny "oops!" expression on her face and the flowers in front of her were all bent over. The other fairies chatting looked like best friends, talking about their fairy magic, and the last fairy looked like she was trying to convince the little bird to fly. It was animated and beautiful.

"It looks just like we wanted," Kristen said, tears sparkling in her eyes.

"There's no time for tears yet, Fields. Get back to work."

They grabbed bottles of edible sparkle dust. Kristen dusted the tree, flowers, and mushrooms with a dry paint brush. Rachel put her sparkle dust in a small machine with a fan to blow the dust to land onto the cotton candy, adding some additional sparkle and shine for when they turned on the lights.

The final countdown began and the girls scrambled to finish what they could on the cake. They didn't have everything done, but when the countdown clock reached zero, they collapsed into each other, proud of what they accomplished.

She looked at each of the kitchens. The other three teams

had incredible cakes with different fairy interpretations and themes.

"Wow," she said, a sigh escaping her lips. "How are the judges going to choose between us?"

"I guess we'll find out soon enough." Kristen handed her a towel to clean off her hands. They watched as each team moved their cake to the judging table. The first team made it just fine. Team two wasn't as lucky. Two of their fairies fell off and shattered on the floor.

"What if that happens to us?" Rachel found Graydon in the audience, who shook his head as if saying not to think about it. She returned her focus to the third cake being moved to the table. A sigh of relief sounded from the audience when everything went smoothly.

"We're up," Kristen said. Two guys came to their kitchen to help Rachel move the cake since Kristen couldn't lift the heavy weight.

She wiped her sweaty palms on her jeans, then gulped away the lump blocking her throat. "On my count. One. Two. Three." The cake was incredibly heavy, straining the muscles in her arms, shoulders and back. "Careful. Careful. Careful," she chanted softly to herself. Inside she thought, *Don't blow it now, Rachel.*

"Lift up, right over the center," she said, positioning it over the table. "A little to the right, now down, gently. Let go."

The cake was on the table. Her knees felt like Jell-O with the heavy weight gone. Rachel reached to the back of the cake and turned on the twinkle lights. An ooh came from the audience, filling her with pride for their design. Kristen gave her a high five. "We did it, Rachel. The rest is cake from here."

"Ha ha, so funny." She bumped her shoulder into her best friend's.

Now, it was time for the competitors to step away while the judges inspected the cakes. All too soon, it was time to face the judges. If she thought her knees were Jello-O before, she wasn't sure what to call them now. Getting ready to face Keegan, John and Kerry was even more terrifying than wondering if she'd fail and not finish her cake.

"Rachel, you've had quite the experience with this whole challenge," Kerry began. Rachel just nodded. "I'd like to begin by commending you on how you and your partner worked together. You had many bumps, some of which other competitors would have used as an excuse to quit, but you persevered and worked your way through them. I'm very impressed with your determination. Not only are you a strong woman, you are a very talented cake designer."

So far, so good, Rachel thought.

Kerry shifted in her seat, then continued. "I like the design changes you made to accommodate the new fondants at the last minute. The twinkle lights add an element of fun and wonder a child would enjoy. Your partner's sugar and molding work is beautiful. If I could change one thing, it would be to have an odd number of fairies on the cake. I know one of your fairy's wings did not turn out, so you opted for four. But I think either three or five would have been better. But overall, I say a job well done."

Rachel exhaled audibly and the judges laughed. She survived Kerry's review and it wasn't as bad as she thought it would be. The rest of the judges' reviews passed by in a blur.

Finally, the competitors stood on the stage while Keegan gave an overview of the challenge, pointing out different strengths and weaknesses of each competitor's creation. Excitement bubbled up inside Rachel like soda pop fizz.

Please, please, please ran through her mind over and over.

Keegan announced second runner up with a silver medal. It wasn't her.

Only three left.

Please, please please.

She squeezed her eyes closed tight.

"And the winner of the gold medal and a check for ten thousand dollars is . . . " There was that hugely long pause, during which her stomach twisted and turned while her heart pounded against her chest. "Rachel Marconi and Kristen Fields."

Her knees went weak, but she couldn't move. Then Kristen rushed over and grabbed her in a tight hug. Keegan brought them up front and presented them with their check. Light bulbs flashed everywhere and the other competitors congratulated them. Everything was surreal, like a movie, except they were somehow caught in the middle of it.

Then Graydon wrapped his arms around her and spun her in circles. His warmth and strength made everything real. "You did it! You won!"

A tremble of excitement flowed through her again. "I did do it, didn't I?"

"I knew you had it in you." And that was the last thing she remembered as his lips settled over hers and the rest of the celebration melted away. With her arms wrapped around him, she realized everything she wanted was right here. Not just a successful career and incredible friends, but a man, who even through their differences, had captured her heart. And she wanted to give it to him. Forever.

Kristen and Todd bumped into the two of them, breaking

their kiss. Heat flooded her face, especially when she saw the cameras still rolling. She hoped Food Network had not just captured their kiss on national TV. Her parents and Kristen's parents joined the celebration until it was broken up when they were needed for the after-competition interviews.

Just before she left, Graydon stopped her. "I need to leave soon for a radio interview, but I'll meet back up with you. I have a surprise planned."

Anticipation flared through her as she returned his intense gaze. She gulped, then nodded. "I'll see you soon," she promised. He stole one last quick kiss before releasing her to join the others on their way to the interviews.

Over the next hour, the adrenalin from the competition slowly receded, leaving her exhausted. Some Food Network employees brought juices, muffins and a variety of fruit for the contestants to keep up their energy. She sighed in relief when it was all over. Kristen dropped an arm around her shoulders. "What now, my friend?"

"Should we start the kitchen clean up?" She dreaded it. Her feet, back, and arms ached.

"We have tomorrow to get it all cleaned and boxed up. I say we take the evening to celebrate and relax. Let's head back to the hotel for showers. Our parents are already there, waiting to meet up with us."

She gave her friend a weary smile. "Can we add a nap to the agenda, too?"

Kristen laughed. They changed from their uniforms back into jeans and short-sleeved tops. Rachel grabbed her cell phone from the top of the locker and slipped it into her back pocket. After applying some lip balm, she pushed the small tube into her front pocket. Right now she was so tired, she was glad she didn't bring her purse to the competition. They went out to the reception area where they met up with Todd, then started toward the hotel entrance.

"Rachel, wait!"

She turned, surprised to see Sheila coming toward her. "Sheila. I didn't know you were here, too."

She waved her hand in the air as if dismissing the comment. "I travel just about everywhere Graydon goes to keep track of his publicity. I was just at the radio station with him. The interview is running long and he asked me to come pick you up."

"Oh. I was just going back to the hotel to shower and rest for a bit."

Sheila chewed her bottom lip. "If you really feel like you need to, we can do that. It's just that it would throw off the timing for the plan." She winked.

Rachel's stomach fluttered as she wondered what the surprise could be. She glanced down at her jeans. At least she had on a nicer top than just a t-shirt. "Will this be okay or do you think I should change clothes?"

"I think you look perfect for what he has planned."

She turned to Kristen and Todd. "Well, I guess I'm going with Sheila to meet up with Graydon. I'll see you guys later tonight."

Kristen hugged her again. "Congrats, girlfriend. Have a great time celebrating with that hunk of yours," she whispered into her ear.

She flushed, but squeezed her friend back. "You, too. And no more puking tonight, okay?"

Kristen laughed as they pulled apart. "I'll do my best," she promised, linked arms with Todd and they left through the hotel front doors.

"My rental is in the garage," Sheila said. On the way, she

asked questions about the competition. When they reached the car, Rachel was happy to finally sit down.

"You look pretty beat," Sheila said from the driver's side. She started the car and backed out of the parking space.

"I'm exhausted and my feet are killing me." Rachel unsuccessfully tried to stifle a yawn.

Sheila glanced over, sympathy on her face. "Why don't you go ahead and rest? It's going to take about twenty minutes to get to the studio."

"A cat nap sounds wonderful. Thanks." She leaned her head back and barely closed her eyes before she was sound asleep.

Chapter TWENTY-THREE

"*R*achel, wake up." Sheila nudged her awake.

She blinked several times and looked around, realizing they were in an underground parking garage. "Where are we?"

"At the radio studio. I know, doesn't look like much does it? You'd be surprised how many stations are run out of old buildings. We've even been to some set up in trailers out in the middle of hickville."

Sheila got out of the car and Rachel followed her example. As she looked around, she noticed the lot was littered with broken bottles and one light flickered, like one of those bug zapper lights. A tingle of apprehension filled her.

"Are you sure it's safe to be here? I don't see any other cars." She edged closer to Sheila, who guided her to a side door.

"It's because it's so late. There's another lot where the employees park, but you can only get in with a key card from that entrance. This is the visitors lot. But yeah, I know what you mean. It could use some clean up."

They came to a heavy metal door covered with peeling paint and nasty words carved into it. Sheila pulled open the door and ushered her inside.

Rachel tentatively stepped over the threshold into the dim interior and looked around. They were inside a stairwell. On a wall was a rusty plaque that said "Processing" with an arrow pointing down and "Management" with an arrow pointing up. The hair on the back of her neck stood up and her stomach knotted.

"Sheila—"

That was all she got out before a heavy black bag swung at her face. She flew backwards, cracking her head against the cement wall behind her. Her vision blurred, her hands gripping the rough wall as she slid down to the floor. She screamed when Sheila viciously grabbed and pulled her hair from the back of her head, dragging her toward the stairs.

Dizziness and pain swirled in Rachel's head when she suddenly found herself airborne, then slamming down the flight of stairs. When she landed at the bottom, all she could do was lie in a motionless puddle. Pain surged through every part of her body.

Sheila's laugh echoed in the stairway. "Did you really think you could have him? That he would actually want to be with you?"

An ominous click echoed off the cement. Rachel tried to open her eyes, to focus, but everything was a blur. Another click, click, click and she realized it was Sheila coming down the stairs. Pain shot through her shoulder when she tried to move her arm.

Click. The sound of Sheila's dress shoes echoed in her mind, making her desperate to get up. She tried to push through the pain and lift up, only to fall into a heap on the floor again.

One last click and Sheila's shoes were in front of her. Sheila leaned over until her breath whispered across Rachel's face. "Ah, is the poor baby hurt?" she asked softly. "Let me make it all better."

Her laughter echoed off the walls as she grabbed Rachel's shirt and dragged her down another flight of stairs.

Graydon shoved through the hotel doors, grateful to finally be done with the radio interview. The DJ had been one of those hash-over-the-glory-days guys and tried to trick him into saying nasty things about former players. Interviews like this took extra focus not to trip up and say something he'd later regret. He wished he could go back in time and change his decision to take the interview Sheila set up. He needed to take advantage of the trip to promote the camps in another area, she told him. Plus, it made the travel costs a business expense. He wanted to say no, to stay focused on Rachel. Instead, he went against his instincts in an effort to fix things with his PR manager.

He rubbed a hand over his eyes as he waited for the elevator to stop at his floor. He couldn't wait to see Rachel and take her out. The elevator doors opened and he rushed to Rachel's room. Finding it empty, he crossed the hall to Kristen's room, assuming they were all together, celebrating. After a minute, he knocked again, then Todd opened the door wearing a pair of jeans and no shirt.

"Uh, sorry, man." He stumbled over his words. "Could you tell me where Rachel is?"

Todd's eyebrows creased together. "I thought she was with you? Didn't she meet you at the radio station?"

Graydon wondered if she tried to surprise him and reached for his phone. "I didn't see her before I left. I'll give her a call and catch up with her. Thanks and sorry to interrupt."

"No problem." Todd started to close the door. "Oh hey, if you can't reach Rachel on her cell, try Sheila."

Graydon swung back around, catching the door before it closed. "Sheila?"

"Yeah, she picked up Rachel after the competition to meet up with you."

"Sheila's not supposed to be here," he said.

Todd gave Graydon an odd look. "She said she's here helping with your publicity stuff, that you were running late and asked her to take Rachel to meet you at the station. "

The muscles in his shoulders clenched and bunched. "She couldn't be—. No, she wouldn't—" he started, then stopped as he sorted out Todd's explanation. Sheila storming out of his office and the conversation with Zack ran through his mind, along with everything that had happened to Rachel these past few months. Could this have all been about him? Not Rachel and Nico? It didn't seem possible, but something inside insisted this new connection was right. That Rachel was in danger—and somehow Sheila was involved. He looked back to Todd, cold fear lancing through him. "I didn't send Sheila to pick up Rachel."

Understanding dawned on Todd's face. He muttered a curse. "Honey," he called behind him. "Get dressed. Rachel's missing."

Graydon hit speed dial, hoping and praying that Rachel would answer.

Rachel curled into a ball on the cold, hard floor. There wasn't an inch of her body that didn't hurt. Part of her wished she would just pass out, another part desperately tried to stay conscious and prayed to find a way to escape. Although that seemed like a dim chance considering she couldn't even lift herself up on her hands and knees.

Across the room, Sheila stalked back and forth near the stairs, periodically checking and rechecking her watch. It had taken a lot of strength for Sheila to haul her down those stairs. She couldn't have the energy reserves to keep it up for long. Or at least Rachel hoped that was the case.

Rachel jerked when the phone in her back pocket vibrated. Someone was trying to call her! She squeezed her eyes shut, hoping desperately Sheila wouldn't hear the slight noise. Sharp fiery pain shot up her arm as she slowly moved her hand. She bit her lip to keep from crying out. Finally, she reached her hip, but the phone stopped vibrating. She had missed the call.

Tears streaked down her cheeks. The phone vibrated again. She looked over to Sheila, who was still pacing back and forth. She reached into her pocket, pulled the phone out, but it slipped from her fingers.

Sheila whirled around to face her. "What was that?"

She remained silent, but the phone was loud as it vibrated against the cement floor. Sheila rushed over and snatched it away. Her face hardened when she read the name flashing on caller I.D. Her fist tightened around the phone, then she hurled it across the room, where it skittered and clattered before coming to a stop somewhere in the darkness.

Sheila turned to Rachel and kicked her in the mid-section. Rachel tried to protect her stomach, but couldn't block the blows.

"You. Can't. Have. Him," Sheila punctuated each word with another kick until Rachel was lying on her side, gagging on the blood and vomit coming up through her mouth. Sheila grabbed Rachel's head and ground it against the cement, rubbing it through her own vomit. She struggled to breathe when Sheila finally walked away and continued to rant.

Flashing lights filled the hotel parking lot. Graydon, Todd, Kristen and the parents answered question after question, while frustration mounted inside him. Rachel was out there somewhere with Sheila and he knew she was hurt. He could just feel it and it was ripping him apart. He had to find her.

"Sir, can you think of anywhere Sheila would have taken your girlfriend? Anywhere at all?"

"No," He shook his head again. "We've never come to Arizona on business together. I have no idea where to go or how to find her." He looked down at his cell phone. The only link he had left with Rachel. He wanted to continue trying to call, but the police suggested he stop so he wouldn't put her in any further danger. What if Sheila heard Rachel's phone go off and went berserk?

The what-if scenarios tortured him.

He refreshed his cell phone screen, thinking maybe he hadn't heard it ring. That maybe Rachel had tried to call or text or . . . He looked at the icons on his phone and the answer that glared back at him.

"He was always meant to be mine. I'm the only one who really knows how to take care of him, help him, love him."

The more Sheila talked, the more unhinged she sounded. Rachel went from feeling fear to nothing at all. Sheila's words filled the empty room, but Rachel barely comprehended them. Her head spun, fuzzy from the constant pain.

"That fool Carissa tried to snare him. She even got him to propose. As much as I love Graydon, I have no idea how he didn't see past her shallowness. She never would have made a good wife. I made sure it stayed that way."

Something wasn't right about what Sheila said, but Rachel couldn't get her fuzzy head to work it out.

"It's amazing the things you can learn on the internet. It was so easy, almost comical really. Poor baby never knew what hit her when the brakes stopped working and she hit that wall. The paramedics said she died instantly." Sheila's hot eyes flicked to Rachel. "You won't be so lucky though."

The click click of Sheila's heels coming closer made Rachel cringe. "The morning he told me he was going to marry you, I knew this was it. You had to disappear, die."

Tears coursed down Rachel's face, while regret filled her. She looked up at Sheila. "They'll know you did it. You're the one who picked me up. Todd and Kristen saw you."

Sheila stopped, her red leather shoes just inches from Rachel's nose. She bent down, so she could look into her eyes. "Tsk, tsk. You haven't been listening." She leaned closer, lowering her voice to a whisper. "I've got a plan."

Just then, the metallic grinding of the door upstairs met their ears.

"And it looks like act two is about to begin." She placed her hand firmly over Rachel's mouth.

"Hello? Rachel, where are you?"

It couldn't be.

"Down here. I'm waiting." Sheila replied, her voice slightly higher to sound more like Rachel's.

Heavy footfalls pounded down the stairs. Sheila removed one of her hands and pulled out a small black gun, then stepped away just as a broad shape came down the last flight of stairs.

"Nico, stop!" Rachel yelled, but the gun fired and he flew backwards to the ground.

Chapter TWENTY-FOUR

*G*raydon stared intently at the blip on the phone screen. "We're almost there. Just up ahead and turn left."

The unmarked police car turned and stopped in front of a set of warehouses. Graydon and Officer Bauer looked around for clues leading to where Sheila and Rachel could be.

The officer scanned the street. "If we can find a car, we'll have a better idea of where to find them."

Graydon peered through the darkness. "What's that entrance, just up there to the left?"

Officer Bauer edged the car down the street to a narrow entrance of an unused parking garage. They pulled through and at the back of the lot, found not one, but two cars parked near a large metal door that was partially open. The officer turned off the headlights, then parked his car directly behind the two cars, blocking them from leaving. He picked up his radio and called in their location to the two other police units that were exploring the area not far behind them.

"Stay here," Officer Bauer instructed. Then he glared at Graydon. "I mean it. Stay right here."

Everything within Graydon rebelled. He wanted to rush to Rachel, but knew he wasn't trained to help her like this officer was. He swallowed the lump in his throat and nodded. "Yes, sir."

The other patrol cars pulled into the lot, each parking strategically to block any possible escape. Officer Bauer opened the car door. A sharp crack echoed through the air. The hairs on Graydon's arm stood up straight. Three of the five officers scrambled to the metal door, barely nudging it enough to get through and begin their search.

Graydon was left with two officers. He heard one report a gun shot and request back up over the police radio. Both remained on high alert. One faced the metal door, the other faced the back of the garage. Fear, desperation, and dread pulsed through Graydon, sweat dripped down his face. His hand itched to grab the door handle and make a run for the metal door and wherever Rachel might be inside, but there was absolutely nothing he could do except drop his head into his hands and pray to a God he hoped was listening.

"Well, well, well. Look who showed up. The stalker boyfriend." Sheila walked over to Nico, keeping her gun trained on him. "Get up, lover boy."

Nico stood, a bit unsteady on his feet, and clutched his arm where blood oozed, dripping through his fingers. Sheila motioned for him to move over and sit next to Rachel. His face turned ashen when he saw Rachel crumpled on the floor. He dropped to his knees and tried to gather her into his arms, but she screamed in agony. Rachel could barely see through the haze of pain, but she felt Nico's hand rest gently on the back of her head.

"Who are you and why have you hurt Rachel?" he asked.

Rachel was shocked, not by the anger in his voice, but by the authority and lack of fear.

"Since you won't be alive much longer, it doesn't matter who I am. But as for your little sweetheart, let's just say she would have been better off if she had stayed involved with you."

"And just what do you think you're going to accomplish by killing both of us?" Before Sheila replied, he continued. "Oh wait, it's obvious, isn't it? The stalker boyfriend, as you referred to me, lured poor little Rachel into an abandoned warehouse and when she wouldn't change her mind about coming back to me, I shot her. Then in grief, shoot myself, too. A tragic fatal love story, but definitely a flawed one."

"Flawed?" Sheila asked incredulously. Rachel wished she could clearly see the expression on Sheila's face.

"Unoriginal. You obviously didn't do your homework. You have no idea who I am, do you?"

"I don't want to hear any more of your babble. You're just trying to stall." She raised her gun and pointed it at Rachel.

"Just know this," he continued. "My family is from Italy and they are very connected, very powerful. Let me assure you of two things. One, the detectives I hired have photos that connect you to Rachel in some rather odd situations and times outside her house and at the bakery. Enough to implicate you if anything happens to her. They know I'm here. Believe me, I'm the type to actually cover my tracks. And two, whatever you do to us will be done a hundred times over to you. Only my family will stretch out the torture for weeks, maybe months, as they make you beg them to kill you just so you won't feel the pain any longer."

Silence filled the room for just a brief moment.

"You're lying," Sheila said, resolutely.

A heavy weight crashed on top of Rachel as gun shots echoed off the walls. She screamed as fire exploded all over her body and the weight pushed down even harder. Shouts, noise and clatter echoed all around the room until the only sounds left were those of her own anguish.

The weight of Nico's body was lifted and as hands reached for her, she finally, gratefully, gave in to the blackness waiting to devour her.

Flashing lights created a dizzying swirl in the damp underground garage. Graydon felt like the walls were wavering and closing in on him. He paced back and forth while police officers and paramedics entered and exited the stairwell. The door that led to Rachel and whatever lay below was full of officers and emergency workers. The sound of gunshots still echoed inside his head but below, everything was silent now. The silence was a thousand times worse.

"Everyone move back. We have three stretchers coming through," said an officer at the doorway. A few officers kept the area clear around the door as the first stretcher came up.

Graydon pushed his way as close as possible. He bent

over in fear when the first stretcher cleared the door. Blood soaked the white sheet in multiple locations. Fear clenched in his chest as the stretcher came closer, closer. Then his breath whooshed out like he'd been sucker punched.

"Nico?" he asked, confusion lacing his voice. The officer next to him turned his head sharply to look at him.

After the shock of seeing Nico, he was unprepared to see Rachel rushed past. He followed, listening as paramedics passed information through their walkie talkies. *Broken leg. Possible fractured arm. Broken ribs with possible internal bleeding. Concussion. Shock.* The words rushed past him, not fully being absorbed but terrifying him nonetheless. Metallic clanks sounded sharp and piercing when they loaded her into the back of the ambulance.

A paramedic blocked Graydon from entering the vehicle. "Sir, you aren't authorized. You need to step back now, please."

"Where is she going?" he demanded.

Officer Bauer returned to his side. "Mr. Green, we need you to help us with a few things here, then I'll take you directly to the hospital."

His hard stare met the officer's. "As soon as possible? No messing around?"

"Yes, sir. I give you my word. We'll leave here for the hospital within ten minutes."

He wanted to rant and say no way. He needed to stay with Rachel, but somehow the rational side of him made it through the warring emotions and knew cooperating was the best thing to do.

The ambulance doors clanged shut, sirens went off and they sped away. Dread clenched deep in his gut. All he could do now was pray she would survive.

She had to because he couldn't face life without her.

"You may want to contact your friends," Officer Bauer suggested.

Kristen and Todd. Rachel's parents. He had forgotten about them. He pulled out his phone and decided a text message would be the best. He didn't know if he could physically tell them what had happened.

G: WE FOUND RACHEL. SHE'S ON HER WAY TO ST. JOSEPH'S HOSPITAL. WILL MEET YOU THERE ASAP.

He pushed send. Before he could pocket the phone, he received a text back from Todd.

T: GOT IT. WE'RE ON OUR WAY. SEE YOU THERE. BE SAFE.

He wished he could jump through the phone and join them, but instead he put it away and followed the officer back toward the stairwell door where another stretcher was just coming up. He stumbled to a stop when he saw the black body bag strapped on top.

No. He had not thought about Sheila since Rachel came out.

"Sir, would you be able to identify her? It's a chest wound, so you'll only see her face."

He swallowed twice before he could get his voice to work. "I'm pretty sure I know who it is."

The officer motioned to the paramedics. Prickles ran down his arms as the stretcher came his direction, then stopped in front of him.

"Are you ready?" Officer Bauer asked.

Graydon couldn't take his eyes off the bag and just nodded. The officer slowly unzipped the bag. Each bump of the zipper matched the electric jolts shooting down Graydon's arms.

First he saw her hair. Thick dark masses, slightly messy. Next he moved his eyes over her tan skin, now tinged an unnatural pale color. His breath whooshed out when he saw her closed eyes.

Why, Sheila? Why would you do something like this?

He stepped back, rubbed his chest, and looked away from his once-trusted friend. Regret and sorrow filled the spot where anger had resided.

"Sir?" Officer Bauer prompted.

"Her name is Sheila Montoyez. She is—was—my PR manager." He turned to the officer. "Can we leave now?"

Officer Bauer nodded. "Yes. Go on over to my car. I'll give this information to the detectives, then we'll go. We can talk more there."

Graydon looked back again as the paramedic zipped up the bag. *May God have mercy on you, because I don't know if I can ever forgive you.*

"Sir, did you hear me?"

He turned and started back to the car. "Yes. That's fine."

But everything wasn't fine. One of his closest friends betrayed him and the woman he loved was fighting for her life. He squeezed his eyes shut, blocking out the barrage of emotions threatening to overwhelm him.

The one thing he couldn't figure out was how Nico fit into this mess. Officer Bauer opened his door and settled into the seat beside him.

But I'm about to find out.

Drip . . . drip . . . drip . . . Graydon stared in a trance as each small drop of solution fell from the IV bag into the connected tube, then flowed into Rachel's hand. Her hand which felt so cold. He gently rubbed it between his two hands as he sat beside her, hoping she could feel the warmth and was comforted.

He dropped his head onto the edge of the bed. She was so pumped full of drugs for pain, nausea and to help her sleep, he had no idea what she could or couldn't feel. But not feeling anything was probably better for her at this point. Twenty-four hours after all the drama and there wasn't much of her that wasn't covered with either a cast or white gauzy bandages.

He looked up and over to the other side of the ICU where Nico was recovering from his own long surgery. A man dressed in a dark suit was stationed outside his door. Earlier, one of the nurses mentioned that it was private security from Italy. Apparently there was a lot more to Nico than he let on.

"How are you, Mr. Green?" Heather, the evening shift nurse, came in to check Rachel's stats.

He sat up and stretched. "Doing as good as I can," he replied. "I assume you're here to kick me out?"

"Sorry, I know the rules stink, but someone can come back in thirty minutes."

"I understand. Take good care of her, okay?"

"Of course." She turned toward a monitor to give him some privacy.

He leaned over and gently trailed a finger down Rachel's soft cheek. "Your parents will be in soon. I'm sure you can't wait for your mom to talk your ear off. I'll be back to rescue you though." His voice turned gruff. He leaned close to her ear. "I love you, Rachel."

He kissed her cheek, then left the room.

Graydon paused near Nico's room. The dark-suited man nodded, indicating that he could go in. The guard stayed in the open doorway, but kept his back to the room. Graydon approached the bedside and looked down. Nico looked like he was sleeping peacefully. After a moment, his eyes fluttered open.

"Hey," Graydon said.

It took a few seconds, but Nico's eyes finally focused on him. "Hey," he replied.

Graydon stood there, not sure what to say next. "I heard your surgery went well. Nothing major got hit."

"Yeah. Lucky, I guess."

"If you can call being shot lucky. Why did you do it?" Graydon looked down at his feet, not sure he could meet Nico's eyes. Afraid of what he might see there.

For a brief moment, only the sound of machines beeping filled the room. "I made a lot of mistakes these past few months, ones I wish I could fix." Nico drew in a sharp breath. "I had a detective following Rachel."

Graydon's head jerked up. "What?"

"Ever since her car was vandalized. At first, I just wanted to know that she was really okay and over me." He chuckled, then winced in pain. His eyes flicked up to meet Graydon's. "That was quickly apparent."

Graydon nodded in agreement, waiting for Nico to continue.

"I planned to call off my detective. I had other projects that needed to be monitored. But at that meeting, he showed me pictures of Sheila that struck me as odd. Sometimes she was with Rachel, other times she was skulking around. I knew something was wrong, so I halted all my other investigations and kept my guy solely watching Rachel."

Nico's eyes filled with regret. "I tried to warn her but did a complete bang up job."

"Why didn't you just tell the police about the pictures?" Graydon asked. The idiot could have saved them all so much trouble.

"I consulted my legal adviser and he said there wasn't enough evidence."

Graydon arched his eyebrow. Legal adviser?

"There's a lot about my family you don't want to know." Nico paused a moment, nodded toward the doorway, making sure Graydon understood before continuing.

"My detective began monitoring Sheila as well. When he discovered she purchased a gun and followed Rachel to Arizona, I flew in from my California corporate office. Sheila made tracking her easier by calling and pretending to be Rachel." He tried to shrug, but only a small motion was possible with the surgical bandages. "That brings you up to date. Before you ask, all of the documentation will be anonymously sent to the police to wrap up any legal questions that may remain."

Graydon held the gaze of the other man who loved his girlfriend. And he knew Nico really did love her, otherwise he would have never risked his life for her. Even though he handled things in a way Graydon disagreed with, he was grateful that Nico had not given up. The jumbled mess of the last few months needed to be forgotten and forgiven. All he cared about at this moment was that Rachel was safe and on the road to recovery. Thanks to the man lying in this hospital bed.

"Thank you," Graydon said. In those two insignificant words, he hoped Nico understood all the things left unsaid.

Nico gave a small nod. "She deserves a life full of love. Take good care of her."

"I will," Graydon replied. It was one promise he was determined to fulfill.

Chapter TWENTY-FIVE

*L*ights twinkled on the tree and laughter floated between the conversations as Rachel's family gathered in the living room for their Christmas Eve gift exchange.

A lump swelled in her throat as she watched each of her loved ones. Adam and Eva trying to rein in the boys, Christopher and Faith so excited for little Emery's first Christmas, her parents content to have everyone under their roof. Kristen and her family joined them this year, too. After their tumultuous experience, her mom wanted to celebrate the joy of family and close friends.

Most importantly, Graydon was there, just as he had been each day since her hospitalization—at her bedside, making arrangements for a friend's private plane to fly her home comfortably, then competing with her mom for the role of over-protective nurturer. Nevertheless, he made her smile and even laugh as he invented reasons why having an arm in a sling and a broken leg was a positive turn of events. Her favorite was when he bought all sorts of fuzzy socks with crazy designs so she could be a trendy foot model.

Throughout her recovery, she came to fully accept the love he offered and her love for him flourished, giving her a sense of comfort and wholeness. He was her rock. There weren't words to accurately express her gratitude that he had come into her life.

Her mother clapped her hands to get everyone's attention. "Alright, everyone. It's time for our gift exchange."

"Presents! Presents! Presents!" the three older boys chanted.

"But first," Natalie continued while Eva shushed the boys. "Your father and I want to say how thankful we are to have you each here, safe and sound."

Tears blurred Rachel's vision as her mother went on to share her love for each of them. Her father led them in a family prayer, then the fun began. Presents were distributed to be oohed and aahed over. Little Stockton ran his new trains around on the floor and Daphne rocked her new baby doll. Jordan and Malone exclaimed over their Lego sets and devised scenarios of how their characters could battle each other.

"Why does everything have to be a battle? Why can't they have a tea party?" Rachel asked her nephews. Jordan pretended to gag and his mom lightly smacked him on the back of the head.

"Respect," Eva reminded him.

"A tea party? With Legos? That's just wrong," Graydon said, then unwrapped a gift from Rachel. "What the heck?"

It was a Lego Friends tea party set. She just smiled. "I thought you could use some refinement and these were just about your age level." The women were the ones laughing now. Graydon extended his hands, threatening to tickle her.

"No tickling the cripple! My ribs are still recovering."

Instead he leaned forward and whispered into her ear. "You know what they say about paybacks, don't you?"

She smirked, enjoying their playful banter. "Bring it on."

He tapped her chin. "Just wait. It's coming."

He had a devilish gleam in his eyes when he sat back and continued his banter with the boys, defending his Lego tea party set. She chuckled and turned her attention to the cozy sweater Kristen gave her.

A little later, her mother called over. "Graydon, I have a present here that says I can't open until you give the okay." She held up a rectangular box.

He leaned over, just so Rachel could hear and said, "This is where the payback begins."

She looked at him curiously as he shifted to face her. The room quieted down with only the sound of Stockton and Daphne playing to break the silence. He took her unbandaged hand and kissed the back of it.

"Graydon?" Rachel tilted her head, trying to figure out what he planned. Instead, he placed a finger over her lips and quietly shushed her. Her heart skipped a beat, unsure where this was leading.

"Today, I'm thankful to be here with you and your family. I know how much each person in this room means to you. They're the foundation of who you are and more than anything, I want to be a part of that foundation, too." He leaned closer. "Do you know what the best part about your broken leg is?"

She shook her head, confused by the change in subject.

"You can't run away." He waggled his eyebrows, while chuckles filled the room. He stood, retrieved something from his pocket, then knelt beside her. She heard her mother's gasp, but didn't look away from Graydon's sincere gaze. Tears threatened as he took her hand, this time with her palm facing him.

"I love how you put your foot in your mouth when you're

nervous." He kissed her pointer finger as light laughter filled the room.

"I love that you were more interested in vanilla bean pound cake than dating when you were in college." She couldn't help but smile as he kissed her middle finger.

"I love your generous nature and positive attitude." He kissed her ring finger.

"I love your teasing and the sound of your laughter." He kissed her pinkie finger.

"I even love how you snuggle up on the couch, then fall asleep during a movie." He kissed the pad of her thumb, then turned her hand over and held it like a prince taking his princess's hand. A few tears streaked down her cheeks.

"I love you, Rachel Marconi. I would be honored if you would share your family, your life, and your love with me forever." He kissed the back of her hand, then asked, "Will you marry me?"

A soft sob broke free from her tear-clogged throat. "Yes," she choked out. "Yes." She laughed, then gasped when he turned his other hand over to reveal a beautiful diamond ring. The design was simple, a gold band with a princess cut diamond. It was classic and just perfect.

He slid the ring onto her finger, then cupped her face. "I love you," he said softly.

She wrapped her free arm around his neck and pulled him closer. "I love you, too. So much." Then she kissed him, starting with a little nibble that turned into a deeper, more meaningful kiss.

"Eew!" her nephews moaned.

"Yeah, come on guys, let's keep it PG rated," Kristen teased.

They broke apart and were surrounded by the family. Hugs and well-wishes took center stage until Jordan asked, "Grandma, aren't you going to open your present?"

"Do I have permission now, Graydon?" Natalie asked.

"Of course, Mom," he said.

Rachel nudged him. "Two words. Suck up."

"I have just one thing to say. Favorite son-in-law."

She rolled her eyes, not bothering to mention he would be the only son-in-law. She turned her attention to her mother, who had unwrapped the present and was lifting the box lid. Her mother started to laugh. First it was a little laugh, then it grew to the point that a few tears streamed down her face. Her father looked over her shoulder, then burst into laughter too. Even Graydon had a huge grin on his face, his shoulders shaking.

"What did you give her?" She wondered what could possibly be so hilarious. Natalie pulled out a book and showed it to the family. *The Wedding Survival Guide For Mothers and Daughters: Tips to Avoid Killing Each Other Before the Big Day.*

Read on for yummilicious Sweet Confections recipes and sneak peek at Saving Dr. Weston Blake, the next book in the Crystal Creek series. Also available in Kindle Unlimited.

If you liked this book, please take a few minutes to leave a review for it! Authors really appreciate this, and it helps draw more readers to books they might like. Thank you!

. . .

Join Danyelle's newsletter and never miss a new release or special sale on her books.

SAVING *Doctor Weston* BLAKE

*J*osephine picked up the volunteer binder and flipped to the back section to scan the list of doctors working that afternoon. More specifically, she was checking to see if one particular doctor was assigned to the pediatric oncology floor.

"Please let him be scheduled elsewhere," she mumbled, her finger running down the long list of names until it landed on the right one.

Dr. W. Blake - Pediatric Orthopedics.

Thank the heavens above, Dr. Doom and Gloom was dealing with x-rays, broken bones, and casts, all of which was a much better fit for his analytical and straight-forward personality. The families on the oncology floor had enough to cope with. What they really needed was a good dose of happiness and hope, not a bunch of statistics.

And that's where she came in, Miss JoJo, also known as Origami Girl.

She had been volunteering at Crystal Creek Children's Hospital for almost ten years, since her own brother's battle with the big C. She knew firsthand how important attitude was. What she didn't understand was why in the world Dr. Weston Blake was interested in pediatrics at all. His personality was much better suited to adults, or better yet, a research lab where he could interact with other like-minded scientists. The one thing she did know was that their aversion for each other was mutual. He couldn't stand her cheery demeanor any more than she liked his block of wood personality.

This made it all the more fun to torment him when they were forced to work near each other. Today, though, she needed a reprieve from Dr. Blake. There were enough stressful things happening in life. She really wanted to focus on the kids today.

Josephine shrugged her shoulders and slipped the cheery, yellow volunteer lanyard over her head and her usual braided brunette bun. She double checked her messenger bag one last time. Crayons, markers, and colored pencils—check. Glitter glue, stamps, stickers, and graphite pencils—check. Coloring pages and sketch pad—check. She closed up the compartments, then slung the bag over her shoulder. The creative coloring project was ready to go!

She felt light as she confidently walked down the hall toward the bay of elevators. For the next hour, she was going to spend time with some of her favorite people on earth. She joined a small group in an elevator and pressed the button for the third floor. It was going to be a great afternoon and the kids would be excited to show off their creations when their families arrived after work.

The doors were almost closed when a hand darted between them. The doors stopped, then slowly slid open again. Her eyes widened when Dr. Doom and Gloom himself stepped onto the elevator, then repeatedly jabbed the already lit third floor button.

He seriously couldn't be going to the oncology floor. Yet he was right there beside her, reaching over to impatiently jab the number three button again.

"Good afternoon, Dr. Blake," Josephine said in her best I'm-trying-to-be-nice-to-the-evil-man voice. She reached over and pushed the button with the close door symbol and the doors slid shut.

Dr. Blake grunted and crossed his arms. He studiously ignored her and everyone else on the elevator. It was just as well, because his ego certainly didn't need to be boosted by the other women's fawning. Postures were straightened, chests thrust forward, and tummies sucked in. Even cell phones were forgotten in the presence of Dr. Blake. While he was all doom and gloom in her opinion, she had to admit he was also annoyingly attractive. The doctors' white lab jackets looked boxy on most men, but his managed to look like it could have been tailored by Armani. With his perfectly coiffed black hair, his dark brooding eyes, and an ever present five o'clock shadow, he was GQ magazine worthy.

But she knew better than to let someone's outside appearance rule her hormones. It was how someone treated others that made them beautiful or an ugly slug of a beast. Where Dr. Doom and Gloom sat on that scale was still murky. After all, wanting to save the lives of children gave him some bonus points.

"How are you, Dr. Blake?" Josephine asked smoothly, wondering if he'd engage in conversation. Thus far, she'd only been successful at wrangling seven words out of the man at one time. He simply nodded in response, so she tried yet again. "It's a beautiful day outside, don't you think?"

He rocked back on his heels, eyeing the elevator's progress, probably wishing he could be beamed up and away that instant. "It's raining," he mumbled.

He spoke! That was two words down. "Ah, but it's wonderful for the tulips and daffodils. We always get that one week of early warm weather that fools the bulbs to start blooming, then a late frost hits them. It fascinates me how they tough it out until they get a boost like today's rain."

Their conversation was interrupted as the elevator stopped on the second floor. Josephine stepped aside to allow the other occupants to exit, while Dr. Blake stepped off the elevator. Was he only going to the second floor? Or had her attempt at conversation annoyed him so much that he decided to take the stairs? Once everyone got off, Dr. Blake stepped back on. Huh. Chivalry. Who knew he had it in him? Josephine shook her head and smiled.

"Something funny?" he asked gruffly, jabbing the third-floor button yet again.

She was almost too shocked to reply. She was fairly certain this was the first time he had addressed her directly since he started working on the oncology floor. "Oh, just thinking about all the fun I'm going to have with the kids today," she replied. "Anyway, don't you agree the rain is a good thing?"

His dark eyebrows scrunched together as he folded his arms tightly across his chest. "No."

That single word was hard and rather final. Josephine tried to come up with another follow up question. She could ask him about his favorite color or TV show. Neither of those would be a good flow from talking about the weather. Ooh, she could ask him if he had a garden! Alas, the elevator dinged and the doors slid open. Dr. Blake quickly exited and turned a sharp left, disappearing down a hall. Drat! She was so close to breaking her record. Oh well. At least he hadn't made her day any worse than it already was.

A few pint-sized patients followed her down the brightly lit oncology hall. "Miss JoJo," little Timothy exclaimed, greeting her with a hug that soothed away the tension of the day. "Did you find Mater?"

She crouched down to meet the six-year-old's brown eyes. "I sure did. I even added something extra special to his picture for you. Let's go to the activity room and I'll find it."

Timothy's wide grin made her heart swell. They walked across the hall and entered the Garrett Family Memorial Activity Center. This was her favorite place in the hospital. The activity center consisted of three rooms. The main room was the general activity center. A mural of campground, tents, and forest animals was painted on one wall, creating a fun adventure theme. Sunshine yellow cabinets held dress-up clothes, board games, and toys galore. The activity tables had cute folding lawn chairs in bright colors for both kids and adults. There was even a tree house in one corner to climb and play in. In addition to the activity room, there was also an education center for kids to do homework and work with tutors, as well as a teen lounge where the foosball table, library, and movie collection was located.

Josephine followed the kids as they scrambled over to a long activity table. She greeted MacKenzie, Dylan, and Tanner as they took places at the craft table, too. It was good to see MacKenzie out of her room and joining the activity. Some of the teenagers felt the projects were too kiddish, so Josephine made special visits to their rooms for some individual time. She secretly loved it when the teens interacted with the younger kids though.

"What's the word on the floor?" Josephine asked while she pulled the craft supplies from her bag.

"I'm on my off week, so I'm feeling much better," MacKenzie said, but then she frowned. "But poor Sarah started her chemo on Monday and she's really sick. I don't remember being that sick when I started." Worry shone in MacKenzie's brown eyes.

JoJo set her craft supplies aside to crouch down next to the young teenager. She squeezed MacKenzie's mocha-brown hand in a feeble attempt to comfort her. "Chemo affects everyone differently. It could be because Sarah is only five, or maybe she's extra sensitive to the meds. It's always hard to see our friends not feeling well, but you guys all know her body is fighting hard. What can we do to lift Sarah's spirits?"

Dylan waved his hand in the air. "I know! We should draw a really big picture of her riding Twilight Sparkle! That's her favorite pony."

"Can you draw one for her, Miss JoJo?" asked Timothy.

"I sure can," she responded. "How about I set you guys up so you can start coloring, and I'll draw something fun for you to color for Sarah."

One of Josephine's favorite things was listening to the kids chatter as they colored. The topics changed as quickly as the direction of the wind in Kansas. They started off with reports of the other patients on the floor. They still had not met Katee, who they reported had moved from yelling to throwing stuffed animals at the nurses. The teen's behavior didn't surprise the kids. They were each familiar with the anger and fear that came as part of finding out you had cancer. Then the conversation turned to TV shows and a magician who came to visit.

Meanwhile, Josephine sketched Sarah sitting astride

Twilight Sparkle with the Castle of Friendship in the background. When it was finished, she tore it from the notepad and handed it over for the kids to color and decorate. MacKenzie got out the glitter glue to make the castle sparkle and shine, while the boys took turns coloring the pony, background, and Sarah. They were finishing up their masterpiece when parents began showing up to collect their munchkins. They oohed and aahed over everyone's art.

"You guys did an amazing job on Sarah's picture. I'm going to take it to the nurse's station, so the glitter glue can dry. Then one of her nurses will deliver it to her. I hope you all have an awesome day tomorrow. I'll see you Thursday for some origami lessons," Josephine said, giving fist bumps and high fives as the kids left with their parents.

When the room was empty, Josephine took the Clorox wipes from the supply closet and wiped down the all furniture and art supplies that she could. She did her best to keep from spreading germs, especially with the kids' weak immune systems. She packed up the craft supplies, then carefully carried Sarah's drawing to the nurse's station.

"Here comes Origami Girl now." Lauren closed the chart she had been working on and leaned against the counter-height nurse's station. "I saw all the happy smiles and knew you wouldn't be too far behind. What's that?" she asked, her pink silk headscarf shifting as she craned her neck to see what Josephine held.

"It's a little something the kids made to cheer up Sarah, but the glue needs to dry before you deliver it." Josephine set the piece of art on the desk top.

Lauren traced her clear-polished fingernail on the paper along Sarah's image. "I love how you captured her expression when she laughs. If I had one ounce of your talent, I'd count myself blessed."

Mary, the stalky floor supervisor, joined them, shaking her head of salt and pepper bobbed hair. "I remember when you were a young teenager in here with your brother. You had a knack for making others happy even then."

"Now that's your real talent," said Lauren. "Infusing your cheeriness with art makes it more fun."

"Speaking of fun," Mary said, turning to Josephine. "I've been asked to have you report to Dr. Mira's office before your shift ends."

Josephine's eyebrows scrunched together. Dr. Mira was the head of pediatric oncology. She'd never been asked to go to her office before. Had she done something wrong?

"No need to fret," Mary said. "I can't imagine you've done anything that she needs to bite your head off for . . . have you?"

"I don't think so," Josephine replied hesitantly.

"Well, then everything should be fine. Although I suggest you don't keep her waiting." Mary gestured down the hall.

Josephine made her way to the end of the oncology floor, then turned down the hall that led to the doctor's offices. Josephine twisted the edge of her shirt around her finger. She did a mental run down of all the patients on the oncology floor, especially the ones struggling. Perhaps Dr. Mira had someone in mind who needed some special cheering up. Still, it was usually one of the nurses who pointed out something like that. She stopped outside the office door and stared at the name plate.

Dr. Mira Stanovski.

She remembered the first time she met Dr. Mira—the day her brother was diagnosed with acute lymphocytic leukemia and was admitted to Crystal Creek Children's Hospital. Her little brother couldn't say the doctor's last name, so she had invited him to call her Dr. Mira instead. It was her kindness and down-to-earth approach that helped her little brother understand his illness and the challenges he had ahead to fight it. An overwhelming wave of sadness filled her as she wondered what her brother would be doing with his life if he had conquered that battle.

She swallowed back the lump that clogged her throat and forced a smile before knocking on the door. Dr. Mira called for her to enter.

The late afternoon sunshine streamed through the windows, momentarily blinding her as she stepped across the threshold into the office—and smack dab into someone else. A pair of strong arms wrapped around her as they stumbled to regain their balance.

"I'm so sorry. I didn't see you." She blinked to adjust to the new lighting, only to find herself in the arms of Dr. Doom and Gloom himself. "Dr. Blake!" She quickly stepped back, tripping over her own feet with the grace of a three-legged duck. His hand darted out to steady her again, then he released her and took several steps away.

Dr. Mira cleared her throat, drawing Josephine's attention away from the miserable man she had the misfortune of sharing the room with.

"I didn't realize you were in another meeting. I can wait until you're finished," Josephine offered.

"No need. Please, have a seat." The older woman gestured to the chairs in front of her desk. Dr. Mira settled into her leather office chair while Josephine hesitantly sat, all the while acutely aware that Dr. Blake stood a few feet behind her.

"How are you, Josephine?" Dr. Mira inquired.

"I'm fine," she replied, confused by the situation.

"You're finishing up art school soon, correct?"

Josephine nodded. "I'm preparing for my debut exhibit at the end of the month, then graduation is in May."

Dr. Mira leaned back in her chair, a small smile on her age-wizened face. "I'm sure you've had offers for employment already though."

"Yes, a few, although I haven't made any commitments yet." Josephine replied. Did Dr. Mira call her down to chat about her future? And if so, what in the world did that have to do with Dr. Blake being in the room?

"That's wise. I'd recommend waiting until after your exhibit. You never know what offers will come after such an anticipated event."

Josephine simply nodded, still at a loss of what to say and feeling more awkward by the minute.

"I believe that you and Dr. Weston Blake know each other," Dr. Mira said, gesturing for him to join them.

Josephine chanced a brief glance at Dr. Blake as he folded his large frame into the chair beside her, casually crossing his foot over his knee with his hand loosely clasping the ankle. A nervous tingle crept up her throat, so she simply nodded to acknowledge their acquaintance.

"Good. Dr. Blake needs some training to complete his residency in six months. It seems his evaluation forms have indicated a need to improve his communication skills with our patients and their families."

Josephine couldn't hold back the laugh-snort that escaped. Her hand clapped over her mouth and her eyes went wide. "I'm sorry," she apologized, mortified by her insensitive reaction.

Dr. Mira simply raised an eyebrow. "I see you are acquainted with Dr. Blake's lack of bedside manner."

Josephine sensed a stillness come over the man next to her. She didn't dare turn to look at him, but from the corner of her eye she noticed his knuckles went white as he gripped his ankle. "May I ask what this has to do with me?"

"Because, my dear, you are to be his tutor."

"Excuse me?" She couldn't possibly have heard that correctly. She searched Dr. Mira's face for some sign indicating this was all in jest, but all she saw were wrinkles surrounding a set of steely gray eyes.

"Dr. Blake and I thoroughly discussed his options for passing this part of his residency. He requested to work with you."

Shocked, Josephine swiveled in her seat to face Dr. Blake. "But you can't stand me," Josephine countered.

He coughed into his hand. She wasn't sure if it really was a cough or if he was shocked she would admit they didn't like each other in front of Dr. Mira. He shifted to face her, his dark brown eyes a shield blocking whatever feelings he kept suppressed inside. "You're a long-time volunteer with a proven track record of comforting children and their families. You are also not a medical peer, which, in this situation, is ideal."

And there you have it. More than seven words at one time and she couldn't even count it as a victory because everything inside her was twisted up into knots.

Dr. Mira leaned back, steepling her fingers together. "The plan is that Dr. Blake will be scheduled off during your volunteer shifts on Tuesday and Thursday afternoons. During that time, he'll help with the activities, observe your interactions with patients during group and personal room visits, and you will also provide him with feedback. Dr. Blake has excelled in every other area of his residency and he is determined to continue in pediatrics. You know personally how important trust and communication is between a doctor, his patient, and the patient's family."

Josephine turned to ask Dr. Blake if this was what he really wanted. After all, there were a lot of other areas in the medical field where he could contribute. Or areas where he could practice his bedside manner, like the morgue. But it all stayed stuck in her head as he studiously avoided her by looking directly ahead. His jaw was clenched. A small eye twitch was the only hint of his awareness that she studied him as she considered the proposition.

Oh man. This was going to suck. How could she possibly volunteer to spend her time with Dr. Doom and Gloom. Not just spend time with him, but how could she try to help him be less Doom and Gloom?

No, it was a torture she wasn't willing to deal with. She had a life, an art exhibit to prepare for, decisions to make for her future. She didn't need this craziness to be piled on top of that. She turned back to Dr. Mira, intending to tell her just that.

"I'm sure you're wondering what's in it for you," Dr. Mira said, before Josephine could give an answer. "If the task is completed successfully, I would be willing to provide you with a letter of recommendation for your volunteer work here at Crystal Creek Children's Hospital, as well as an introduction to the chairperson for the National Children's Hospital Network. I do believe that you applied for their artist in residence program." She sat back in her chair, eyeing Josephine.

Whoa. Josephine's head filled with a million thoughts all

at once. A letter of recommendation from Dr. Mira was worth its weight in gold. Her recommendations were few and far between, making it a huge status symbol for medical residents. Plus, a personal introduction to the chairman of the national children's hospital network - that was huge. Both of those combined might be enough to secure a spot in their coveted Artist in Residence program, giving Josephine the opportunity to design and create murals and art for hospitals with all the work paid for by the network's grants.

"Taking that into consideration, are you up to the task of tutoring Dr. Blake?"

It almost made the next four-to-six weeks of Dr. Doom and Gloom seem bearable. She drew in a deep breath, then let it all out in a whoosh. "I'll do my best."

Dr. Blake's head swiveled towards her and his dark brown eyes met hers. The determination there was hard and glaring. Was it all about conquering a challenge, to prove himself worthy of being a pediatric doctor? Or was he as annoyed as she was to be caught in this trap?

Either way, she was committed—hook, line, and sinker. She just hoped she didn't end up drowning in the process. She stood, shook Dr. Mira's hand, then turned to her nemesis. "I'm teaching origami lessons on Thursday. You might consider looking up some YouTube tutorials if you haven't done it before."

He inclined his head in acknowledgment. "Duly noted. See you Thursday, Miss Jorgensen."

"And please, call me Josephine, or better yet, JoJo when we're around the kids."

"JoJo." His nose crinkled as if the name left a bad taste in his mouth.

And with that, she left the room wishing she had let the sucker drown in his own dreary pond.

Ready to binge read the Crystal Creek series?
Available in ebook, Kindle Unlimited, and paperback.

- Confessions to the Girl Next Door
- Crazy for the Sweet Confections Baker
- Saving Dr. Weston Blake
- A Best Friend's Guide to Love
- How to Woo a Billionaire in Ten Days (coming soon!)

Sweet RECIPES

Chocolate Lava Sundaes

Ingredients:
    1 box of your favorite fudge brownie mix
    Ben & Jerry's Phish Food ice cream
    1 jar of hot fudge
    Real Whipped Cream (recipe below) or 1 can of whipped cream
    1 chocolate bar

Directions:
Follow the box directions to make the fudge version of your brownie mix, so the brownies are thick and moist, not light and cakey. Let cool until just warm.

Top with scoops of ice cream, drizzles of hot fudge, and lots of whipped cream. Use a peeler or paring knife to trim shavings off the chocolate bar.

HOMEMADE WHIPPED CREAM

Ingredients:

1 cup heavy whipping cream

1 Tbsp confectioner's sugar (granulated sugar works in a pinch, too)

1/2 - 1 tsp of vanilla (depending on how flavorful you want it)

Directions:

Chill a clean metal bowl and the whisk attachment of your mixer in the freezer for 10 minutes. Add all of the ingredients to the bowl and whisk on high speed until medium peaks form, about 1 minute. Be careful not to over beat—the mixture will turn chunky and buttery.

Whipped cream is best served immediately, but you can make it in advance by whipping the cream to soft peaks and refrigerating it for up to 2 hours. When ready to serve, continue whipping the cream to medium peaks.

Dark Chocolate Cake with Peanut Butter Frosting

Ingredients:
- 1 box of your favorite chocolate cake
- 1 box dark chocolate or chocolate fudge instant pudding
- 1/2 cup chocolate chips
- Peanut Butter Frosting (recipe below)

Directions:

Follow the cake mix directions, plus add the instant pudding. Mix well. Fold in chocolate chips. Bake according to box directions. Cool completely before frosting.

Peanut Butter Frosting

Ingredients:
- 1/2 cup butter, softened
- 1 cup creamy peanut butter
- 3 Tbsp milk
- 2 cups confectioner's sugar

Directions:

In a medium bowl, beat together the butter and peanut butter with an electric mixer. Gradually add in the confectioner's sugar. When it begins to get too thick, add the milk 1 Tbsp at a time, until all the sugar is mixed in. The frosting should be thick and spreadable. Beat for 2-3 minutes to make it fluffy.

Peanut Butter Chocolate Chunk Cookies

Ingredients:

- 1 1/2 cups all-purpose flour
- 1 tsp baking soda
- 1/4 teaspoon salt
- 1 cup creamy or chunky peanut butter
- 3/4 cup (1 1/2 sticks) butter or margarine, softened
- 2/3 cup packed brown sugar
- 1/3 cup sugar
- 1 tsp vanilla extract
- 2 large eggs
- 1 3/4 cups chocolate chunks or chips

Directions:

Preheat oven to 350°F.

Combine the flour, baking soda and salt in a small bowl, then set aside.

In a separate large bowl, beat peanut butter, butter, brown sugar, sugar and vanilla extract until creamy. Add eggs, mix well. Gradually beat in the flour mixture. Fold in the chocolate chunks. Drop by rounded tablespoons onto ungreased baking sheets; press down slightly.

Bake for 9 to 12 minutes or until golden brown. Cool on baking sheets for 2 minutes; remove to wire racks to cool completely.

Almond-Lemon Shortbread Cookies

Ingredients:

   3 sticks of butter at room temperature
   1 cup sugar, plus a little extra for sprinkling
   1 tsp vanilla extract
   1/4 tsp almond extract
   zest from 1/2 of a lemon
   3 1/2 cups all-purpose flour
   1/4 tsp sea salt

Directions:

In a large bowl, use hand mixer to cream the butter and sugar together. Then add the vanilla, almond and lemon zest. Mix together well. Add salt, then gradually add flour while mixing on low-medium speed. The dough mixture will be dry and possibly a bit crumbly. Continue to beat until all the ingredients are well combined.

Use your hands to shape the dough into a ball. On a clean, floured surface, reshape the dough into a flat disk about 3 inches thick. Cover with plastic wrap, then chill for 20 minutes.

Preheat oven to 350 degrees. Remove the chilled dough and roll out on a floured surface until it's 1/2 inch thick. You can either cut it into fingers, circles, or use large shape cookie cutters. If cutting into fingers, I prefer to use my pizza cutter and make them about 3"x1" rectangles.

Place cookies on a baking sheet lined with either a Sil-Pat or parchment paper. Sprinkle the cookies with sugar, then bake for 20-25 minutes until the edges begin to brown. Let the cookies cool for 5-10 minutes before moving.

Makes about 30 finger shortbread cookies.

ACKNOWLEDGMENTS

EVERY BOOK HAS A BEHIND-THE-SCENES CAST AND CREW. MANY, MANY THANKS TO:

Amy Day, for taking me to my very first hockey game, which inspired Graydon Green's character and led me to write this story. Crazy for the Sweet Confections Baker wouldn't be here today without you.

My fabulous writing group friends (you know who you are!) for loving Rachel and Graydon, laughing when appropriate, getting caught up in the angst and providing essential feedback to strengthen the story.

Heather Tullis for coming up with the awesome idea to set our two series in the same town with cross-over characters. Be sure to check out her In the Garden series.

A big thank you to all our fans who helped us name our town - Crystal Creek!

To my munchkins for feigning excitement about yet another Whatever Dinner Night when I worked too late to actually cook the meal we planned. I love each of you infinity plus a hundred million. =)

And most importantly, to my hubby, John. Thank you for being my best friend, my true love, and more. I'm so grateful I have you to share my life and dreams with. xoxoxo

ABOUT THE AUTHOR

Danyelle Ferguson is author of the award-winning Crystal Creek sweet romance novels. She loves writing stories that feature strong women conquering difficult challenges and finding love along the way. When she's away from her laptop, Danyelle enjoys dancing in the kitchen with her family, all things pink, and is obsessed with pretty pens. Follow her online for IRL goofiness, cat photobombs, and writing updates.

ⓐ amazon.com/~/e/B004LHL0FC
🅱🅱 bookbub.com/authors/danyelle-ferguson
ⓘ instagram.com/danyellefergie